D1104132

CAUGHT

MP
class
of
2017

SULLI GILES

ISBN: 0692496386
ISBN 13: 9780692496381

PROLOGUE

The man smiled as he took his newborn son from the nurse. The baby was light and fragile in his arms. He had plans for his children that would affect them their whole life, and he couldn't wait to get started.

The man recalled the memory in vivid detail. He had been sitting in his college dorm room, the door shut firmly, doing psychology homework about siblings. Ideas swarmed around his mind. He had theories. Oh, did he have theories.

The plan didn't come together in one night, but over the next four years, bits and pieces started to slide into place. The plan would take him decades to complete, and he couldn't do it alone. He needed access to information that he couldn't obtain as a civilian, and there had been one way to do that. He needed a position of power and planned to obtain one. It was a golden opportunity when the CIA and Ares took an interest in him.

Now he had more plans. The plans were so complex and knotted that he could hardly keep them straight.

The man whispered to his child, "The final piece. Oh, I've waited for this moment for so long. It was almost too late. Your brother is growing. His memory is getting stronger by the day. That is dangerous for me."

The baby began to cry.

The man glanced back. His oldest son sat in a chair, gnawing on a cookie, with the bag at his feet. The man smiled again and passed the baby to his unsmiling wife. She knew the plans he had for her children, but she would not say a word. The man knew this and was proud of the progress he'd made with her over the past few years. Such delightful progress.

He wished she had given birth to a girl. He would have liked to see how a girl would handle the life he'd carefully planned for the second child, but he supposed he would have to settle for the boy.

These two children were such minor pieces to a bigger and darker plan, which had numerous variables. These children were just two of the more *delicate* variables.

He walked over to his older son and sat him on his lap. He had already picked out a perfect family for this one to live with. He didn't need to bother with his other son. The baby would not be permanently placed with a family, but he would still live within twenty miles of his older brother. The man wanted to see if the two would interact. He chuckled. Oh, he was so excited.

CHAPTER 1

I sat at the edge of the water on a crowded beach, where most people hung out with friends and family. But not me. I came here to hide.

I was alone and in a lot of trouble. More than I thought I was and definitely more than I cared to think about.

A lot of fugitives might have stayed at a beach that was less populated, but I thought it was safer at crowded beaches. It was easier to melt into a crowd, but I still felt like eyes were constantly on me. I stood and started to walk away from the beach. I didn't stay in one place for too long. Even though I was up and moving, my nerves were still fried, and I looked over my shoulder more than I should have. I walked past a group of people who listened to loud music and ate hotdogs.

I bit the inside of my cheek until I tasted blood. I would have killed for a hotdog. It took everything I had not to turn around and ask for food. That would raise too many questions, and I wasn't that hungry. Not yet.

That's why I came to town. I was out of food.

Unfortunately, I didn't pay too much attention to the things around me. My eyes were focused on the ground in an attempt to keep my bare feet away from anything sharp. I looked up just as I ran into a cop. The man dropped his phone and cup of soda, and the liquid splashed on both of us. I grimaced and wiped the sticky soda off my arms.

"Sorry! I wasn't looking where I was going," I quickly apologized as I realized who this man was.

"Neither was I," the cop answered and looked at me closely.

All I wanted to do was turn around and run.

"You look familiar. Do I know you?" he asked.

My stomach lurched.

"I don't think so, no."

Run. All the cells in my body willed me to move, but I didn't. I stood right there. The hot pavement burned my bare feet. Why was a cop on the beach? Had someone called and told them I was back in town? Who had seen me? When? Had it been someone from school?

I weighed my options. If I ran, the cop would run after me on the assumption that I had something to hide. I just needed to act cool. *Just act cool and everything will be fine.*

The cop looked at me a little longer, and I saw the recognition dawn on him. He would have had a hard time forgetting me. The cop tried to reach for a pair of handcuffs without my noticing, but before he even had a finger on those death traps, I was gone.

"Stop him!" the cop yelled out of impulse. Dozens of heads turned to see what the sudden outburst was all about, but no one made a move to help.

I started to blindly run toward town. I could already imagine the pain of the stone bruises that I would feel later. I had no idea if I should continue to run or hide, but I knew I couldn't let that man catch me.

Cars slammed on brakes, and I took advantage. Most cars drove slowly around this area of town, so I wasn't hesitant to run in the middle of the street. A few cars beeped, but it barely registered. The cop was right behind me, but I wasn't going to turn around and check to see how far he was. I soared over the top of a hedge and hit the ground running. My next objective—after I got away from this guy—was to get a pair of shoes. My feet were being torn to shreds by the rocks and pavement. I ran into a parking lot and hid behind a black car, its metal burning my fingers as I grazed it.

I could see through the windows; it didn't seem like the cop had seen me, but he walked into the same parking lot. He would see me in a few seconds if I didn't hide. I took a breath of fresh air and went under the car, which reeked of gasoline. I shut my eyes and held in a cough, but opened them when I heard footsteps. I half expected to see the cop's face. Instead,

I watched the cop's black shoes stop right in front of the black car. Without a second's hesitation, I shimmied out and started to run yet again.

"Stop right where you are!" the cop screamed at me, and I felt like he probably had a gun in his hand.

But of course I didn't stop.

I made a mad dash for the closest café, threw open the door, and side-stepped a lady with a baby in a stroller. I got a lot of glances from diners as I raced for the bathroom like my life depended on it—and in a way, it did.

In the men's bathroom, I was greeted by smells of decayed seafood and sewer water. I realized I'd backed myself into a corner. There was no way out of this. I couldn't run back out of the café or the policeman would catch me, but I couldn't stay here.

I needed an idea and I needed it now. I whipped around. A window. I knew I barely had ten seconds before someone came into the bathroom to get me. I could already hear the footsteps.

I couldn't get caught now. The only thing on my mind was getting that rusty window open and getting out. I could barely see out of it; bugs were imprisoned in a sticky substance in the corners. I gave the window a hard shove.

Nothing happened.

Another shove. Still nothing. Panic squeezed my empty stomach, but I wouldn't give in. I pounded both fists against it.

It squeaked and budged.

Relief rushed over every pore of my body.

After one last shove, it finally came loose. I jumped as high as I could and squirmed through the ridged opening. I felt shards of hard metal scrape against my legs. I was halfway out when the policeman burst through the door, and I felt his hands wrap around my ankles. I lashed out with my bare foot and connected with his nose, and his grip loosened. I fell to the ground and landed on something hard. The policeman tried to get his large frame through the window, but it was no good. I stood, laughed, and ran.

CHAPTER 2

The walk back to my hideout wasn't pleasant. For starters, I was still hungry and thirsty, and now my leg was bleeding. My hair wouldn't stay out of my eyes. The walk was at least three miles, and I was without shoes.

My hideout was an old house behind a park, set way back in the woods and out of sight. No one had been in that house in a long time. Last week, some kid from the park tried to follow me back into the woods, and I had to wait an hour before he finally left.

I winced. If I stepped on one more pinecone, I was going to scream. I had five blisters on my right foot and three on my left. Last night, I'd had to pop the biggest one and enough water to drown the world poured out and then I had to tear off the dead skin. I would have killed for a pair of shoes. Two plastic water bottles and two rubber bands would have been fine. I would have even settled for a pair of Crocs.

I was paranoid. This much I knew. I still couldn't bring myself to just walk up to the abandoned house without walking around the perimeter at least twice. I had to make sure no one was there no matter how much my feet screamed at me to stop. I constantly felt like I was being watched. And not just by a squirrel.

I surveyed my surroundings from the porch, and everything seemed to be in order. There was a big clearing in the woods where the house had been built some years ago for reasons unknown. The wooden house rested on ten-foot stilts. A window was busted and let in all the bugs, especially the mosquitoes. I'd done my best to repair it, but I didn't exactly have much to work with. However, the busted window did give me a shard of glass, and I kept it close when I was here.

I pushed open the front wooden door and stumbled inside. I knew at once no one had been in the house, because I'd put a small leaf in the doorway that hadn't moved.

The house was one big room, a dysfunctional bathroom, and one bedroom. At least I had a bed. To be honest, I had it better than most fugitives.

But that didn't mean that I wasn't going to complain.

I went through the cabinets one more time, although I knew they hadn't changed since I left. They were still empty, along with my stomach. I was mad that I hadn't been able been able to get food in town. That stupid cop ruined my chance.

I sat down on the couch and put the only thing that was mildly entertaining in this whole house on the coffee table. The previous owners had left a deck of cards, although there were only fifty cards left. This made playing solitaire fairly difficult.

I looked at my leg. It was scraped, but I didn't see any glass. I licked my finger and tried to get the dried blood off.

Three games of solitaire and two blister pops later, I yawned. My run-in with the cop scared me out of my wits. The cop had caught me, even if it was only for a few seconds. I needed to be more careful. I walked into the bedroom, flopped onto the bed, and took a much-needed rest with the shard of glass two feet away.

———

I woke up suddenly but had no idea why. I hadn't dreamed and hadn't poked myself with the glass, which had happened more times than I cared to admit. Then I heard the sound of a cabinet being slammed shut. Someone was in the house.

Weapon in hand, I slowly crept to the window and saw that there was not a patrol car in my line of view, but that didn't mean there wasn't one.

My only option left was to go into fight mode, but I didn't have a chance. The door swung open, revealing a startled teenage girl, who screamed.

"Wasn't excepting any visitors today."

The girl gawked at me, her eyes wide in fear and face red with shock. She was my age with dark-blue eyes and dark-blond hair, borderline brown. She had her phone in one hand, and the other hand covered her mouth. She wore an old T-shirt and running shorts with tennis shoes. She had an athletic and lean body. Her muscles looked fairly tense.

The girl backed out of the room without letting me out of her sight. I couldn't let her leave. I had to convince her that I was waiting for my friends or something.

"Who are you?" I asked. I positioned myself in between the girl and the front door. She backed away and put the counter between us.

"Listen, I sat by some pot head in eighth grade and behind a kid who was sent to YDC for reasons still unknown, so don't think for one second that I won't..." She trailed off and eyed my shard of glass.

I dropped it to the floor, and she seemed to relax.

"What are you doing here?" I asked.

"I just moved here, and I was looking around town. I saw the park. I was looking through the woods and I just..." Her eyes searched the room and then landed on me.

"You just thought it would be completely fine if you walked yourself in here and checked the place out? Didn't somebody ever teach you differently? I could easily be a killer."

"The house looked pretty abandoned to me. Why are you here?" she asked me.

"I'm waiting for my friends to show up."

"Right."

Before I had time to respond, I heard the sound of a car. I looked out the window again and picked up the shard of glass. The police had arrived. There was a dirt road that led from the west side of the park back to the house, so overgrown it had mostly been forgotten. Mostly.

I wanted to scream. Everything that could go wrong was going wrong right now.

"You need to leave."

"Why?" she asked and walked toward me.

"Just leave."

She looked out the window and gasped. "Did you really kill someone?"

"What? No," I said defensively.

"What did you do?"

"What makes you assume they are after me?"

"Because *I* didn't do anything!"

I knew I couldn't keep up the act any longer. It was too much of a desperate situation. "You want to know what you can do? You can walk out of that front door and pretend you never saw me. You can then explain that there is no one in here. No one at all. Just a boring house."

"I don't even know your name. Why would I do that?" she said and crossed her arms.

"Because it would be the nice thing to do. It's Chase, by the way. Now, please. Please. I'm begging you here. Please go and stall that man while I get out of here."

I ran back into the bedroom, my mind in a panic. Had they followed me? How was this happening? How had I been seen? I'd been so careful…I grabbed the sheet that was on the bed and tied it around the bedpost. I pulled the bed closer to the window and gave the sheet a quick tug. It seemed like it would hold. It would make the drop to the ground a lot less painful.

"I haven't agreed yet," the girl said as she entered the bedroom. Her cheeks were flushed, and she bounced around on her feet.

"I'm not waiting around."

A few seconds after the girl left the room, I started my slow descent to the ground. I dropped about three feet and landed on a sharp rock. I grimaced but remained silent. I looked at the bottom of my foot to find that blood had already formed around the edges of the cut. I glanced upward and saw the cop's feet on the stairs. I had to run now and worry about myself later.

I got a few dozen feet into the woods before I picked a fallen tree to hide behind. I couldn't manage to run anymore. I looked behind myself to make sure I wasn't leaving a blood trail. If I was going to get caught, I was just going to get caught.

I knew I couldn't trust that girl. She had probably already ratted me out. The sheet hanging out the window probably wasn't working to my advantage either.

I heard a stick crack under someone's foot and froze. I couldn't risk a glance back. Instead, I sank lower to the ground. I had to get a better hiding spot—I was way too exposed. I turned my head to the right and assessed that the fallen tree had probably been knocked down in a storm, which meant its roots were still attached. It would be a fine hiding place.

I heard footsteps and knew I had to move. I belly crawled to the base of the tree and tried my best to remain silent. A few feet away, I discovered a hole under the tree that looked like a wolf or a wild dog had made it. It was perfect.

I went in head first and half expected to be transported to Wonderland. I drew in my knees to my chest and tucked in my head. It was a tight squeeze; I was lucky I'd dropped about ten pounds. The tree pressed down on me like a heavy weight, but I kept my breathing steady. This was not the time to develop a fear of tight spaces.

The footsteps sounded heavy and close. I shut my eyes, mostly to keep the dirt out.

"Chase. Come on, I know you're here. The girl told me, and you snapped pretty much every branch you walked by. Did you really think you could stay away from us this long? You're hurt. I saw the blood. You're probably hungry and thirsty as well. How does a cheeseburger sound? Or a soda?"

The policeman continued to try and draw me out by describing numerous fast-food specials, and his voice faded until I couldn't hear it. Not that it mattered. Nothing he said could make me come out. Still, my mouth watered at the sound of a cheeseburger and a soda.

I stayed in the hole for another fifteen minutes before I had the audacity to get out. I poked my head over the fallen tree. Nothing. The policeman had moved on.

I was too worried to return to the house. I figured that the police would come back. Maybe not today, but they would be back. I was making them look like a bunch of circus monkeys because I was teenage boy they couldn't catch.

I shook the dirt out of my hair and decided I needed to get my priorities straight. First, I needed to clean the wounds on my foot and my leg. I didn't exactly know how, but I knew I needed clean water so I couldn't exactly go and dip into a creek. I'd heard about the flesh-eating bacteria stuff. Then I needed food, water, and shelter. A pair of shoes wouldn't have been too bad.

The cut was on the arch of my foot, so it didn't hurt much when I walked, and the bleeding had stopped. It stung, but I would be fine. As I limped, I started to feel thirsty again. I was sick of having to find my own food and water. The fact that I was broke put a real damper on things.

That left one option.

Stealing.

I knew stealing was wrong. Blah, blah, blah. If there were another option, I probably would have done it.

Probably.

I wasn't walking back to town. That was way too far and my feet couldn't handle it. The police were probably still hanging around the area, but I needed water. The Florida sun blared down on me, and I wasn't sweating anymore. That was a problem.

I made a wide arc around the house and came out of the woods to the side of the park. I planned to steal a couple of dollars out of a woman's purse while she tended to her child on the playground. It'd worked before and there was no reason it wouldn't work now. Then I saw the best thing I'd seen in a long time. Some kid was having a birthday party. There was a big inflatable waterslide with about twenty rambunctious kids around it. There wasn't one kid around the table of food. My stomach growled.

I carefully walked up to the table, trying not to become too distracted by the smell. Some kid fell and scraped his knee, and the two adults gave attention to him, making this act easier to complete. I grabbed a few chicken nuggets, stuffed them in my mouth, and washed them down with a bottle of water. I even snagged a cupcake. I didn't remember the last time I'd had something sweet.

I glanced up as I ate a chicken nugget to check to see if anyone was coming. The coast was clear, so I grabbed a Coke out of the cooler and carefully backed away with more nuggets in my pocket. I passed a bench, and out of the corner of my eye, I saw a purse with a few dollar bills on top of a wallet. It was almost too easy. I looked around to make sure no one was watching, and there was nothing but a tree and some little kid within fifty feet.

I walked past the purse, grabbed what I could, and stuffed it in my other pocket. I hadn't even broken a stride. I walked another fifteen feet before I heard heavy feet that pounded the ground, and before I could react, my wrist was twisted as I was spun around by a strong force.

I grimaced at my stupidity. This was a park. Kids obviously played hide-and-seek with their parents, who most likely hid behind trees and looked to make sure their child was safe. In this case, a husband saw me stealing from his wife's purse while he was hidden behind a tree.

And as I looked over the man's shoulder, I could see the wife coming straight toward me. The man still had my wrist at an odd angle, and his fingernails dug into my skin.

"Did you honestly just take money out of my wife's purse? What's wrong with you?" the man screamed, drawing attention. I figured he would have started to cuss at me, but there was a small boy holding his mother's hand by his side.

Great, the whole family was here.

I knew I couldn't get out of this one with lying. He'd caught me red-handed.

"Take it out of your pockets right now," he spat at me, and when I didn't respond, he drew me closer to him.

"I think you're breaking my wrist," I murmured.

He released some of the pressure but still had a fairly strong grip.

"I'm not going to ask again."

I quickly handed him the money, which turned out to be four dollars. I felt physically sick, and not just because of my situation at the moment. Those four dollars could have easily bought a water bottle and a hotdog at the beach.

The wife looked confused. "Why four dollars? Why not more?"

The husband answered for me. "Because he likes to steal for the thrill of it. Isn't that right?" The man loosened his grip, and I broke away.

I didn't waste a second. I turned and ran.

The man didn't run after me, but I still hopped a fence and landed in someone's back yard, ignoring the pain in my feet. I slipped out of the back fence and kept walking. I needed to put as much distance between the park and me as I could. I walked toward the end of the road before I finally stopped.

There weren't any cars in the driveway of the closest house, so I figured no one was home. I sat down, glad to be off my injured foot. I turned on the hose and let the cool water run over my leg and foot. I washed out my hair and tried to spray down the rest of my body to get the dried salt, blood, and dirt off. I couldn't even think of the last time I'd taken an actual shower.

I thought about that girl. I'd been stupid to tell her my name. The cop wouldn't have bothered to look around the woods if I hadn't told her my name. And now the police knew that I was back in town.

Wonderful.

CHAPTER 3

The chicken nuggets and cupcake proved to be the only food I was going to eat for the next two days. I hated being hungry because it was a problem that could be easily fixed, which made it even more frustrating. I didn't feel great, but the water from the hose kept the real fatigue at bay. That hose was a gift, and I took advantage of it, but it didn't take away all the sharp edges of the hunger pains.

I decided it was time for a little trip to the grocery store, and I made it to town without a problem. My foot was slightly swollen, but there was nothing I could do about it. The infection would surely fix itself.

I had a headache. I wasn't sure, but it might have had something to do with the crime I was about to pull off. I'd stolen before. Nearly every kid had. I'd never done it for fun though, contrary to what that man believed. It left a bad taste in my mouth, and I'd learned to mask that by eating what I'd stolen. I'd thought about pick-pocketing, but the square wasn't crowded enough. It would be too easy for someone to see me.

I didn't have any second thoughts as the grocery store came into view. I had faith in my abilities.

A few locally owned stores that had paintings of sunsets in the windows and sculptures of mermaids and dolphins surrounded the grocery. There were a few fast-food restaurants, and the places seemed to be packed to the rim. That's why the square was empty. Everyone was eating.

Lucky.

I knew exactly what I planned to take. Peanut butter and bread. That was important when you were about to steal. Always know what you are going to take. As I walked by the recycle bins outside the doors, I took a grocery sack that belonged to this particular store and stuffed it down my shorts. No one glanced at me when I walked in. Tourists filled the grocery store and crammed products into their carts. It seemed more like a feeding frenzy than a grocery store.

I had to wait forever for the isle with the peanut butter to clear out. It was only clear for about seven seconds, but that was plenty time for me to grab what I needed and start to leave. I didn't think anyone saw me.

I hoped not.

I started to causally walk out of the grocery store, my heart pounding. I had the bag, so no one glanced at me. I think they were happy to see people leave.

Still, I had to get out of the general area. I calmly walked until I was well out of the parking lot and then jogged to the beach so I could make two peanut butter sandwiches in peace. My headache eased a bit as I wolfed down the food, and I let out a shaky breath. I stuffed the stolen goods under a log and walked to the water's edge. There weren't many people there. I glanced over at the lifeguard, who was on his phone. The waves were choppier than I'd seen them in a long time. There was a storm out at sea, and the wind was strong and made the waves even more brutal. I dove into the water and wished the waves would wash away the guilt I felt. I didn't understand. Why did I feel guilty? The bread and peanut butter all together probably cost less than seven dollars. It wouldn't make the grocery store go bankrupt. That's when I realized it wasn't guilt I was feeling.

It was anxiety.

That feeling should have clued me in that I should leave.

CHAPTER 4

That's when I saw the girl. Maybe that's why I didn't leave.

She stood above the breakers and studied the storm that was building. I looked around to see if her parents were there, but as far as I could tell, they weren't.

I would probably be in police custody if she hadn't stalled the man for those few moments. Sure, she'd ratted me out, but if I were in her place, I would have done the same thing. I couldn't place my feelings for her.

I went out a lot farther so she wouldn't notice me.

The ocean got rougher with each wave, and the wind grew stronger. The girl had her back turned to the waves and started to swim back to shore. There was a wall of water that approached her. I tried to warn her about the wave, but the words died in my throat. It broke on top of her, and she disappeared from sight.

On that note, I immediately started to head to shore. I could feel the current pulling me out and had no intentions of getting hit by another wave like that.

The girl still hadn't come up for air when I reached a little way above the breakers, which had taken about ten seconds. The waves came in harder, and another big wave pushed me down. The water was barely up to my knees, but you only need about three inches of water to drown someone.

Another five seconds passed, and she still hadn't come up, which slightly concerned me. The wave that had taken her down had already retracted back into the ocean. She'd been under for quite a while.

When I was about ready to search for her, she popped out of the water twenty feet away and started to cough up seawater. Another wave came and slapped her in the back of the head. She hauled herself a little closer to shore and managed to get herself to her feet. She stumbled until she was completely out of the water and landed on the sand.

I walked over to her and ignored the instinct to flee. "Are you?" I asked when she looked up at me. Her face flickered with recognition.

"Something cut my leg." She turned her leg over, and I saw a long cut on the outside. It bled, the blood mixing with the waves that lapped at her feet.

"How do your lungs feel?"

"I'm fine, but I would love water. Is there a water fountain near?"

"Yeah. There's one over there by the shower." I held out a hand, and she took it and pulled herself to her feet. Great, I was in deep now.

I started to think about jail as I walked the girl over to the shower and water fountain. Maybe it was because if the girl said anything that gave my identity away I was bound for jail, but perhaps I was being a bit too self-obsessed. Not everyone in this town knew or cared why I'd been sent to jail.

If I went back to the same jail, the inmates would kill me before I could blink. I was the one who'd escaped. They had probably received a punishment, maybe tighter security and less food—and less food meant more fights.

The girl introduced herself as Macey Mallory when we were a few feet away from the water fountain. I knew she wanted me to tell her my name, but that wasn't happening. We both knew she knew who I was. I just chose to ignore it.

Macey drank some water and then splashed some on her leg, and the bloody water pooled at her feet.

"Well, I have to go. My parents will get mad if I'm not home before this storm hits." I backed away and turned around, completely unaware of the sand castle that obstructed my path. I fell flat on my face and ate sand. I groaned, spit out the sand, and turned on my back. Macey was right above me and laughed. I stood up and balanced on my good foot. I was too embarrassed to feel too much pain.

"What's it going to take to keep your mouth shut about this?" I asked harshly, my expression set hard. She'd seen me bust it on a sand castle.

A *sand castle.*

"What? Keep my mouth shut about you falling over a sand castle?" Macey asked.

"Right." I turned around and walked away from her. She followed me.

"It wouldn't kill you to answer a few of my questions."

"It probably would," I told her.

"Where are you goin'?" she asked me.

"Where do you think? I'm going home," I said and didn't turn around to face her.

"Where is home?" she asked and ran to catch up with me. I knew she hoped for me to give false information in my story, but I was determined not to let that happen. She knew I wasn't going home, but I knew she wasn't either until I told her what she wanted to hear.

She caught up to me, spun me around by my shoulders, and made me look right into her eyes. "Why were you asleep in the house, and why did you run off when the police showed up?"

"Why did you tell on me? This isn't fourth grade. That cop knew exactly where I was because of you."

"Oh, please. I find a strange boy asleep and alone in a house in the middle of nowhere. He's as skinny as a stick, and he tells me he could be a killer—then the police show up. Excuse me for being a little concerned. Now, tell me why you ran."

I couldn't run. I felt too weak. Besides, she would catch up with me again or start screaming and yelling until the cops showed up to whisk me back to jail. I was starting to think I deserved to be there.

She stood and waited for an answer, seemingly enjoying making me uncomfortable. Her arms were crossed over her chest, and she had a slight smirk on her face. She had on a long, thin shirt and bathing suit bottoms. I had to focus to keep my eyes on her face.

"I really don't see what you're making such a big—" I stopped mid-sentence. A patrol car pulled up in the parking lot. There weren't many reasons a cop would be here, but I was one reason.

The policeman hadn't seen me, but if he came over, I'd be thrown in the back of the car before I even had a fighting chance.

I needed to get away.

Before I knew what I was doing, I slid my hand into Macey's and pulled her in the opposite direction of the policeman.

"What are you doing?" she asked me.

"Listen, Macey, can you just play along for ten minutes, please?" I pleaded. "I don't want the cop following us." I looked over my shoulder.

"Okay, I will…if you tell me what you did that was bad enough that the police are after you," Macey said and glanced at the cop.

"What if I don't?"

She smiled. "Then I'll get the cop over here. Duh."

"Swear you won't say a word to anyone?"

She nodded, and I began the lie. I knew I didn't have to lie. I thought it was fun.

"All right…At school we have the kind of lockers where you can take off the lock, right? More than half of the school doesn't even bother locking their locks. There weren't enough lockers, so I let my best friend, Justin Patterson, share with me. We never went to our lockers at the same time because it got too crowded, and we worked out a schedule so we didn't have to go at the same time. One day, there was this drug search at school. They found meth in my locker. Only problem? I don't do drugs."

"Justin put them in there?"

"I don't think so. He might have let someone else put them in there. The locker was registered to me, so I got in trouble. Big trouble."

"What happened?"

"I was taken where they take all young, dashing delinquents. Juvie. The happiest place on earth." That part was true. I flipped my hair, which was constantly in my eyes.

"What happened in there?" Macey asked.

I laughed. "The worse you were, the better. Most boys were thieves, druggies, and drug dealers, and all of them were in gangs and dumb enough to get caught. Then there was me. The Pretty Boy." That part was true.

"Pretty?"

"I don't know. Pretty Boy. That's what they called me. The rest of them were horrible criminals, and I was PB who was convicted of a crime he didn't do. I was stupid enough to tell them that too. They had a field day. I should have told them I killed someone." That part was true.

"Field day?"

"Every guy there was five inches taller than me and had arms as big around as my head, but it was partly my fault. I guess they would have laid off me more if I would've learned to keep my big mouth shut and leave the basketballs alone." That part was also true.

"Didn't your parents bail you out?" she asked. Her voice was full of curiosity.

"I don't have parents." That part was true.

Macey nodded her head.

When I didn't say anything more, Macey kept on coming with the questions. "What about the people that you were living with, then? What did they do?"

"I wasn't in a foster home then, and the state wasn't willing to do anything. Ticked me off."

"They can't be the only people you were mad with. Who else?" Macey said, sounding a lot like Dr. Phil.

"Justin. He told the teachers and police that he didn't share a locker with me. He told them he just carried his stuff around with him. I stayed in juvie for about two weeks before I escaped while taking out a water bottle for one of the guards."

"They didn't see you walk out?" I could tell that she had a hard time believing me, even though it was true.

"They weren't paying attention to a scrawny kid with a busted lip and a black eye. The detention center was in Tennessee, so I've only been here..." My voice faltered. I had no clue how long I'd been back.

"Do you think the police will come again? To the house, I mean?" she asked.

"Hope not."

"What happened to your foot?" she asked as she glanced down.

"Don't worry about me. How are you? You almost drowned. You should probably go and see a doctor about your leg. How's the cut?" I tried to get off the subject of myself and tried not to limp.

"Oh, shut up. I'm fine. Your foot is swollen. I'm no doctor, but that can't be good. You're the one that needs to see a doctor."

"Can't go to the doctor," I informed her sternly. That would be suicidal.

"Fine. My house is just a little ways up, and you're coming with me. My mom bought a mini-ambulance, and it's somewhere in my room." Macey grabbed me by the elbow and started to drag me. I didn't much care where I was as long as the cops didn't follow me. A little medical attention wouldn't hurt, and I could probably get some food.

"What are you going to tell your parents if they see me?"

"Hopefully, you'll stay hidden enough that we won't have to tell them anything. Besides, you seem to have plenty of experience staying out of sight. But hey, they still might be doing the errands."

We walked in silence the rest of the way, which wasn't far at all. When we got to Macey's, the bottom of the storm dropped out, and we ran inside, but not before I made sure there wasn't a car in the driveway. Her house wasn't far from the park, which explained why she'd been there that day. It was right on the beach, still in the nice part of town, and it was a soft pink with seashells surrounding the doors and windows. Very homey. We walked in the house and were greeted by towers of unopened boxes shoved against the walls. I stopped in the kitchen and stared at the fridge. As if on cue, my stomach growled. Loudly.

"Are you hungry?" Macey cut her eyes toward me.

"Starving," I said, my eyes still locked on the fridge.

Macey walked over to the fridge, opened the doors, and looked in. "Chase, you're in luck. We've got turkey, bread, and mustard. You up for a sandwich?"

On my request, Macey made me three sandwiches and one for herself. She eyed me as I crammed the sandwiches into my mouth. I knew I would be sick afterward, but my first priority was to get this food into my mouth, and the pace didn't matter.

"Do you have a problem?" I said, through a mouthful of sandwich.

"When was the last time you had something to eat, Chase?"

The question caught me off guard. "Um, a hour ago, but before that, it's been two days."

She nodded her head.

After I finished the last of the sandwich and had more to drink than I probably should have, I asked her a question that concerned me.

"I think you're kind of weird. What kind of girl invites a strange guy into her house?"

"The kind of girl who knows a tad bit of karate and where her family keeps the knives and guns. Besides, I feel like if I breathe too hard near you, you might fall over. And if you wanted to hurt me, I think you would have done it by now, but I probably would have killed you first."

"Thanks," I muttered.

A few minutes later, I limped up the stairs behind Macey in the quest for the small ambulance. She searched in the unopened boxes for a few minutes.

"Where are you from?" I asked suddenly.

"Take a guess."

"Alabama? Tennessee? Georgia?" The stacks of boxes surrounded me from every angle, and the room was completely empty except for a lamp and a bed. Downstairs hadn't been much better. She hadn't been lying when she said she'd just moved here.

She looked guilty. "The last one. Is it my accent?"

"No, not at all."

She looked at me a little harder.

"Yeah it is."

"Thanks," Macey said sarcastically as she tried to get the blood from the cut on her leg off her hands.

"You can say the whole word. It's not that hard."

"Oh, be quiet." She smiled and reached her hand farther into the box she had her hand in. "Found it."

I'd actually been expecting a mini-ambulance with medical supplies in it. I was dismayed to see that it was just a regular first aid kit.

"You swear you won't tell anybody that you saw me, especially your parents?" I asked as she approached me.

She laughed. "No, I don't think I should get them worried. Telling them about you would require me to tell them about my wandering in the woods and near-death experience in the water."

I smiled. "Pinky swear?"

"Trust me. I can keep a secret," She said and ignored my smile.

I smiled inwardly. I knew I shouldn't be worried about her. I had plenty more things to worry about. "Hey? How would you like to donate to a charity called the Feed Chase Miners Fund?" I asked. "Or FCMF for short."

"Here, I grabbed you this Pop-Tart and five bucks. Enjoy."

I nodded and thanked her.

Macey waved off the thanks and instructed me to sit down. She bent down with some sort of cream in her hand and picked up my foot with the other. Her face looked confused.

"Where's the cut?"

"On the bottom."

She lifted my foot up and grimaced when she saw the damage. "Ouch. And you still don't have any shoes?"

"No."

"That's smart." She applied the cream and wrapped it with a bandage. I was surprised about the lack of pain I felt as she handled my foot. She handed me a pill that I assumed to be a painkiller, and I chugged it down with a bottle of water.

"Here. Keep the cream. Put it on every five hours or so." Macey wrapped a bandage around my foot and tied it off. I didn't bother to tell her that it was too tight.

I stood and tested my foot. It hurt just as badly as usual, but at least the bandage would keep the dirt out. "Thanks again," I said, gesturing to the Pop-Tart, cream, and money in my hand. "But I really need to go. I forgot to get my stuff at the beach," I said, remembering that I'd left the stuff I'd stolen under the log. I walked down the stairs, but Macey stopped me before I could leave.

"Hold on. Here." She tossed me two pairs of socks. "I would give you shoes, but I don't have any that will fit. It's the best I can do."

"It's much appreciated," I said, one foot outside of the door. The rain had stopped.

"Wait, what's your full name?"

"Already said it." I smiled and left, knowing that was likely the last time she and I would encounter each other. It was time for me to skip town.

CHAPTER 5

The director sat in his office and read over the report in the newspaper. There'd been a murder of a single dad in his thirties. The body was beyond recognition. It'd been torn to shreds and all the blood drained. The only thing that led to the body's identification were the tags around the man's neck. He'd fought in Iraq. Authorities were begging anyone with any information to come forward.

A small smile crept over the director's face. The job had been done. The agent would bother him no longer. He supposed he should send something to the agent's children. Flowers, perhaps? Candy?

He moved the paper aside and looked at the two folders in front of him. His plan was in motion, and there was nothing that anyone could do about it. He couldn't help but feel a little honored that his partner had let him orchestrate all of this. That meant everything had to go off without a hitch. The director knew that Chase Miners was suspicious of nearly everything, and he might not believe the story that Brandon would tell him. It didn't matter if Chase believed Brandon or not. He just had to be at the pier when Brandon was. His partner insisted. The director couldn't entirely wrap his head around all of this. His partner's work had caused Chase to be mistrustful, and now it could backfire on him. His partner was working against all he had done to the boy and was hoping it would work.

The director thought it would be best if the boy came alone. There didn't need to be any others, but his partner thought otherwise. His partner thought they should kidnap a girl with a relation to Chase to use as leverage.

The folder showed everything that was known about both of the boys. It included all of their medical files, school records, and sports records, even drawings from when they were younger. Anything that would help the director and his partner break both of the boys.

The director's phone rang and he answered it.

"Chase Miners's whereabouts have been reported to the local police just like you requested," the voice on the other end said.

"And the video was sent to the police?" The video had been his partner's idea.

"Yes, sir. A while ago."

"And Brandon?" The director asked.

"The agent will be going to his house soon."

"Everything else is in order?" he asked as he rubbed his forehead. Everything *had* to be in order. One mistake could mean the last fifteen years were for nothing. His partner would not be happy.

The person on the other end paused, and the man instantly knew that something was wrong. This person had made a mistake. Mistakes meant death. Sometimes worse.

"Not everything. Dawson Williams still claims that his children are dead. He might not believe that Chase and Brandon are his sons. That means one thing. He may be too far gone to care that two kids are being tortured, and we may never get the coordinates out of him."

The man on the phone (and the director) thought that Dawson Williams was the real father of Chase and Brandon.

"And the lie detector tests? Do you have the results yet?"

"Every single number he has told us has been different and seems to be unrelated to each other, but the lie detector shows that he's telling the truth. He has become an excellent liar. The best I've ever seen."

The director checked the clock and closed his eyes. His private plane departed in a few hours, but they would wait for him. Or death would follow.

"Turn the air conditioning back on in his cell, and make sure he gets at least two thousand calories a day and plenty of water. Give him something to keep his mind occupied. Books, TV, music—anything that you can think of. Don't hurt him anymore, and make him as comfortable as possible."

"But sir" The person on the other end started, but he quickly stopped. He knew it was best not to question the director's motives.

CHAPTER 6

I picked up my stuff, walked out of the beach area, across the parking lot, and onto the sidewalk that led into town. I walked about ten yards before I made sure I wasn't being followed.

I was.

It was a patrol car. I quickened my pace to a slow jog, but I could almost feel the cop speeding up too. No. No. I heard the patrol car park and a car door slam.

The cop closed the gap between us, and I was forced to decide whether I should sprint or keep my pace.

I choose option A when I glanced back and saw the cop was after me. I slung the grocery bag over my shoulder and flew, burning my feet on the pavement. I should have put the socks on. I dodged tourists, and a car nearly hit me as I ran through the street. The other cars slammed on brakes and blew their horns at me.

I made a bad decision of running down a dark alley. I thought it had been one where I could easily climb a ladder at the end and run onto the roof. There was a roof like that near the pier, but I was at least three miles away from there.

The alley came to a dead end, and I banged my hands against the wall, pushed off, and automatically looked for a place to hide. I could see the long shadow of the policeman as he approached the entryway of the alley. There was only one place to hide and I *wasn't* happy about it.

A Dumpster.

I nearly threw up when I realized how badly the Dumpster smelled. I put my fingers on an unidentified green, sticky substance as I lowered myself. I took one more breath of fresh air and closed the lid. Now I was in complete, utter darkness filled with a stench that brought tears to my eyes. I heard something crawling in the far corner and held my breath as the policeman walked by. Had he heard me?

Probably.

I heard his shoes walk near me, and my heart filled with false hope, but then I heard his shoes stop right in front of my hiding place.

"I know you're here. Make it easier on the both of us and come out." He opened the lid slowly.

I made another split-second decision to charge out, which took the policeman by surprise. The lid of the Dumpster took a few layers of skin off the back of my leg as I leaped out and completely knocked the policeman out of the way.

I ran as fast as I could with the policeman in hot pursuit. I couldn't help but feel a little stupid as the grocery bag whirled around me. I approached an old building with a gate around it; hopefully, this would provide enough time to plan an escape route. My fingers latched around the fence, and I began to climb. My lips slowly curved into a smile, as I thought this just might not be the end. I might get away, but I would have to move quickly. I might even have to leave town tonight. Yes. Definitely. Maybe farther down the coast? A place where people didn't know who I was.

Then it happened. At the top, I lost my footing and fell to the ground with a thud, my body twisting in the process. My forehead cracked against the pavement, but I managed to roll onto my back. I saw white dots for a few seconds.

I stood up and grabbed the fence for support, but the world swayed back and forth. I blinked a couple times to make the dots go away, but that only seemed to make the nausea worse. I could scarcely hear pounding behind me. Something warm trickled down my upper lip. I wasn't sure where I was.

I looked behind me and saw the policeman coming closer and closer. I knew I had to get away. Now. I took one step and then another, but the world wouldn't stop spinning, which was profoundly annoying. There was a pounding in my head. My muscles went slack.

I don't remember hitting the pavement.

CHAPTER 7

When I woke, I didn't try to figure out where I was. There was too much pain.

"Do you know where you are?" a voice asked.

I tried to sit up, but the policeman easily pushed me back down. I didn't have the strength or will to try to sit up again.

"How long have I been out?" I asked.

"About two hours, but the doctor gave you something to make you sleep. Do you know where you are?" he asked again.

It took me a few seconds to respond. "A hospital. Tell me what happened."

"You tried to climb that gate and lost your footing and fell. I have your peanut butter and bread over there. And socks," he said, almost comically.

"And it was your brilliant idea to bring me here?"

"You lost consciousness for about ten minutes. I thought I might as well bring you over here. Just to make sure. You lost consciousness again when I carried you in here. You know you're pretty light for a boy your height and age?"

"I'm on a diet called 'I have no money.' Great for weight loss. What did the doctor say?"

"You have a slight concussion and an infection in your foot. The doctor gave you a shot, but you'll have to stay on medication for ten days."

I nodded. My head pounded, and I felt like I needed to throw up. I wondered who would be paying for the medicine. The state?

"Wait. The drive to the hospital is at least twenty minutes from where we were. You said I was only out for ten minutes. What happened in the gap?"

"You don't remember?"

"I wouldn't be asking if I did."

"Not much," the policeman started. "You started talking about a big wave, a kid's birthday party, and a girl named Macey. Another reason I brought you here. It made no sense."

Macey. A girl named Macey. My mind fought to recall a girl. It felt like I was waking up from a dream and was attempting to remember it. The memory was just out of reach. There had been something about a mini-ambulance.

A few seconds later, the memory came back in bits and pieces. I remembered that I'd gone to Macey's house to stay away from the cops and then she'd fixed my foot. But that was it. I could remember bits and pieces of meeting her, but I couldn't place a face on the name, which concerned me.

"When can I leave?" I hated the smell of hospitals, and I wasn't a fan of needles. Then again, I don't suppose anyone was.

"The doctor said you could leave in the morning."

I groaned. I didn't feel like staying there another second, much less the night. "Leave to go where?"

"That brings us to an interesting topic…" The man's voice trailed off when there was a knock on the door. I studied him as he turned his head. The policeman was probably about thirty-five years old, fit, but with thinning hair. He had his gun strapped to his belt. Now that I thought about it, he probably had a higher clearance than an average cop. Would they be the ones talking to me about where I was going? Didn't they need a social worker for that?

A doctor walked in and smiled at me and nodded to the policeman, who excused himself.

"I take it you've had a rough week?" the doctor asked, which was a weak attempt to get me to smile. It wasn't going to happen.

I didn't answer. I felt like crawling to the end of the bed and going to sleep.

"How's your head feeling? I hear you took a nasty fall."

I took a breath and lied. "Fine."

"A few more days and that staph infection would have been out of hand. You're lucky."

"That's up for debate."

Instead of replying to my comment, the doctor handed me a bottle of water. "How did you cut your foot?"

"A rock."

"Must have been a fairly sharp rock to have done that kind of damage." he said under his breath and then instructed me to drink the water. As he put something into the bag that was connected to the IV in my arm, he told me that the medicine would knock me out again.

I didn't appreciate his wording.

———

I woke up the next morning and felt a lot better than I had in a long time. My head didn't hurt, and my foot didn't sting too badly anymore. A nurse walked in, bandaged my head, gave me breakfast, and walked out. She didn't say a word to me. Either she knew who I was, or she really hated her job. Maybe both.

About half an hour later, the same policeman who caught me walked in the hospital room.

"How are you feeling?" he asked me.

"Like a bad movie," I muttered.

"In that case, you've been released."

"But I have to come with you, right?"

"You can't exactly go back to the way you were living. We both know that. But you're going to be happy when I tell you this. Your case has been reopened. There's been new evidence."

"What new evidence?" I asked. I sat up too quickly; black dots appeared in front of my eyes, and I winced. My heart pounded faster and faster. "What new evidence?"

The policeman didn't answer my question directly. He told me that we were leaving the hospital and nothing else.

I changed back into my regular clothes, which were covered in holes and dirt. I looked down at my bare feet and yearned for a pair of shoes. I came out of the bathroom and found the policeman sitting down, a bag by his feet. He handed it to me.

"What's this?"

"Look inside."

I peered in and saw a shoebox and a pair of socks. I managed a smile.

"Sorry if they don't fit."

I slid on the socks. I laced up the running shoes and stood. "They fit fine."

"I couldn't have you without shoes much longer. Especially with your foot."

"Thanks," I muttered, majorly embarrassed but certainly grateful. "Did you buy these?"

"My son is a little older than you. I had him drop these off earlier this morning."

"Oh." I hated when people I didn't know did nice things for me. I felt like I owed them.

"Right. Well, let's get going."

I asked about the new evidence more times than I cared to admit, but he wouldn't tell me anything until we arrived at station. I'm not sure the man realized how important this was. The ride there took a month.

"Will you at least tell me your name?"

"You will refer to me as Officer Edge."

We finally pulled into the police station, and I got out of the car before he put it in park. He hadn't bothered with the handcuffs, and he didn't make me sit in the back. When I asked why, he shook his head and said he didn't see any use. I wasn't sure if I should be offended or grateful.

The police station was a small and unimpressive building. It went unnoticed by a lot of people. I was led into an office in the back of the station. The walls were completely white, and there were no pictures of family or certificates on the wall. It looked like it hadn't been used in years. There was a desk with a computer and chairs in front. I was told to sit down in the chair that was in front of the computer. There was a paused video on the screen.

"Press play."

"What is it?" I asked.

"It's the new evidence," Officer Edge explained to me.

The video showed a bridge I was familiar with, and a few seconds passed before two kids came into view. That's when I realized what this video was. It was the night my ex–best friend, Justin Patterson, fell off the bridge, and my life crumbled around me. It was the true reason why I was sent to jail.

I couldn't bear to watch as Justin and I stopped to talk about the party we'd just been to and who the hottest girl had been. There was no volume to the video, and I was partly glad you couldn't hear what Justin and I talked about now. The bridge was known for having a fantastic view of the sunsets. Directors often recorded the sunsets and sunrises there. It hadn't been a mistake that we'd stopped there.

Then it all started to happen. Justin leaned over the rail, and I turned to him and told him that he was going to fall. Honestly, in that moment, I hadn't believed that he was actually going to fall. Stuff like that only happened to other people.

I couldn't handle it anymore. Why were they making me watch this? I had to live it. Why did they think I wanted to see it again? I tried to get up, but the officer put his hands on my shoulders and eased me back into my seat. I understood. This proved I hadn't pushed him. But don't make me *watch* it.

"Just give it a minute."

I didn't want to give it a minute. I didn't want to give it two more seconds, but I couldn't leave. Officer Edge had made that clear enough.

I tried to look away but couldn't. Justin leaned over the rail as the sun was about to set. His feet lifted off the ground, and he fell. I saw myself trying to grab his feet as he toppled over, head first. I'd made contact with his shoe but failed to get a solid grip.

I watched myself stand there, back turned to the camera, which was positioned over us. I remembered it all too clearly. Justin hadn't come up, and I just stood there, which didn't help me very much during the trial. Frankly, I'd been too terrified to move, and that was something I still regretted. Ten seconds later, he still hadn't come up for air. Thankfully, a man had been fishing under the bridge, and he jumped in to save Justin. He turned into a local hero overnight and had countless interviews from the newspapers and local TV channels. He hadn't been modest.

I pressed pause.

"Now we know. You didn't push Justin Patterson off the bridge. He fell when he leaned over the railing. All the charges have been lifted," Officer Edge said.

"This would have been great sooner. But seriously, I want to commend this police department for all its success. Really. Good job. I'm so proud."

My snide comments were ignored.

"There was a man trying to get footage of the sunsets and sunrises. He needed them for a class he was taking. I believe he was an artist. Anyway, one night he fast-forwarded and watched all the sunsets. Something about color change in nature over a period of time. You could imagine his shock when he found this. He sent it in to us because he had a feeling that this was important."

"You guys said that the security cameras over the bridge were broken."

"Yes. They'd been damaged by a storm earlier that week. This camera was put out the day after, when the storms had cleared.

"How convenient."

"I agree. You are lucky that the man picked that bridge."

"What about Justin's parents? What about his brother, Brandon? They're not starting a riot?"

"Oh, that brings us to another topic. As we just saw, it's clear that you didn't push Justin. It was completely his fault. Obviously, Justin's parents would naturally believe their son over you, but that doesn't excuse Justin from withholding information. He also lied to the police when he told us that you threatened him. He still claims he doesn't remember that night."

"Have I mentioned he's a liar?"

The policeman nodded, and I knew then that he didn't believe the bull Justin fed them. Justin knew I didn't push him. He just didn't want everyone to find out *why* he fell. So he'd blamed me.

But it hardly mattered to me anymore. I would never talk to him again. The only interaction we would ever have again would be when I put my fist into his face.

Everyone knew that I wasn't out to kill anyone and that the Patterson family was awful. I was completely ecstatic. There wasn't a word in any language that could describe the feeling that ran through me. I felt like jumping up and down.

"You still escaped from juvie and resisted arrest, and who knows what other crimes you committed since that time. It was decided that your case would be taken up with the judge directly. He felt bad that you were sent to juvie falsely accused, so he's not going to give you a punishment. If I'm being honest, which I think you deserve, this was the judge's last case before retirement. He wanted out of there. We both had a feeling you went through enough, especially when you walked from Tennessee to Florida. How did you manage that?"

"Carefully."

"Were you barefoot?"

"Most of the way."

"Did you hitchhike?"

"Can't say."

"I knew you wouldn't talk."

"What about now? What's today?"

"The eighth," Officer Edge said.

"Of what month?" I asked.

"Of June." Officer Edge asked me. "Are you feeling all right?"

All right. I wasn't sure I knew what that meant anymore. I hadn't had a decent meal in months. I'd been stuck in the same clothes for a month. The last time I slept in a bed that didn't smell like puke and blood was, besides last night, a month ago. I'd just found out that I wasn't being thrown back into a black hole. I had the worst headache, and I didn't know where I would be sleeping that night. All of these things tend to leave a person on the opposite side of "all right."

At least, I felt like saying that.

"I'm fine. Where am I staying?"

"Right, that's already been arranged," Officer Edge said.

"How? When?"

"When we viewed the video and learned that you were back in town, we contacted some foster families to see if any would be willing to take you. The state and courts thought it would be best not to send you to a group home. There was only one willing couple, and even they were hesitant. Their names are Stacey and Joshua Haney. I suggest you respect them. They are being gracious to take you in on such short notice. I wouldn't push my luck much further if I were you."

The last part of his minispeech rolled over me like a weak wave. I knew not to push my luck. The Haneys had to be slightly insane to take their chances on me.

"Do you have anything you want to take with you?"

"No. When are we leaving?" I'd thrown the peanut butter and bread away. Macey would be fine without the socks.

"Now, if you want to. I'll just call social services," Officer Edge said. He stepped out of the office to place the call.

CHAPTER 8

As much as I tried to act like a toughened teenage boy, I couldn't deny that I looked forward to a dinner. It didn't even have to be a good dinner. I just wanted dinner. I also looked forward to a hot shower. I couldn't remember the last time I hadn't felt salty. I really needed a haircut too. My hair was always in my eyes. I thought of cutting it myself, but I'd probably end up sticking my eye.

The Haneys' driveway was long and uphill. Their house was at the end of the neighborhood and about a ten-minute walk to the beach, and it was relatively close to Macey's house. Maybe this wouldn't be horrible.

I got out of the back of the car, took a deep breath, and tried to gear myself up. Why did I feel nervous? I could do this. They should be the ones that were nervous. Not me. I was just along for the ride.

Still, I hoped that they weren't like some other foster families I'd stayed with, but even if they were, I was older and stronger. I could handle myself. The social worker that had replaced Officer Edge never stopped attempting to make conversation with me, even as we walked up to the front door. I finally interrupted him with my own question.

"Do they know everything? Have they seen the video?" I asked.

"Of course they have. They know just as much as we do."

"That makes me feel a thousand times better. You guys took quite a while to find out the truth."

The Haneys walked out of the house and watched us walk up to the screened-in porch. I didn't even have to think before there was conversation.

"It's nice to meet the both of you," Mr. Haney said. It was corny, but there wasn't anything much better to say. He clapped me on the back, and I winced. I couldn't recall it, but I'd probably landed on my back when I fell.

Mr. Haney was a six-foot-tall, skinny man with brown eyes and thinning hair. His teeth were a little crooked, and his white tennis shoes with the long, white socks weren't doing too much in his favor. His wife stood about five feet seven inches. She had curly red hair with green eyes and pale skin. She had perfect teeth, but unlike her husband, she could have lost a few pounds. "Chase, why don't you head upstairs while I talk to Mr. and Mrs. Haney?" The social worker asked me.

It was a rhetorical question, and I knew I couldn't say no. Mrs. Haney directed me upstairs. I walked up the brown-carpeted stairs, looking for a bathroom. I was in desperate need of a shower. I walked down the hallway and entered a bathroom that was off of what I guessed to be my new room. For the time being, anyway. They would get sick of me soon enough.

I looked into the mirror for a long time. The cut on my forehead wasn't deep and had already scabbed over, but it hurt to touch. The mirror wasn't full length, but I still could easily see my top ribs through the skin. I would need a Big Mac and a milkshake to fill that out. I hardly looked like the person I remembered.

I took a greatly needed shower and smelled less like a homeless drug addict after. I grabbed a towel and walked to the room that I guessed was mine. I pulled on my shorts and didn't bother to put the shirt on because it was covered in my blood. I didn't think the Haneys would appreciate that. I looked in the drawers for something to wear but came up short. I knew I couldn't go downstairs half naked, so I unwillingly put on the shirt and walked downstairs.

I thought about Macey. I wanted to see her for a reason I couldn't place a finger on, and it annoyed me. I didn't have the time or energy to deal with that kind of stuff. My life had started to fall back into its own messed-up order, and I intended to keep it that way. I walked into the huge kitchen, where the Haneys were cooking dinner.

"Hey," I said. I leaned against the wall and looked down at the floor. I liked to pretend I had more confidence than I actually did. They both turned around, shocked that I'd made an effort to talk to them. Honestly, I was just as shocked as they were.

"Hello," they answered back.

"What's cooking?" I asked.

"Um, steak, potatoes, rolls, and yellow rice," Mrs. Haney said.

My mouth watered at the sound of the words, and the smell made me weaker than I already felt. I hugged around my midsection to distract from how freakishly skinny I was.

"Do you like that?" Mr. Haney asked.

"I haven't had a meal that good in months," I told them, which might have added a bit more tension. "This will be great."

They laughed nervously, and Mrs. Haney messed with her ring on her finger. No one in the room had made direct eye contact.

"Thanks," I said quickly, hardly believing what I was about to do.

"Pardon?" Mrs. Haney questioned.

"For letting me staying here. I know you guys probably don't want me living with you. I wouldn't want me living with me. I don't know what the police told you—probably that I'm a thief and a liar. Those things are true, but I only steal when I'm really hungry, and I only lie when needed. You don't have to count your silverware. I know that doesn't sound too reassuring, but I'll try not to get in a situation where I need to lie or steal. Honestly, I just want to fly under the radar for the rest of my life. I'm sick of all the running and attention, and I'm sure the police are tired of running after me. I honestly can't believe that you guys agreed to this."

They stared at me a few more seconds and told me that it was no trouble at all. I knew that was a lie.

The smell of the food was about to make me go insane. I couldn't stop biting the insides of my cheeks. The food was on my plate, and Mrs. Haney and I waited for Mr. Haney to sit down. I willed him to hurry, but he seemed take his sweet time. When he finally sat down, I immediately started to eat. The food tasted ten times better than the chicken nuggets and cupcake.

"What did you do to your forehead?" Mr. Haney asked.

"I fell off a fence," I answered, and I had a feeling that wasn't the last question. It never was.

"And your foot?" he asked.

"A rock cut it."

"I got the medicine for the staph infection. You need to take one after you eat," Mrs. Haney said.

"Did insurance cover it?" I asked.

"You don't need to worry about that," Mrs. Haney told me.

"How did you get the blood on your shirt?" Mr. Haney asked me.

I looked down at it and wished I had been able to change. I wondered if they would buy me new clothes. Did I have to ask for that kind of stuff with them? I probably needed a job.

"I'm not entirely sure," I admitted.

"That reminds me. I went shopping. I didn't get you too many things because I wasn't sure what you liked. The guy in the store tried to help me, but I don't know if I did a good job. The clothes are upstairs. Did you find your room? It's the one that's connected to the bathroom," Mrs. Haney rambled.

"I did."

After a few minutes, Mr. Haney cleared his throat and started to speak. "Look, with every foster child, we ask them what they need from us. It tends to make things a lot easier, and we know you've been through a lot. Especially these past few months."

I put down my fork. Was he serious?

"Nothing, thanks."

We ate in silence after that.

CHAPTER 9

A few mornings later, I finally looked through the bag of clothes that Mrs. Haney bought for me. Until this point, I'd just grabbed whatever was on top. I've never been one who particularly cared what the label on a shirt was, but my heart did skip a beat or two when I pulled out the clothes that had been given to me.

They still had the price tags on them, and I added them up in my head. The number came out to about one hundred seventy-five dollars.

The cost of all the clothes I'd ever owned probably didn't come close to that number.

Life wasn't too bad.

My foot was a lot better than it had been, and I only had five more days until I was through with the horse-sized pills. The cut on my forehead was pretty much gone, and the headaches were less severe and frequent. Macey's face was clear as ever in my mind's eye.

I'd also gained two pounds.

I walked downstairs to find breakfast on the table. I ate the toast, biscuit, and bacon while I thought about how I'd gone the past month without any breakfast. It was almost an unsettling change, but I could adapt to this without complaints. Mr. and Mrs. Haney walked in the dining room, and I sat up straighter.

"Are you guys doing anything today?" I asked.

"We were thinking the three of us could go out to lunch. A new restaurant opened up on the beach, and it's gotten some good reviews," Mr. Haney said.

"Fun." The Pattersons had taken me to a few restaurants over the years, but that was it.

"Okay, then there's no way Leo's can let you down."

I'd gotten along okay with the Haneys. The tension had really declined within the past two days, and we were nearly comfortable with having a real conversation. They asked a lot of questions, but I couldn't blame them too much. They had a right to know about the strange kid who woke up screaming in the middle of the night. Not that I told them the truth.

They'd even enrolled me in the tenth grade at the high school. Though it had only been a few days, I could tell this couple wouldn't turn around one day and hit me for no reason. There wasn't a smell of cigars in the house, and the fridge was free of beer. I'd checked. Unless I did something to really make them mad, I would be fine. It would be a nice change from previous foster homes I'd been so *privileged* to stay in. Now, if I could only stop flinching every time they raised their hands. They'd noticed.

———

We walked into Leo's and sat at a table for three. There was a string of restaurants on the stretch of beach and a few stores mixed in, so the area was lively. I could easily get lost in the crowd, which I found comfort in. I could smell the ocean.

Both adults ordered water, and I ordered sweet tea. That was one of the many things I hadn't had in ages, and I got my hands on a glass whenever I could. I looked around the restaurant for anyone I might know, but I came up short. Good. I didn't feel like talking or explaining anything to anyone. People loved to jump to conclusions, and I was in no mood for that.

Then I looked down to the beach where, as fate would have it, I saw a girl that looked strangely like Macey. Or what I imagined Macey to look like.

"Can I go down to the beach really quickly? I think I see one of my friends," I asked before I realized what I'd said. "Please? I'll be quick, and I'll try not to pull a gun on anybody. Swear."

"Go on ahead. I'll call you over when our drinks get here," Mrs. Haney said and waved me off.

I quickly thanked them before they could change their minds. I jumped down the stairs and started to walk toward Macey. I wasn't sure what I was doing or what I would say to her.

But my ego took over, and I called out her name. "Hey, Macey."

She turned around and the wind whipped her hair. "We keep running into each other. You're not followin' me around are you?" she asked and smiled.

"Of course not. Are your parents down here?"

"No. They're up there eating," she said and pointed to another restaurant up the beach. "What happened to your forehead? That wasn't there the last time I saw you."

"I fell."

She rolled her eyes at me. "Thanks. But how?"

"Fighting hybrid aliens."

"A hybrid alien? Okay. I'll play your game. What kind of hybrid alien?"

I smiled as coolly as I could, but my mind raced. I had no idea what the heck hybrid meant. I'd just seen it on car commercials and thought it sounded cool. "What kind of hybrid alien? You want to know? It's classified information. The CIA said I couldn't say anything about it."

She narrowed her eyes at me. "You have no idea what hybrid means, do you?"

"No clue."

"A hybrid is a mix or cross of something," Macey said. She took a few steps into the water, and I followed her. "And I'm fairly certain the FBI would handle that kind of case."

"Fine. Um, a hybrid shark alien thing," I said. We stood in about a foot of water. It was murkier than usual, but I didn't think about that too much.

I looked to make sure no one was around. "Actually, a cop came after me, and I took off. I would have gotten away, but I made the stupid mistake of climbing a fence, and I fell off. That's how I got this thing on my forehead. I actually passed out for a long time." I paused for effect. "The charges were also dropped."

I was about to go into more detail, but a big wave came, and I felt something wrap around my leg. There wasn't any pain for a few seconds but then it felt like I was being shocked. I fell down and swallowed a gallon of salt water. I coughed and wiped the water off my face. I lifted my leg out of the water and saw a jellyfish with long tentacles wrapped around my leg. I hauled myself out of the water, ripped the jellyfish off, and threw it across the sand. I wanted it as far away as possible.

"Chase!" Macey screamed as she jumped out of the water. "What happened?"

I pointed to the jellyfish a few feet away. I didn't trust myself to speak.

"Are you all right?" She thrust down her hand and pulled me up.

"I'm fine," I said. My head was down, and I fought back tears. I needed to get myself under control. It was just a sting. Only a sting.

"What is that?" Macey asked. She cringed as she looked at the creature I had thrown. It was a brilliant blue and lay motionless.

"I don't know. Some kind of jellyfish, I guess. Listen, I have to go back. The Haneys didn't even want me come down here in the first place. See you around." I quickly turned around and walked away. My leg urged me to quit with every step. It felt like it might give out.

The Haneys greeted me as I sat back down, a fake and pained smile plastered on my face. What had that thing been? My leg stung and throbbed. I gripped the table.

"Who did you see down at the beach?"

"Oh, just someone." I bit the insides of my cheeks. My leg. Oh. My leg. It burned now.

"From school?" Mrs. Haney asked. She tried to make small talk.

I couldn't stand it anymore. I felt like throwing up. "Listen, I got in the water and this thing stung me. It hurts. Like, really hurts." The burning worsened.

"Did you see what it was?" Mrs. Haney asked, and concern filled her voice.

I was about to answer when a wave of nausea crashed on me. It felt like electricity was zipping up and down my body, and my heart felt a little funny.

"I think I might need to go to the hospital."

The rest of the time was a blur. Mr. Haney threw a ten-dollar bill on the table, and I limped out of the restaurant (turning a few heads) and dragged myself into the backseat of the Haneys' car. We drove to the hospital, and the burning never let up. My leg was inflamed and splotchy. I kept my head between my knees. We pulled into the hospital parking lot, and I was quickly given a room. The doctors asked what happened, but I couldn't get my thoughts together. What had happened? I could feel my heartbeat against my chest, and it got harder to breathe. It felt like my throat was closing up. I couldn't get enough air. There was a buzz of noise around me.

———

I woke up slowly. I was in a hospital bed, but I still had on my regular clothes. My body felt heavy, and my head pounded. I looked down at my hands and instantly wished I hadn't. Angry red welts popped, out and they itched and stung at the same time. Tiny dots of red blood seeped out. I tried to rub it away but to no avail. My leg wasn't wrapped, and I guessed that was a good thing because it felt like all the skin had been ripped and shredded through a meat grinder then thrown to the wolves for a snack and then sewn back on. I could have been stabbed by a thousand knives, been beaten, thrown in a volcano, and not known the difference. But perhaps I was being a little dramatic.

I sat up and felt woozy just as the door opened, and the Haneys walked in.

"Hey," I offered.

"What happened?" Mrs. Haney demanded. "Why in the world would you get in the water? We were supposed to be having lunch. You scared us half to death."

Mr. Haney shot something back in my defense. "You were the one that let him go out in the first place. He would have been perfectly fine if he would have stayed at the table."

Mrs. Haney shot a death stare at her husband, and I could tell a fight was about to start. All because of me.

"Come on, guys. Let's not play the blame game here. I'm fine. Honestly."

"You're not fine. The doctor thinks you were stung by a Portuguese man-of-war and that you might be allergic to the toxins, judging by what happened and how quickly. It's supposed to be extremely painful."

"I second that," I said. "How much longer do I have to stay here?" I was ready to leave. I was in the hospital way too much, and I'd never gotten that sweet tea.

"We'll go and check with the doctor." Mrs. Haney eyed Mr. Haney, and I had a feeling their fight about whose fault it was wasn't over. They excused themselves and left, but I could still hear the bickering when the door closed.

I lay back down. Why did I have to mess everything up with everyone I met? It felt like some sicko controlled my life from behind closed doors. Every time something went the slightest bit right, something had to go horribly left.

Then I got a visitor.

At first, I didn't speak. I didn't trust my eyes. Maybe I was hallucinating. Maybe I was allergic to the toxins, and it had messed with my head. Why would he be here? Out of all people, why him? How did he know?

"Brandon? What are you doing here?" I asked. Brandon Patterson was Justin Patterson's (my ex–best friend's) older brother. I immediately felt more defenseless than I had in a long time. He had no business there.

Brandon had helped me a lot over the years and had given me a lot of his old stuff. I had worn his old clothes and shoes and used his old book bags. He had always been the one who remembered to leave the back window unlocked so I could climb in if I needed to. He always seemed to be more concerned with my well-being than Justin was. But that didn't excuse the fact that he believed I actually tried to murder Justin.

He saw my weariness. "Don't worry," Brandon said and checked behind himself. "Justin and my parents aren't here," he said. After a pause, he asked, "Have you seen the video yet?"

"Yeah. Why are you here? How did you find me? Are you mad? Because I swear if you take one step closer to me, I'll scream and get you arrested."

"No. Don't do that. Do you know what stung you?"

"A jellyfish."

"What kind?"

"A Portuguese man-of-war."

"That's not even a jellyfish."

"Whatever."

"Who are those people?"

"What people?" I asked.

"The people you're staying with."

"You mean my foster parents? Come on, Brandon. We've been over this. It's not a bad word. I'm not going to start crying because you bring that detail up."

"It's a pretty big detail that you don't have parents."

"Thanks."

"Right. Actually, that might not be completely true," Brandon said. "That's what I need to talk to you about. Just try to keep an open mind."

"That's not going to happen. You do come from a family of compulsive liars."

"And you don't lie? Please, Chase. That's the whole foundation of your bad-boy reputation."

"When I lie, it doesn't ruin people's lives and end them up in jail on false accusations. I lie to survive."

"I'm not the one that lied, Chase. Stop treating me like I was the one that did."

"Then tell everyone to stop treating me like I tried to murder my best friend," I shot back.

"Justin agreed to tell everyone the truth."

"Isn't he delightful? But if my memory serves me right, he's a liar."

"He says he learned how to lie from you," Brandon said.

"Obviously, he didn't take notes, because he got caught."

"There was video proof."

"A good liar makes sure all the loose ends are tied up."

"I believe we're getting off track here."

"Do stand on the tracks. I think I hear a train coming."

"Funny," Brandon said and crossed his arms.

"I thought you had something important to tell me."

"Right. But please do try to keep an open mind. All right? Okay. I guess I should start at the beginning. Or the only beginning I'm sure about. Don't ask questions till the end. All right? I hardly believe this myself. A man came to my house while I was home alone and told me that he worked for the CIA. Obviously, I didn't believe him, and I threatened to call the police. Then he started talking about my mom and dad. Apparently, when I was around three, the Pattersons adopted me, but I didn't even know this until the man told me. Sure, I thought it was weird how I didn't look like them or Justin, but there are plenty of kids like that. Can you believe it? All these years, and they never told me. He showed me a picture of Mom, Dad, you, and me. I think we were in the hospital after you'd been born."

He tried to find the right words. He'd always been a bit awkward. Especially when he was lying. Like now.

"Chase, we're brothers. Our dad worked for the CIA, and no one knows where our parents are now."

I rolled my eyes. "Anything else?"

"That's what the man told me. He texted me about thirty minutes ago and said that you were here. He insisted that I come and tell you everything. I told him you wouldn't believe me. He said that it was time we found out. He said we needed to prepare because stuff was about to happen," Brandon explained. He'd used too many pronouns for my liking.

"How could I believe you? Is this your idea of a joke? Did Justin put you up to this? We're not brothers. Your parents are the Pattersons. Justin is your brother, not me. No CIA agent talked to you. Do you think I'm an idiot?"

I was furious. I wanted to get up and punch him in the face until his nose broke. It was the dumbest and the most haphazardly put-together story I'd ever heard. It was almost funny that he thought he could get to me. Once drama ended with this family, they stirred it right back up again, and I always seemed to be the main ingredient.

And it was awfully sick to tell an orphan he had parents.

Still, he seemed nervous. He was checking over his shoulder and talking quietly, like he was expecting someone to jump out of the supply closet and attack him.

"Please believe me. You and I look more alike than Justin and I."

"Prove to me that we're brothers."

"How am I supposed to do that?"

"I don't know. That's your problem, not mine," I told him matter-of-factly. He couldn't prove it because we weren't brothers. The CIA? Please. The story would have been more believable if he told me that an alien had told him all of this.

"Why don't you believe me?" he asked me.

"I don't know. Maybe it's because the rest of your family are obsessive liars and like to ruin lives. Are you even listening to yourself? That story is insane. I don't have any family," I said and rolled over so my back faced him. I didn't want to see his face.

"Fine," he said to my back. "Don't believe me, but listen to this. You don't know a thing about your real family. They could be royalty for all you know. But they aren't. Our father worked for the CIA. Why would that agent come and tell me? And how did he know you were here? Why didn't he tell me sooner? Like years ago? Why didn't he tell you too? Why didn't they take us in for protection? And don't you find it a little odd that all of a sudden there's evidence that puts you in the clear?"

I turned back around.

"Something bigger is going on. If our dad worked for the CIA, don't you think that he would have made some enemies? What if he knew some big secret? What if criminals think we know something? The agent said something about an underground terrorist group called Ares, but he had to leave because my parents pulled up in the driveway. My parents," Brandon said, disgusted. "I can't believe they never told me. Cowards. Anyway, the underground group—I don't even know what that is, but it sounds pretty awful. Before he ran out the back door, he told me to meet him at the pier on Monday. He instructed me to bring you."

"Are you even listening to yourself?"

"You still don't believe me," he said, miserably. "I'm trying to help you."

"Don't act surprised that this isn't working out for you. For all I know, I could be hallucinating. You need to leave now." I hoped Brandon would leave before Mr. and Mrs. Haney came back. That was a discussion that I was not geared up for.

"Fine. Be there around one on Monday. I'll be there, and the guy can explain everything ten times better than I did," Brandon Patterson said. "I don't think we're safe, Chase Miners." A few seconds later I heard the door slam, and he was gone.

I had already decided to go the pier.

Although this could be a dream—and I was half convinced it was—he seemed really miserable that I hadn't believed him. It didn't look like he had lied either. When people lie, they usually have a tick. I knew Brandon's: he shifted from side to side. But he hadn't done that. So, maybe he had told the truth. Or maybe he had become a good liar. Just like his brother.

But still. Could my dad have worked for the CIA?

Nah, that was stupid. My parents were probably young druggies. They weren't CIA agents who knew some big secret. That was outrageous.

The doctor was different from my last visit at the hospital. She came in, and immediately her eyes flickered to my forehead. I groaned. I wished it had been the same doctor so I wouldn't have to explain everything. Doctors were the nosiest people.

"What happened to your forehead?"

"I fell."

She narrowed her eyes. "How?"

"Off a fence. I already came here about that."

She inspected my hands and leg. As fate would have it, the leg that the Portuguese man-of-war stung was the same leg that had the staph-infected foot.

"All right, what happened there?"

"I jumped out of a tree and landed on a rock," I lied.

"Barefoot?"

"I was at the beach."

The doctor seemed to buy it. After all, it was partly true.

I was released from the hospital forty minutes later with bottles of painkillers and the instructions to come back if it was hard to breathe. During the car ride home with the Haneys, I didn't say much. My mind was in a restricting haze. If I talked, I was afraid I would spill everything, and the Haneys would think I was crazy. I wasn't even sure what "everything" was. I played back the conversation I'd had with Brandon over and over, and a thousand more questions hit me every second. I'd never been told what happened to my parents. It had never bothered me too much. I wasn't sure I wanted to know why they hadn't been able to take care of me. No reason could make me forgive them. It wasn't likely the CIA had employed them—they hadn't even been able to take care of a baby, after all—but it wasn't impossible.

I wished it were.

When we got into the house, I grabbed a Pop-Tart and limped upstairs before Mrs. Haney went into lecture mode. I'd gotten an earful on the way back.

I hopped into the bed and screamed into the pillow. When had my life gone completely haywire? This wasn't fair. I tried to do the right things. Obviously, I hadn't tried hard enough. If I had been smart, I would have never gotten into the habit of sneaking out and stealing. Maybe if I hadn't had a record, I wouldn't have had to go to jail after the whole bridge incident. I closed my eyes. I wanted sleep desperately. My leg and hands were on fire, and I thought going to sleep might numb the pain. The pills the doctor had given me decreased the swelling and eased some of the pain.

My mind drifted to my walk from juvie to Florida. I remembered always being hungry, thirsty, and sunburned. Of course, the time I lost my shoes to a muddy swamp wasn't something I could easily forget. All attempts to find the shoes were in vain. It was bad luck if you were just taking a stroll down a road and happen to lose a shoe. It was horrible luck if you were in the middle of Georgia and still had miles and miles to walk. Barefoot.

I had to walk slower to avoid injury to my bare foot. Nonetheless, I still managed to get my foot cut, and that made it a challenge to walk.

I'd been forced to hitchhike with an empty stomach and a dry mouth. I'd had a headache and was extremely irritable. My own breathing got on my nerves. I hadn't even meant to hitchhike, really. I had been walking along the side of a dirt road that was mildly busy. I didn't have enough energy to jump into the cover of the woods every time a car came by. At that point, I had almost hoped that the police would find me so I could get out of the sweltering heat. Cars always sped up when they passed me, like they were ashamed not to pull over and help the kid that hobbled along the side of the road. Or maybe it was the orange jumpsuit that was turning people off.

There were two pickup trucks that slowed down, and one was just to toy with me. The driver acted like he was stopping, but at the last second he stepped on the accelerator and sped down the road, kicking up a lot of dust.

The second truck slowed down, and I anticipated he would speed off like the last one. When he pulled over, I was greeted by loud country music that blasted from the stereo. The passenger was a guy who looked to be about nineteen.

"It's a little dangerous for such a young kid to be walking alone," he told me.

"Aren't you a little young to have a beer in your hand?" I shot back.

"Fair enough. What happened to your shoes?" he asked as he looked down at my bare feet.

I pointed behind me. "Miles back and three feet underground."

"Where are you headed?"

"Northern Florida."

"That's a pretty long walk for a kid in an orange jumpsuit missing shoes. Did you break out of Upwards? I did a few months there a few years back. Hated every second of it. Is Mr. Haneswroth still there? I hated that man," he said.

"Are you going to give me a ride or not?" I said.

The passenger looked over to the person in the driver's seat. "I don't know. Hey Phil, You feelin' Florida?"

The driver leaned over to get a look at me. "I thought we were going to the movies."

"Come on. The poor kid is barefoot and a pile of bones. We can't leave him out here. It's about to rain," the passenger said to the driver. "Anyways, he's a fellow Upwards man."

"Which means he's a convicted criminal. Excuse me if I don't want him near my brand-new truck."

"You let me in here, and I'm a convicted criminal. And what is he going to do? Rob us? The kid is like ten, dude," the passenger said back. "We can take him. Think about it. How happy would you have been if someone had given you a ride if you broke out of Upwards? And northern Florida isn't that far. Two and a half hours if we speed, and we can hit up the beaches."

"Remember what my little cousin did when she was ten? Set the house on fire. And she had a broken arm," Phil said. He casually put his foot on the gas and started to inch forward. "Anyway, helping an escaped convict is against the law."

"So is having an open beer in the car," I said quickly. I was desperate.

"Really?"

"Yeah. The fine for being caught is a minimum of eight hundred dollars. Probably more if you're underage. They might even put you in jail for a few nights. It would be really bad if the police got a call saying that someone had broken the law, don't you think?" I checked the license plate and tapped my head. Hopefully they knew that I'd memorized the sequence.

The thunder rumbled in the distance.

"Fine. Get in," Phil said and waved me to climb into the backseat.

I snapped my eyes open. Enough with the memories.

———

The next morning, my leg was stiff and still stung. I didn't want to get up, but the sun was bright. It must have been around eleven, and my stomach growled. I literally rolled out of bed and limped down the steps to the kitchen, which was brightly lit with brand-new steel appliances that most people only dreamed of owning. I wondered what these people did for a living. The whole house screamed Florida. It was painted with bright and happy colors inside and out. The fridge was as wide as my arm spam and filled with all different sorts of food. I grabbed some milk and drank it from the carton. I snatched two bagels and ate them cold.

I heard the Haneys' footsteps, and I quickly put up the milk and bagels. One of the families I'd stayed with didn't appreciate things being left out or the fridge being open for too long.

"Did you sleep well?" Mrs. Haney asked.

"Okay."

"How is your leg?" she asked.

"It could be better."

"The doctor told me that you should take it easy for a few days," Mr. Haney told me.

"I can just sit around here and watch TV?"

"I suppose so," Mr. Haney said and sat down across from me.

"Can I see your leg?" Mrs. Haney asked.

I brought my leg out from under the table and showed it to her. It had red welts up and down that kind of looked like a spider web had blown onto my leg and cooked it. Honestly, it looked worse than it should have.

"Oh my. I burned the tip of my finger last month and I cried for days," Mrs. Haney laughed. "I can imagine that hurts quite a bit."

After a few moments of awkward silence, I told them I was going upstairs to take a shower. As if it would wash away my problems.

I thought about Brandon. Was I sure he had been lying? I didn't see why he would lie to me. I hadn't pushed Justin off the bridge, and he knew that. There was really no reason for him to be mad at me. Actually, he had no right to be mad at me. I had all the right in the world to be mad at his family. And I was.

I had till Monday to figure out the whole pier thing. How was I going to get there? Surely, I would be able to walk better by then. I couldn't exactly bring the Haneys with me. What if Brandon or this (possibly pretend) agent tried to talk to me?

No. I had started to believe the lie, and that couldn't happen. If I started to believe the lie, then Brandon would win. I needed to come back to reality. My parents weren't entangled with the CIA, and Brandon wasn't my brother.

I turned on the shower.

Still, I wanted to see if Brandon would show up at the pier. Would he bring one of his friends to play the part of the agent? After all, this did seem like a game to him. I had to go to the pier.

I decided to bring someone with me so the agent wouldn't try anything, but I didn't exactly have any friends that I was dying to see. Then I remembered Macey. I knew I'd freaked her out yesterday. One second we were both perfectly fine and then the next second, I was going crazy. Who knows what she thought of me now? Not like she'd had a good impression of me the first go around or the second. She probably thought I was insane, and I couldn't have that.

I decided that I would take Macey to the pier. If Brandon was there, he would think I was at the pier because of her, not because I believed the outrageous story he'd told me. Anyway, I wanted to see her again. Surely, nothing bad would happen. Brandon had been lying. Hadn't he?

CHAPTER 10

I watched TV on Monday morning. I watched it every morning, but today was different. I desperately wanted it to be one o'clock. It was only nine thirty, and I hadn't planned to go to Macey's house until twelve. I was anxious to see if Brandon would go through with his lie.

I was anxious about a lot of things.

I told Mr. and Mrs. Haney I was bored and needed exercise around twelve. I took Mr. Haney's old bike to go riding. I told them that moving around helped relieve the soreness in my leg, which wasn't a complete lie.

Thankfully, my leg didn't sting as much as it had been, and my hands were almost back to normal. I was pretty much up for whatever.

I got to Macey's house with no problem. The ride didn't take more than fifteen minutes.

I had about twenty dollars in my pocket, but there was no way I was going to need all of it. The food at the pier was dirt-cheap, and it tasted that way. My heart started to beat quickly. What if Macey wasn't here? I hadn't even thought of that.

I was about to knock on the front door when I heard Macey in the backyard. Good. She was here. I didn't want to knock on the door and face whoever answered it. Her parents probably wouldn't be keen to see me.

I walked around the side of the house and called out. "It's Chase. Nobody shoot."

"Speak of the devil," Macey said sweetly. "What happened to you?"

I held up my hands and turned my leg so she could see the damage.

"Ouch. Looks like a spider web."

"Yeah. I had to go to the hospital."

"Really? Why?"'

"Something about intense and excruciating pain and being allergic to the toxins."

"Are you okay now?"

"I'm good," I answered.

"Do you know what kind it was? Jellyfish, I mean."

"Portuguese man-of-war."

"Chase, that's not even a jellyfish."

"I seem to be the only one that doesn't know that," I muttered and thought of Brandon. "You play soccer?"

She looked down at the soccer ball at her feet and back up at me. "I don't know."

"Soccer is a great sport," I said. I took a seat on the grass and waited. All of a sudden, I really didn't want to go the pier. I just wanted stay here and forgot the whole thing. It was easy to forgot troubles when the sun was so brilliant and the wind was cool. Then I thought of Brandon. That look on his face...

"Really? Most people say different."

"If you're a girl," I finished.

That didn't go over well with Macey. I knew it wouldn't. That had been the point in the first place. She picked up the soccer ball and heaved it at my head, and I ducked at the last second. "I guess a soccer player's hand-eye coordination isn't that great, huh?"

"Go jump in a hole."

"You read that on the Internet too?" I teased.

"You come over here for any reason? Or are you still stalking me?"

"I was going to challenge you to a little match. I'll get two of my friends and you get two of yours, and we can have a little soccer match. We'll see who wins."

"Please, I don't know anyone besides you. But when school starts, I'll find two other girls that can play, and you can get your baseball buddies to play two forty-five-minute halves, and we'll see if you say soccer is a 'girl's' sport after."

I smiled. "Deal. But first, how about you and I have lunch on the pier? You can explain the rules to me there."

Macey ran inside and told her parents that she was going to ride her bike around the neighborhood. I wasn't exactly sure why she lied, but I didn't bother to ask why. Luckily, she had her bike in the garage, so she didn't have to ride on the handlebars of my bike. I've always found that a bit awkward.

The pier was alive with tourists. Half of them were wearing "Salt Life" T-shirts, which had always been funny to me. Most of them only came to the coast for a week every year.

We didn't have to wait long to get a table at the front of the pier. This wasn't exactly a big, fancy structure, just a few planks of colorful wood that jutted out over the ocean, but "the pier" was what all locals called it. It was roughly one hundred feet long and about twenty feet wide with about twenty tables spread around it. Off to the right of it was a restaurant where people sang karaoke. Off to the left was a hotel with bathrooms by it, separated by an alley. The atmosphere was lively, and there were people everywhere. The day was clear, and the sunlight bounced off the water. It was completely safe. So why were my hands shaking?

I looked behind Macey. There was a man who immediately stuck out to me. He wore a tight black shirt and khaki shorts. He didn't have a tan and seemed like he was searching for someone. Not that that was too weird. Maybe he'd been stood up by his date. He noticed me and looked away. He must be the fake agent. Brandon was running late.

I was frankly impressed with Brandon. He'd come through with his little story.

Maybe I could act like I knew the man and talk to him. I could get him to confess that this all was a big hoax and then laugh in Brandon's face, but then Macey would probably want to follow me. Where was Brandon? He was coming, right? He had seemed so intent in the hospital.

"Dude," Macey said and interrupted my train of thought. "The only thing I know about you is nothing. Besides that you have a problem with lying and the police. A smart girl wouldn't have come to the pier with you."

"What? We know each other perfectly," I defended, distracted. I needed Brandon to get here. The guy in the black shirt was starting to freak me out.

"I don't think we do."

I don't think she meant to, but her eyes flashed to my wrist and then back to me.

My face reddened. She was the first person to notice them. Or at least the first to confront me about it. I slowly retracted my arm and looked away. I hadn't done it for attention. I didn't see anyone for days after I put them there.

"Chase, can I ask you something, and you have to swear that you won't lie?" Macey asked.

"Shoot." I thought she would ask about the scars and why they were there. I didn't want to talk about it.

"You know I don't really believe the story about why you were sent to juvie, right?"

"You don't?" I asked, slightly relieved.

I looked over at the pretend agent, mostly to stall for time. He looked at a boat that was anchored about two hundred feet away from the dock and looked around once more.

She shook her head. "It's a little off. It sounded like something a teenage boy might come up with."

I rubbed my hands on my face. Now that I was proved innocent, I wouldn't mind telling her the story. The whole story.

"I was hanging out with a guy named Justin Patterson after a party, right? School was just about to let out, and on the way to his house, we stopped to watch the sunset on a bridge. This bridge has the best view of the sunsets every night, and half the time there's a sighting of porpoises. That's why we went on that bridge. Justin was being an idiot and leaning over the side of the bridge, trying to make me laugh. I wasn't exactly having a good night. I told him to stop, but he didn't listen. He got top heavy and fell. Head first. I swear I tried to stop him from falling, but he was too heavy.

"The bridge was at least forty-five feet off of the water, so the impact hurt. It was low tide. I didn't jump in after him. I didn't want to get hurt. Besides, I thought he was okay. I thought we were going to laugh about it. I didn't know he was hurt. There was a guy fishing under the bank, and he got Justin out of the water."

I paused and looked over my shoulder. The fake agent's drink had arrived, but he didn't touch it. He stared right at me.

When I didn't say anything else, Macey looked at me a little weird. "That's all? That can't be all."

"You want more?" I wanted to get up and run.

"If you can believe it," Macey said sarcastically.

"Okay, well then I called nine-one-one. I was carrying Justin's phone in my pocket because his shorts didn't have any. I nearly threw up when the fishermen brought him up the bank. He'd hit the stumps of trees. It was more blood than skin, but they told me later that his nose was bleeding, so that made it look worse than it was. They let me ride in the front of the ambulance. After the x-ray, we found out that he had a broken leg and arm and that a vein had busted in his arm. He hit his head on the side of the bridge on the way down. Then his jacked-up parents pressed charges. They thought I'd tried to kill him. They never did like me too much. They thought I was a bad influence. It made it to the juvenile's court and everything. All the evidence looked like I was trying to kill him. They said that jealously pushed me to shove him over the bridge. The orphan killing his friend that had it all. I was told to plead guilty so I would get some counseling or something, but I pleaded innocent, yelled at the judge some, and boom. Juvie for little ol' me."

"Justin didn't say anything in your defense?" Macey asked as she threw a fry to a bird while a waitress gave her a dirty look.

"No. He told them that I'd been mad at him because he was going out with some girl that I liked. Like I would try to murder someone over a girl. Worst of all, there *was* a girl that I sort of liked, but she informed me that she only went out with boys that had a good family, so we never had a chance at a relationship. Then Justin started to go out with her. I wasn't mad at him for that. I had no interest in going out with a girl like that."

"Did you guys have a fight about it? Come on, someone just doesn't throw himself over a bridge and blame it on his best friend for no reason."

"There was no fight. Nothing. Justin lied to the police, and thankfully, they know about it now. Two other guys—Sam and Cam—I'd been friends with them for a long time too, and they actually thought I wanted Justin dead. No one believed me. My record didn't exactly do wonders for me." I decided to come completely clean with her.

"So, why did Justin lie?"

"Because he didn't want his parents to know that he had been drunk. That's why he fell off the bridge. There was no way he was telling his parents that he had been so drunk that he fell off a bridge. His parents would most likely send him to an institution. He made the decision that he would rather send his best friend to jail than explain to his parents that he wasn't perfect.

"During the party, Justin drank three cans of the beer in the bathroom while a couple of junior guys convinced me to have a few sips. After that, because beer was unquestionably disgusting, I drank a whole bottle of water.

"Peer pressure had a score of one. I had a score of zero.

"At that time, it hadn't been that big of deal. Looking back, I wish I'd stood my ground and not had anything to drink. A few hours after Justin woke up, he already decided that he was going to throw me under the bus. He told police that I had been drinking and pushed him over the bridge. So the police interviewed some kids that had been at the party to obtain evidence. One girl told them that she'd seen me drinking. That killed my case. I wasn't sure if Justin actually remembered a lot of the night. Either he'd had more beer than he cared to admit, or he actually didn't remember the night."

"You didn't tell anyone that Justin was drunk?"

I shook my head. "It didn't work. And Justin was in the clear because he claimed he didn't remember anything."

"Justin was one of your best friends, right?"

"Now he's more of the guy who ruined my life. A splinter under my nail. A lash in my eye."

Macey nodded her head. "I'm with you. I hate Justin and his parents. Why did they press charges?"

"I already said they thought I was a bad influence. They just didn't know that Justin was the one that came up with all the stupid ideas. Anyway, I wasn't staying in jail. The food was nasty."

"So, how did you escape?" she asked.

"Walked out."

"But how? I've seen those TV shows. They have guards everywhere," Macey said and tossed another fry in her mouth.

"Not everywhere. It's not exactly like TV. I was the youngest kid there, and at the bottom of the totem pole. Besides, I don't exactly look too threatening. I was the delivery boy for the guards. That gave one more thing for the other guys to hate about me. One day, I had to take some document to a guard, and I saw a blind spot between two towers, so I just walked out and ran until I was in the woods."

"How do I know you aren't lying?"

I shrugged my shoulders. "You don't."

"Fine. Assuming that you are telling the truth, weren't you scared half to death? I would have been if the police had been chasing me. I couldn't handle it," Macey said.

"I didn't handle it."

I had been so caught up in our conversation that I almost didn't notice when the fake agent walked by our table. He ducked in the alley between the hotel and the bathrooms.

I looked around for Brandon.

Nothing.

I quickly excused myself to go to the bathroom and started to walk toward the alley. I had to find out what he was doing. I paused directly outside of the bathroom, which was right next to the small alley, and acted like I was waiting for someone. I heard the man talking on the phone.

"Yes. Yes, sir. No, sir, Chase still doesn't know anything. Yes. His brother is here. Yes. I have been keeping an extremely low profile. Yes—yes, sir. I am aware you are concerned, but these things are harder to complete than you think."

There was a pause while the person on the other side spoke. I was too far away to make out what the person was saying, but all of a sudden I thought Brandon really might have been telling the truth, and my stomach cramped with fear.

"Three days," the man continued. "That's all I need."

Before I could process what this man had said, he was standing in front of me. My heart somersaulted into my stomach. The man's body was way too big for his head, which was oddly small, so he looked like a bobble head. Under ordinary circumstances, I would have laughed and not thought the man was very tough. But the gun that stuck out of his waistband halted any laugher or humor.

Nope. Definitely not one of Brandon's friends.

He blocked all my exits like a football player, and I knew I wasn't going anywhere.

I spoke with my back against the red brick wall. "You're not friends with Brandon?"

He looked down at me. "Why were you eavesdropping? You know it's considered rude."

"No one ever told me that."

The man smirked. "You shouldn't be concerned with my conversations."

"I shouldn't?" I saw the gun again. "I think I should. It's good to be curious. Helps not get into unwanted trouble."

The man regarded me. "You will definitely get your father to talk." The man smiled and grabbed my arm.

I didn't register that his hands were on me. "My father? What are you talking you about? What will get him to talk?" With every question, I grew louder until the guy put his hand on my mouth.

"Shut up." He raised the gun, pushed it in my stomach, and put a pair of dark sunglasses on me; immediately, I couldn't see anything. "Walk, or I'll put two bullets in your back. You scream, and I'll put a bullet in your girlfriend's head. Your choice."

CHAPTER 11

I felt the cold, hard metal in my back and couldn't believe that I managed to get both of my feet to move. What was going on? I couldn't see where I was and nearly tripped over my own feet. The guy had both my hands in an iron grip behind my back, which meant I couldn't do anything about the sunglasses.

I probably looked like a regular kid getting in trouble by his regular father, but I had a feeling if I got a punishment that it might have something to do with bullets and blood. I felt unsteady ground beneath my feet. I was on a boat. He let go of my hands, and I threw the sunglasses off.

"Chase!" I heard someone yell. I think it was Brandon. "Stop! It's a trap! Jump! They made me tell you to come here! They would have killed Justin!"

Honestly, he was a little too late for my liking.

I tried to call for help, but the sound of the motor drowned out anything I had to say. I was slammed into the back wall when the man gunned the boat. I almost went into the water to get ripped apart by the motor, which would have put a real damper on things. The floor of the boat was almost too hot to tolerate.

"What was that about?" I asked after I regained my balance. I stood up and walked toward him. I looked back to see if I could see Brandon, but he was lost among the crowd of people.

I turned around quickly when I heard footsteps and the phrase: "Take care of him."

Two men seized me by my shoulders and threw me to the floor. They wrenched my arms back, put handcuffs on my wrists, and then jerked me up and put me on one of the seats. One of the henchmen grabbed the handcuffs and twisted them, tearing my skin. I saw a small fishing boat near and yelled for help, but one of the men punched me hard in the stomach, and my words died. I doubled over in pain and gasped for breath. I lashed out with my foot and made contact with one of the man's knees, and he stumbled. I started to go for the other guy, but some kind of metal tool was thrashed into my head and I saw stars. I stumbled back and landed back on the seats.

The man with the body too big for his head tossed the other guy duct tape, and he wrapped the lime-green tape around my mouth three times. I resisted as best I could, but the guy held my pounding head straight. I struggled against the handcuffs, but they held tight.

"I see you've met my coworkers." The man gestured to the two men behind him. The man came up close to me, took my chin in his hand, and held it tightly. "It's great to have you, Chase. I do believe this is the part where I tell you why you're here. It would be explicitly rude if I left you in the dark. As Brandon might have told you, your father worked for the CIA as a field agent and made many enemies. Powerful enemies, I might add. When he was much younger, your father came across important information. Now, if the information is used to its fullest power, it could change the world. Your father realized the importance of the information and hid it. That was his first mistake."

"The Krabby Patty secret formula could change the world. A lot of things could change the world."

The man looked at me strangely but continued to enlighten me. "It's easy to hide a few pieces of paper, but it's harder to hide people, especially for a long period of time. Your father went into hiding for quite some time after discovering the information. For protection, he put you and your brother into the foster system. He thought you would be adopted, and you would be safe from people like myself.

"Obviously, he thought wrong. We caught your father, and now we have you. We knew that he was the one that hid the information. We have people in the CIA. We've been trying to get it out of him for some time. See, your father thinks his sons are dead. He thinks he has nothing to lose but his own life. He believes that *you* are dead. Oh, but how bittersweet he will feel when he sees you. You will get him to talk. Of course, the only way to get him to talk is to harm you. Then after he tells us, we will kill you and make him watch. It is well worth it. One life is such a simple thing to pay for the chance of world domination."

One of the henchmen unwrapped the tape from my mouth, and I sucked in air. "You want to take over the world? That's the most idiotic thing I've ever heard, and I go to public school. You don't even know what the information is about, and you never will. My father won't talk. You guys can't prove that I'm his son. You can't even prove to *me* that I'm my father's son. I could just be some random kid that you picked up off the side of the road. He'll never believe anything that comes from you. And even if he did talk, you idiots would never be able to figure out how to use the information. You're raging psychopaths," I rambled. I was too terrified and frantic to stop.

The kidnapper signaled one of his henchmen, and I got slapped in the face. Hard.

"When your father sees you on the ground writhing in pain, he'll break. He'll believe that you're his son. And you want to know why? Because you'll be the one telling him."

"And why would I do that?" I asked. "How do I know I'm his son?"

"I don't want to ruin the surprise." He smiled sickly, and I quickly remembered Macey. He said he would harm her if I didn't do as I was told.

"Please, feel free to indulge me. I don't want the secret to hurt your pathetic and fragile brains."

I should have kept my mouth shut. The henchman made another move toward me, and I flexed my stomach, but I don't think it did any good. His fist felt like a rock. I'm surprised a rib didn't crack. My vision blurred for a few seconds, and I felt like throwing up.

"We have to have him alive." The one that had held the gun to my back said, slightly annoyed. I looked around and noticed a few fishing boats around us and started to yell for help. I briefly wondered if I should throw myself overboard, but I wouldn't be able to swim far with just my legs. I would have to get the handcuffs off first.

One of the men put the stupid duct tape around my mouth again. He grabbed me around the back of my neck and walked up to the man with the gun. "Take him below?"

The man nodded.

Apparently, below meant a storage room that wasn't built for anything alive. I couldn't stand straight in it. The room was three feet wide, four feet long, and probably three feet tall. It was dark except for the light that came from under the door. I tried the door several times, but obviously it was locked. The tape and handcuffs hadn't been removed.

I could feel the boat moving, but I couldn't tell which direction. I started to feel a bit seasick and wondered if I was going to throw up. I knew I couldn't. If I did, I would suffocate. I willed myself to take deep breaths and calm down. My brain felt like it had been thrown through a blender. I was petrified. Where were we going? Where were they holding my father?

Father.

I never had a real reason to use that word. It felt weird just to be thinking about it. Was he okay? How long had they had him? While I was terrified for myself, I was also scared for him. What would happen if he spilled the information? I knew it wasn't possible for them *to take over the world*, but information was powerful. It could be a formidable bartering item.

I was in the room no longer than a minute before I started to get hot. It had to be at least ninety-four degrees outside and the humidity made it feel ten times hotter. I was stuck in a small, dark room with no windows, and I couldn't even wipe the sweat off my face.

I started to panic a few minutes later. It felt like the walls were closing in on me. I tried to take in slow, deep breaths to calm myself down, but the air was so hot it made my lungs burn. I started to kick the door to see if I could get it to move, but it didn't budge. I figured the noise would at least annoy the men on the deck.

I sat down and wiped the sweat off with my knee and thought about breaking down the door. That would at least solve the problem of it being five thousand degrees in here, but it wouldn't solve the problem of my hands being bound or of the three men who had no problem with kidnapping and torturing sitting on lawn chairs fifteen feet above my head.

But there still was the looming fear that I might die if I didn't get out of this room. I began to throw myself against the tiny door. It was more difficult than it should have been because I was on my knees and couldn't put my head up straight without it hitting the ceiling.

By the fifth try, my shoulders killed me, and I was lightheaded. I closed my eyes for a few seconds before hearing footsteps. I had a couple guesses of who it might be. Fear coursed through me again. I backed up as far away as I could from the door.

I sat up and waited as the door creaked open. A man bent down and his face was grim. It was the guy I'd kicked in the knee.

"I suggest you come with me."

I shook my head. It was safer in here.

"Come here now, Chase."

The man's hand shot out and grabbed me by my foot. He pulled it, and in a matter of seconds, I was out of the room.

He took the tape off my mouth and unlocked my handcuffs. At first, I thought he just wanted to free me because he wanted to show just how much stronger he was.

But he didn't hit me.

"All right, Chase. Listen up. We don't have much time, so don't ask questions. All you need to know is that I'm an agent for the CIA. I have a bomb and a getaway boat, but we have to act quickly if we want to live."

The second the sentence was out of his mouth, the bomb that he had taped to the side of the boat exploded, creating a hole about two feet high and one foot across. The explosion made me jump, as if my nerves weren't already damaged enough.

"How are we supposed to get out of that?" There was no doubt that the men upstairs heard it. We had about ten seconds before they got down there and shot us both.

"Like this." He grabbed a fire extinguisher and threw it at the hole in an attempt to make it bigger. It worked and water started to pour in. I heard footsteps again and whipped around to see the two other men running down the stairs, and they didn't look too happy.

"If you jump, I'll find her, and I'll kill her," one of them warned.

I didn't have time to react to the threat. The man who claimed to be a real CIA agent grabbed me and threw me out of the boat. The cool water was refreshing, but I didn't have any time to enjoy it. The man bounded in after me and screamed for me to swim. I didn't need to be convinced to swim away from the boat that was now being swallowed in red-hot flames and had two crazy men with loaded guns. He must have started a fire.

"Down!" he screamed. I took a deep breath and dove down into the water. I opened my eyes so I could see where I was going. A bullet zipped in the water a few feet away from me.

The men in the boat still needed me. Alive. That meant they weren't shooting at me. They must have been shooting at the real CIA guy. That meant I had to get away from him. The people on the fishing boats had to have noticed the enormous boat that was on fire and the gunshots that went off every few seconds. People were either going to come closer to the burning boat or drive away. I doubted they could see me as I bobbed around in the water, and I didn't plan on getting eaten up by a motor. I needed to get away.

I surfaced and looked around for the boat that the man said he had nearby. I saw it a few dozen feet away and was immediately fearful again. It was a tiny fishing boat with a small motor on the back of it. It would have been my last choice to get me out of a tight situation, but it was all I had. I quickly swam over to it, clutched the motor, and pulled myself up. I heaved the anchor up and set it beside me. The man came up out of the water and gasped for breath. I knew I needed to go and get him. I couldn't leave him there to die. He was the only one that knew what was happening.

By now, the fire had engulfed the sinking boat, and the men who had kidnapped me were gone. Had they escaped the burning boat or died? Did someone help them?

The man stuck his hand up in the air and yelled for me to come over to him. I had no clue how to drive a boat, which became an even bigger problem when I saw the kidnappers with their newly acquired speedboat. They'd probably pointed their fancy guns at the people in the speedboat and made them jump. It looked much faster than the one I had.

I located the keys and quickly stuck them in the ignition. I pushed down the throttle a little too fast—the front of the boat went up, and I almost flipped. I eased down on the throttle and turned the steering wheel so that it was facing the CIA agent. I didn't want to go too fast and accidently run him over, but the kidnappers were getting closer to him. They would kill him and then kidnap me again. I couldn't have that.

The spray of the ocean made it hard to see, so I bent down about a foot and a bullet ripped over my head. So much for needing me alive. They were trying to kill me now. The men in the other boat could see I was having trouble so they increased their speed. I choked back a scream and pushed down the throttle. I had to beat the men to the CIA agent.

The throttle was pushed down as far as it would go, and I was pretty sure I was screaming, but I couldn't hear myself over the reverberation of the motor. I said something that might have been a prayer and willed the small boat to go faster.

The kidnappers were incredibly close to the CIA agent, and I knew I had to do something. If I didn't, they would beat me to him. Adrenaline rushed through my veins, and my heart felt like it pumped a thousand gallons of blood a minute.

I saw one of the kidnappers take a gun and aim it at the agent in the water. He was going to shoot him right here. The only logical thing to do was to crash my boat into the side of their boat.

The crash was deafening. I covered my ears with both my hands, but it did little to drown out the sound. Both of the men were thrown out, and for the second time in less than five minutes, their boat caught on fire. I crawled to my boat's controls and felt the heat from the fire on my face. I put the boat in reverse and gunned it backward until I was fifty feet away.

The kidnappers were desperately trying to find something to hold onto so they wouldn't drown, but I wasn't too worried about them. For now, anyway. I was more concerned about the agent.

I screamed at the CIA man, who seemed to be in shock, to swim over to me. He took one last look at the boat that was on fire and started to swim toward me. I breathed a sigh of relief. Maybe I would get out of this mess alive. Once he was close enough, I helped him get in the boat, and he didn't even try to thank me for saving his life. He ran to the steering wheel and turned the boat around. The men in the water screamed and yelled at us to stop. There were more threats regarding Macey.

I hadn't even noticed, but people screamed. We'd caused quite the scene. I saw a boat in the distance that had flashing lights.

Oh no.

I didn't see how we would be able to squirm out of this one. Thankfully, they were headed toward the men and the burning boats, but they were sure to come after us once they realized that the men were fine. Or dead. After all, I had pretty much broken every boating law in the book. Our boat slowly picked up speed, and for a minute I thought it might break down and we would be stuck, stranded in the middle of the ocean, with everyone and his brother trying to catch us, but it kept going along.

"You're welcome," I said. We had been riding now for five minutes, and I still didn't know where we were going.

"We're not secure yet."

"But you're not floating face down in the water with a bullet lodged in your back. A thank you is in order."

The man didn't answer me. A few more seconds went by and then the motor made a few spurting noises and started to smoke. We quickly lost speed and came to a stop about three hundred feet away from the shore.

"That's not good. I'm surprised the motor even lasted that long."

"If you hadn't wrecked the boat, we might not be in this situation," he said and looked around for life jackets or something we could use to make it to shore. He handed me a pink lifejacket with a flower on it, and we put the lifejackets on and jumped into the water.

"If I hadn't wrecked the boat, we would be in a situation worse than this one," I said. This man was starting to anger me. I'd just risked my life to save his, and he hadn't even acknowledged that. "They weren't after me. They were after you. You were doing the exact thing they wanted you to do by going toward them."

It was all right if he wanted to believe that. I'd saved him, and he knew it. Best not to gloat.

"What now?" All I really wanted to do was act like this never happened.

"We go to Virginia."

"Virginia? What's in Virginia? Why do I have to go there?"

"The CIA headquarters is in Virginia. Well, the one the public knows about, anyway. You have to go because you can't wander around out here anymore. It's too dangerous. Today was a close call, and a lot of things went wrong. We have to get your father, secure the information, and then put a stop to the people those men work for. We can't even think about doing that if they have Brandon or you."

"What does the information concern? Nuclear launch codes?"

The man laughed. "It's something much more powerful and delicate than that."

"So no hints?"

"Information is dangerous, Chase."

It had been worth a shot. "You really work for the CIA?"

The agent paused.

"Not technically."

"What do you mean?"

"I work for a secret branch of the CIA."

"Like a spy?"

"Not exactly."

With that, I took off faster for the shore. I didn't know if I could trust this guy, and I didn't plan on sticking around to see if I could. What did he mean? A secret branch?

"Listen to me," the man started, but I didn't pay any attention to him. I was on the shore and had every purpose of booking it until I got home. Then I was going to get under the covers and hope this all was a dream. Then my leg started to sting again. It felt like tentacles were wrapped around my leg all over again. I bit the insides of my mouth. I was exhausted. I just wanted to go home.

"If you don't come with me, you, the Haneys, or Macey, will be killed. Or worse. There are things worse than death."

I didn't answer.

"If they don't kill you, they will kill your friends and the Haneys."

"I'm not going anywhere until you explain this whole 'I work with the CIA, but not really' thing."

"To my family and friends, yes, I do work with the CIA, but that's not the whole truth. Are you familiar with the Cold War?"

I shrugged my shoulders. "Not really. I've heard of it."

"In a simple explanation, it was basically just a threat of war between the United States and the Soviet Union. People were scared about the spread of communism, and they were especially terrified of being accused of being a communist. Do you know what communism is?"

I gritted my teeth. I wasn't stupid. "Yeah."

"Then you understand how damaging it would be to someone's career if they were accused of this. The FBI helped in the conviction of twelve leaders of the American Communist Party. Everyone was terrified of being accused by Joseph McCarthy and the House Un-American Activities Committee. It was known as the Red Scare. Rights were being restricted. Then groups like the NSA, CIA, and the FBI started to get nervous. The NSA and CIA had just been founded, and policies were still being developed. If the government started to restrict these groups, our nation's security would be at risk. The Applied Research Group was formed so if the government rendered these groups useless, America would have a backup agency."

"Applied Research Group? Boring name."

"No one cared to find out what the Manhattan Project was, and we know how that turned out. If you heard someone talking about the Applied Research Group, would you want to find out what it was?"

"Not really."

"Exactly. Some of the most dangerous groups in the world have the most uninteresting names."

I nodded.

"This group contains three branches: the NSA branch, the FBI branch, and the CIA branch, which is the largest. They all have operatives that work in the Applied Research Group, or ARG. The ARG combines information from the three organizations and deals with the problem accordingly if the original agency can't fix the problems. There are so many rules and regulations that it's hard to do pretty much anything without the media scrutinizing every move."

I stared at the man in front of me.

"You seem confused."

"A bit. You work with the CIA, but that's basically just a cover so you can work with the ARG, right?"

"In a sense, yes."

"So, all the ARG does is give information to another agency if they need it?"

The man nodded. We stood on the shore. I shook out my hair and sent water everywhere.

"Among other things," the man whispered.

"And you got assigned to rescue me? How?"

"Your father worked with the CIA, which mainly deals with foreign intelligence, but he wasn't a part of ARG. He became involved with a domestic group that liked to cause quite the stir. That's the FBI's territory. I looked into your father's case and submitted it to the ARG because it involved him, which involves the CIA, and domestic issues. Right now, the ARG expects me to bring you back to the CIA headquarters."

"Why the CIA? Won't people ask questions?"

"People know better than to ask questions. Besides, the ARG doesn't have a headquarters fit for a kid. We barely have a headquarters. The CIA knows I'm bringing you back. My supervisor is with the ARG and the CIA so he knows what's going on. Right now, we have to go to Langley."

"I'm not sure I'm into that."

"You don't have a choice. Come on, we can't talk about this here. We have to go the airport now if we want to catch our flight and stay ahead of the people who tried to kidnap you."

At the time, I didn't find it strange that our plane tickets had already been reserved without him having to place a call. "You're not going to tell the Haneys?"

"They wouldn't let me take you. Besides, we don't have the time. It's better if they know less."

The man pulled me toward town. I still didn't know if I trusted this guy completely. Obviously, he had been working undercover with the men on the boat. But for how long? Had he helped them plan my kidnapping? Who made Brandon tell me to come to the pier? Had he known it was all a hoax?

CHAPTER 12

A mile's worth of walking later, I was in the man's patrol car and on the way to the airport. When I'd asked why he had a patrol car, he informed me that policemen didn't stop other policemen if they were speeding. And he planned to speed.

"The Haneys are going to think I ran away. They'll call the police," I said.

"Don't worry about it. They've been taken care of."

I tried to press the subject, but the man refused to say any more. At this point, I still had questions that I wanted answered, but I knew my mind couldn't process anything else. Besides, I really didn't want to know what he meant when he said the Haneys had been taken care of. I closed my eyes for a few minutes and tried to settle my thoughts. I felt uncomfortable in my wet clothes and wished we could swing by the Haneys' house so I could change.

We had been in the car for a few minutes when I noticed a familiar figure on the sidewalk.

It was Macey. I recognized her shirt.

I immediately sat up. "Hey, there's the girl I was at the pier with. Macey."

The agent cut his eyes her way.

"Shouldn't we do something? Warn her?"

"About what?" he asked.

"They threatened to hurt her. Even you said that they would try and kill her if I didn't come with you. I'd actually prefer she didn't die."

We were probably about four hundred yards away from her when we saw the black Hummer.

The agent groaned, like he had just noticed he was low on gas or something.

"What?" I asked.

"Ares," he whispered.

"Ares?" Brandon had mentioned that name.

"The group that went after you. They call themselves Ares."

"Where did they get a Hummer?"

"I don't know. It might not even be them, but I would bet my job it is," he whispered. "Why is she flagging us down?" he asked and gestured to Macey, who was waving her hands.

"Stop and see what she wants. She might know something. They don't even know it's us, so maybe they'll pass us. I need to tell her to lie low for a few days," I said.

I didn't think he would stop. He hadn't listened to anything I'd said so far, but he slowly pulled up to Macey and blocked her view of the Hummer. I rolled down the window and smiled at Macey, and she blinked a few times.

"Chase? What—what did you do this time?"

"Not important. Listen, did anyone come up and talk to you after I left?"

"No," she said quickly. "Chase, what's going on? What happened?"

"They want to know more about Justin Patterson. It's no big deal. Why were you flagging us down? Did something happen?"

"Yeah, some jerk stole our bikes. I was just going to tell the policeman about it…" She turned her attention to the agent next to me, but before she could say anything, a bullet ripped through the air about ten feet above her head, and we screamed.

The Hummer was only one hundred yards away.

"We have to go," the agent said.

Another shot was fired.

Macey flung open the door and tumbled inside as another rain of bullets came down. She had no intention of waiting on an invitation, and the agent didn't have time to object to his new guest. The Hummer drew closer, and the sound of the engine shook the air. And my nerves. The agent stepped on the accelerator, and the Hummer did the same. Now we were in a foot race. A wheel race. Whatever.

But it was definitely Ares.

Macey's face was completely white, and she took deep breaths. I probably didn't look much different. We were both in the back.

"Chase? Care to explain?" she screamed.

"Um..."

Before I could even think of something to tell her, the black Hummer crashed into the back of our much smaller car, and we jutted forward. I slammed my head against the back of headrest and groaned.

"Go!" I screamed at the agent, and I think we caught air for a second.

I heard the agent mutter something and then he smacked his forehead. "Chase, hand me the duffel bag."

I grabbed the bag next to me and handed it to the agent. He took his hands off the wheel, rummaged through the bag, and produced a green object.

"Is that a bomb?" Macey asked, shock rising in her voice.

"Yes," Agent Dotson said as he pressed a few buttons and threw it out the window.

I didn't turn around to watch the initial explosion, but I heard it. Macey and I then whipped around and watched the events unfold. The Hummer tipped over and started to tumble and gain speed.

I screamed something unintelligible.

Thankfully, the agent was smart enough not to try to outrun the huge truck. He veered off to the right of the road, and the car crashed into a swampy area.

The front of our car was quickly submerged in the water, and the rest of the beaten-up car followed. We'd missed hitting a tree by a few inches. The agent rolled down the window in the front and quickly climbed out. There was a lot of screaming, yelling, and confusion as water started to seep into the car. Macey shimmed out onto the roof, and I followed her. Twenty seconds after the crash, all three of us were on the roof.

Macey nudged me out of the way and then leaped onto the bank.

"Hurry up, Chase," she warned. "It's sinking."

The agent and I copied her technique, but I didn't complete it as gracefully as I would have liked. My feet slipped into ankle-deep mud, but that was the least of my worries. I turned around and watched the police car sink to the bottom of the swamp. Now we didn't have a car, and my feet were muddy.

Macey turned around and stared at the smoldering truck that was about a hundred yards back. "Would someone care to explain what just happened?"

"Well, I—" I started to explain, but Macey didn't give me time.

"Where did you go? And don't even try and give me that story about this guy wanting to know more about Justin. I'm not that stupid. I sat on the pier by myself for half an hour. Do you know who paid the bill? Some Canadian couple on their honeymoon, Chase. What happened? Where did you go?"

"Allow me to answer that," the agent said. "Chase was kidnapped by the men that were chasing us. The CIA sent me."

"But Chase is the one that left the table. No one took him."

I answered for myself this time. "When I was in the hospital, Justin's older brother came to visit me. His name is Brandon. Long story short, he told me that my dad worked for the CIA and knew some big secret that a group called Ares wants to know. Some guy snuck into Brandon's house earlier and told him about my dad and who knows what else. That man really worked for Ares and was just trying to get Brandon to the pier so he could kidnap him. Or me. Or both. I really don't know why he didn't kidnap him at his house. Ares probably wanted Brandon to tell me about my dad so that I would come to the pier too."

"Wait, stop for a second," Macey commanded me. "Why didn't someone stop the kidnapping before it actually happened?" She gestured to the agent. "You should have been the last resort. And how is Brandon in any relation to you?"

Words caught in my mouth. "I sort of found out that Brandon is actually my brother."

Macey squinted her eyes at me. "Wait, is Justin your brother?"

"No," I told her. "Brandon was adopted into the Patterson family. Thankfully."

The agent beside us grew restless. "I *was* the last resort. The first and second resorts were killed." He looked away, and I wondered if he had known the first and second resorts. I stared at the agent and waited for him to tell more of the story, but he seemed to be done answering our questions.

"Come on. We need to make sure those men didn't survive."

"There's no way," I insisted. "That truck flipped at least three times. And you threw a bomb at it."

The ARG agent didn't listen to me. Instead, he walked toward the truck. Macey and I glanced at each other.

"Well, I'm not standing here and waiting for more crazy people to come." She also walked toward the truck, and I had no choice but to follow.

Even from dozens of yards away, I could see the smoke billowing from the truck that had been reduced to twisted pieces of metal.

"Where are the bodies?" I asked out loud.

"That's quite the movie line," Macey said with slight humor. She slowly stepped away from the truck. I wondered if she was about to throw up. I thought I was.

"I was just wondering the same thing, Chase," the agent said. He kicked what looked like a door, and it clambered to the ground.

"Do you think they could have jumped out?"

"It's a possibility. You'd be surprised what some of those Ares men are capable of. We need to move, and move quickly. We still have a flight to catch." He looked back to Macey, who had her back turned to us. "Now, I just have to figure out what to do with her."

"I guess dropping her off at home is out of the question?"

"No, she's seen and knows way too much." He lowered his voice. "Don't mention the ARG. Your friend is already in a lot of danger because of you. Don't make it worse by burdening her with information."

"Because of me? Are you kidding?"

The agent opened his mouth to respond, but Macey turned around and asked, "What happens now?"

The agent glanced at me and shook his head, as if this was my fault. "First, we'll need to rent a car somewhere and get to the airport. Then I'll call headquarters and tell them what happened and get an extra ticket. I assume that local authorities should be informed of the wreck, but we should be far away from here by the time they get out here."

"Wait," Macey protested and moved in front of us. "What do you mean, *we*? Don't you mean you and Chase?"

"Sorry. You have to come with us. Protocol," the man said.

"Protocol? Are you serious?" Macey inquired.

"Of course," he answered. "Now come on, we have a plane to catch. I'll have someone call your guardians and parents and tell them that you're going to be a part of the Witness Protection Program for a little while." The agent set off in the direction that we had come.

With the agent out of earshot, Macey turned to me, her face red. "Chase, is this guy serious? He can't possibly believe that I'll just hop on a plane and go with you guys. My parents will freak! What am I supposed to tell them? 'Oh hi, Mom, yeah it's Macey. Where am I? At the airport. You want to know why? Well, you see, my friend turned out to be the son of some secret agent and was kidnapped, so then I kind of got caught up in the whole enchilada. There's no need to cook dinner for me tonight or any other night for the next three weeks because I'll be busy hiding from psychopaths. Love you.'"

"I mean, I guess you could say that, but I would come up with something that wouldn't freak your parents out as much."

Macey squinted her blue eyes. "What did you tell your foster parents?"

I shrugged my shoulders. "Nothing."

Macey shook her head, and she ran to catch up with the agent.

About twenty minutes later, we'd arrived at the Rent-A-Car place. I walked inside the small lobby and into the single bathroom. I locked the door, sank down to the floor, and ran my hands through my salty hair. What was happening? What *was* happening?

I stood up abruptly and walked to the sink. I turned it on and watched it run for a while before I put my hands under the stream. I watched the water turn a soft pink for a few seconds as it washed off the blood from the cuts on my wrists. I splashed water on my face and tried to get my breathing under control. I felt like I might throw up.

I told myself to calm down and shook my blonde hair.

"Chase? Come on. Hurry up. We have to go. Mr. Agent is getting all agitated."

Calm down. *Calm down.* It felt like I was going to have a panic attack. I'd had a few, mostly when I had been younger, but I had no intention of having another. I took one more deep breath and walked out of the bathroom.

Macey frowned at me when I looked at her.

I smiled. "Then let's go. No need to get that man's panties in a wad."

I followed Macey out of the car rental building and into the parking lot, where the man waited for us in the car. We pulled out of the rental place and onto the busy interstate.

"Make sure no one follows us. I don't think Ares has enough backup here yet, but they'll be angry now," the agent said. "That tends to give people motive."

"I'd be pretty mad if I let a CIA operative into my little crime ring," I muttered.

"Wait, wouldn't this be more of a case for the FBI?" Macey asked and leaned forward.

The agent looked in the rearview mirror. "Why would you say that?"

"I mean, correct me if I'm wrong, but the CIA deals with foreign cases. and the FBI deals with domestic cases."

"Chase's dad worked for the CIA. That makes this our territory."

Macey sat back with a frown on her face. She didn't look like she believed him, and she was right not to. I knew he lied. It bothered me that he didn't tell her about the Applied Research Group.

———

Macey had just finished speaking with her parents. The agent then took the phone from Macey and continued the conversation, but I wasn't too sure what he said. I wasn't sure I wanted to find out.

"They wouldn't try another Hummer. It would be a regular car. See if anyone is following us." Macey made no move to look out the back window of the car.

I turned around. "How am I supposed to know if someone is following us?"

The agent pulled over to another lane.

"Anyone switch lanes?" he asked.

"You probably should have told me that I was supposed to look for a car that switched lanes before you switched lanes," I said dryly. "I don't exactly watch action movies religiously."

"Those action movies don't exactly give a true picture of what spying and Special Forces do."

"Seems pretty close to me," I mumbled.

A few minutes passed before Macey leaned over to me. "What did they do?"

"Not much, really. Regular kidnapping, I guess. Tied me up, hit me, and locked me in some dark room," I told her. I lifted up both my hands so she could see the cuts on my wrists from the handcuffs.

"Did they want to kill you?" she asked softly.

"They wanted my father to see me, who is alive by the way. Who knew? They want some information, and he's the only one who knows it. I guess having me would help them achieve that somehow."

I didn't tell her the part about the part where they told me that they would torture me. She didn't need to know that.

"This is serious, isn't it?"

I nodded my head.

"I won't wake up in Georgia?" she asked halfheartedly.

I shook my head.

"What if they don't figure it out? What if you and me are stuck with this guy forever? What if we never get to have a normal life again?" Macey raised her voice enough that the agent looked in the rearview mirror. "I mean, do you even know this guy's name? Are you sure he even works for the CIA? Have you seen a badge?"

"Four things, Macey. One, lower your voice. Two, I've never had a normal life. Three, I have no clue what this guy's name is. Four, I'm trusting that he does work for the CIA. He was the one that rescued me."

"I promise you kids I'm an agent for the CIA. I would have killed you by now if I weren't. My name is Agent Dotson," the man in the front of the car said.

"A little eavesdropping?" I asked. "I guess that's a good quality in an agent."

"Listen," Agent Dotson said. "The CIA denied my request for a private jet, so we'll have to take a regular plane. It might be safer that way anyway. They'll be less likely to blow up a plane with civilians on it. That would too messy of a situation. Anyway, they want you alive."

"Blow the plane up? What?"

"This isn't a game. I don't know if you haven't noticed that yet. When we get to the airport, please try to act natural. Chase, don't tell anyone anything. The same goes for you, Macey. Don't draw attention to yourself. The CIA has already gotten our tickets. Hopefully, no one will say anything about our lack of bags. Our best bet is to lay low."

We parked in front of the airport, and I got out. People breezed in and out with smiles on their faces. I envied them like I'd never envied anyone else. They didn't have a care.

After the somewhat invasive security check, Dotson told us that we had about half an hour before we started to board. There was no way I was going to sit there for thirty minutes posing as Agent Dotson's malcontent son. I asked for money so Macey and I could get something to eat from the McDonalds around the corner. I was starved.

After paying for our order, we sat by one of the windows that overlooked the planes taking off. The roar of the planes was slightly comforting.

"Are you scared?" Macey asked me.

"I would say no, but then I'd be lying. Macey, you should have seen the way those guys looked at me. They really looked like they wanted to kill me. They probably would have *really* hurt me if Dotson hadn't gotten us out of there. We actually caught their boat on fire. Twice." I managed a laugh on the last part.

"I would have been too terrified to move," Macey said and leaned over the table.

"I passed so many people while the guy took me to the boat. None of them noticed what was going on. He put these weird sunglasses on me so I couldn't see anything, and he threatened to kill you if I made a move to escape."

"This guy just grabbed you and took you on the boat? In front of everyone?" Macey asked. "That's crazy."

"I know."

"Nothing like this has ever happened before?"

"Have I ever been kidnapped and then rescued by a federal agent? Nope."

"That's not what I meant," she said. "I meant, have you ever noticed anyone watching you? Anything weird happen like that?"

"Macey, the police had orders to look for me for a third of my life. It always feels like people are watching me." I paused. "Don't look at me with that look," I told her. There was pity in her eyes.

"What look?"

"That look. The one you just gave me. Don't feel bad for me. I hate when people give me pity. It's not fun. I feel like people don't take me seriously."

"Chase, you were just kidnapped."

"I still don't like pity."

Macey checked her watch. Dotson told us that if we weren't back five minutes before they began to board, then he was going to call a lockdown on the whole airport. I didn't think he was joking.

"You can hardly blame me, Chase. Come on, we have to go. Don't want to miss the flight."

I'd never ridden on a plane before. I didn't like the fact that there were just a few inches of metal between death's bite and me. I felt my stomach hit the floor and bounce back up into my chest when the plane took off.

"Is your stomach going as crazy as mine?" I asked Macey after my ears popped for the fourth time. She sat beside me. Agent Dotson was somewhere in the back of the plane. I thought back to what he had said. No one would really try to blow up the plane, right?

"Not really. I've flown before."

"Macey, what Dotson said about the people and the 'thing.' That doesn't make you nervous?" I didn't want to mention the word *bomb* on a crowded airplane.

"They need you alive, Chase. Not dead."

"That doesn't exactly make me feel all warm and bubbly," I told her.

"It's the truth," she said. "Now quit talking. A plane is like a library. You just don't talk."

But I wasn't finished. I had to get some of these things out.

"The first and second resort. They died. For me. The same men that are after us killed them."

"I know." Macey took my hand and squeezed it, which was probably the best thing she could have done.

I turned away from her and looked out the window. The ground below looked like a puzzle piece that had been laid together carefully. Everything seemed so orderly and precise, like nothing was out of place.

I woke up when Macey shook my shoulder. "We're here," Macey whispered.

"I'm ecstatic."

Macey and I waited for the agent outside the plane. He walked past us and didn't even glance our way.

"Weirdo," Macey muttered as we followed him out of the airport.

Once we were out of the airport, Agent Dotson paused and looked around for a moment. Macey and I stood and waited for his instructions. "Follow me. We need to go and rent a car."

Once we had a car, our trek to the CIA headquarters began.

We had to go through a checkpoint when we got closer to the headquarters. The car was checked for bombs and anything else that might explode. We were allowed to pass once the security men had been assured that neither Macey nor I had any intention of blowing up the building.

"And you have to go through that every day?" Macey asked.

"Yes. We don't take chances when it comes to security," he answered blankly.

"And I suppose that's why I was kidnapped? You know what, why didn't you guys intervene in my life when I was like seven or something?" I asked. "You know, before the criminals kidnapped me?"

Again, there was no answer. Dotson pulled into a parking place and unlocked the doors, which had been kept locked from the inside the whole time. "When we go in there, the two of you won't touch anything, talk to anyone, look at anyone, question anything, go anywhere without permission, or do anything that would bring the slightest attention to yourself. It isn't going to go smoothly with the boss to know that the mission didn't go as planned. I wasn't supposed to have a second passenger. Consider this an honor. Not many kids know what the inside of this headquarters looks like."

Macey and I looked at each other and rolled our eyes. This guy was ridiculous.

We were whisked fairly quickly through the main lobby. I barely was able to glance at the huge abstract paintings that lined the walls of the massive building. Agent Dotson told us that the campus covered 1,400,000 square feet and sat on 470 acres of land. And that was just the number released to the public.

"I know the two of you have had an exhausting day. It would do the both of you good to go and get some sleep. It's almost seven o'clock. I'll get someone to bring you food or something. Don't come back up unless someone tells you it is okay." Agent Dotson put us both in an elevator and selected a number. The door closed before we could ask any questions.

"This is insane," Macey said. "There's no way this is even remotely legal."

"Do you realize something?" I asked her as the elevator descended.

"That everyone here is insane? I've caught on," she said dryly.

"No. Macey, we're going down. We're going underground."

Macey groaned and sat on the floor of the elevator. "Now I have to sleep underground? Great."

"Try to keep your excitement to yourself." Then, in a deeper voice, I went on. "Don't do anything that would bring the slightest attention to you. Oh, and this is an honor. All the other kids in this nation are safe at home, but you get to see the CIA headquarters."

"Careful," she warned me. "You know that this place has cameras everywhere."

"Please. What are they going to do to me? Kill me?"

Macey shrugged her shoulders and yawned. "You never know."

The elevator dinged and opened to a floor that resembled a college dormitory.

"Oh, man. This is weird," Macey said.

"I thought it would be a little more impressive-looking, you know?" I asked as I took in the white and narrow hallway. "Maybe guns and national secrets painted on the walls?"

"I didn't have high expectations. I'm taking a shower and then I'm going to try and sleep." She walked a few steps, then turned to look at me. "But wake me if the food comes."

She walked to the third door, opened it up, and disappeared inside.

I walked down to the second door and opened it. The first door just felt too close to the elevator. If someone came downstairs, I wanted a little time to react.

Inside there was a bed, a closet, a desk with a lamp on it, and two chests of drawers. The walls were painted a metallic gray. Nothing screamed CIA or Applied Research Group, which I was eager to learn about. There was a door on the far left side of the room, and I guessed that it led to the bathroom. I opened the door and saw two sinks, two toilets, and two showers.

There was another door on the other side of the bathroom, and I heard someone on the other side. Was that another agent? An Ares member? I felt the blood in my veins contract. No. It wouldn't be an Ares member.

I walked in.

That was my first mistake.

The person turned around faster than I could blink and kicked me hard in the shoulder. I stumbled against the wall but didn't fall. On instinct, I threw up my hands, but they might as well have been noodles trying to stop a tornado. The person approached me again and hit me once in my stomach and then in the face. I doubled over, and the attacker's foot made contact with my chin. My head shot up, and I felt hot pain and tasted blood. The person grabbed my neck, lifted me off the ground, and reeled back his fist. He was getting ready to knock me out.

"Stop! Dude, chill out!" I yelled before my oxygen was cut off completely.

I shut my eyes and waited, but the final blow never came. The attacker dropped me on the ground.

"That hurt," I whispered. I grimaced as I breathed in air and spit blood out of my mouth.

"Stay on the ground and put your hands up."

I lifted my hands limply and sucked in air. "Just chill. Just—just chill."

"Who are you? Why are you here? Who sent you?"

"Dotson," I said, and my voice cracked. I'd lost count of how many times I'd been hit today, but at least this kid hadn't pulled a gun. This was a teenager, maybe a little older than I was.

He lowered his fists. "You're bruising pretty fast there."

"Really? And whose fault is that?" I felt a warm gush of blood running down my wrist. I thought back to the henchman and how he'd twisted the handcuffs on my wrists and caused the skin to tear. The cut must have reopened when I had been slammed up against the wall. I pressed my left hand around my right one to try to stop the flow of blood. No need to make this guy mad about getting his carpet bloody.

"Why are you here?" He put out his hand to pull me up. I didn't take it. I didn't trust my legs to support my weight.

"My name's Chase."

"I didn't ask for your name. Why are you here?"

"Where did you learn to fight like that? I barely even saw you coming." I rubbed my mouth and was relieved to see that teeth didn't fall out.

"Here. Now answer my question before I punch you again. Why are you here? And tell me the truth. I can tell when people lie." The boy handed me a cloth to wipe my bloody mouth.

I doubted that, but I didn't dare say anything. "Long story," I answered. I stood and backed a little bit into the bathroom. I wanted to be as far away from this manic as possible.

But he wasn't having any of that. He took me by the shoulders, pushed me to the bed, and slammed the door. I knew resisting wouldn't get me anywhere. He pulled out a chair from under the table, sat down, and stared at me. "I'll ask you again, Pretty Boy. Why are you here?"

Pretty Boy. Who was this guy? He was around sixteen or seventeen, but he knew how to fight so well that I might have guessed that he had been training for that long.

"Um, I..."

"Spit it out. Now."

I saw him clench both his fists, and the muscles in his arms rippled.

"Okay, okay. I will. Just chill."

"Talk, and I will."

"Earlier today, I was out on the pier, and this guy came at me with a gun, and before I know it..." I paused again and tried to find the right words to use.

"You're pushing it," he warned me again. He stood up and took a few steps toward me, and it took everything I could muster not to back up even farther. "Do you want a repeat of what I just did to you?"

"I got kidnapped by a couple of criminals," I told him.

"Keep talking, or I'll push your head into one of those toilets and flush."

"They put me on a boat and tied me up," I said to please him. "They started to punch me and talked about my dad and brother. I didn't know my dad was still alive until a few hours ago, and I didn't know that I had a brother until a few days ago. Then they start talking about how they need me so they could make my dad talk. Those men need information, and my dad is the only one who knows what it is, but he won't tell them. Dotson brought me here because he thinks that I need protection."

Just like I did with Macey, I didn't tell this kid about the torture part. Best left unsaid.

"That's all I wanted to know."

"Yeah, well," I said to him. "You can pack a punch."

"I went easy on you, Pretty Boy." The kid moved the farther away from me, and I watched him unclench his fists.

"You really hurt my neck," I told him. I could already feel the angry welts on my neck, and my shoulder hurt. By the time this was over, I was going to be one big bruise. My whole body ached, and I was exhausted.

The teenager was about six feet tall with dark black hair, tan skin, and brown eyes. He had light freckles across his nose, muscular arms, and broad shoulders. He wasn't the type of guy I wanted to be in a fight with.

"You scared me half to death. I'm not used to people being down here," he said.

"So, if someone comes down here, you automatically decide that they need to punched, kicked, choked, dropped on the ground, and interrogated?"

"No. Just you. Considering you're the only one stupid enough to sneak up on me. Bad day or not."

"I didn't anticipate to get beaten again when I walked in here."

"Uninvited," he said defensively.

"Right. Because you guys send out invitations."

"Get out."

I got off the bed to leave and hadn't taken two steps when I felt woozy and nearly fell. I would have fallen flat on my face if the kid hadn't steadied me. He put me on the bed, and I didn't have enough energy to sit up, much less stand up and walk out of there with the tiny shred of dignity I still had. My wrists stung and my head pounded. The sting on my leg felt like it was on fire again. I needed sleep. Black dots swarmed my vision.

"You don't look so good, Pretty Boy," he told me.

"I don't feel so hot either," I muttered through closed eyes. Another wave of nausea hit me, and I realized that I was about to throw up. That wasn't good. I mustered up every bit of strength I had left and ran to bathroom and threw up in the toilet. Acid burned my throat, and my headache still wouldn't let up. It could have been from my concussion, the blow to the head I'd received on the boat, or the punch from this guy. Who could tell?

The guy looked a little disgusted, but he also looked anxious. It occurred to me that he could get into trouble. "Do you want me to get something for you? Like a doctor? Your eye looks pretty bad, and I'm pretty sure I didn't do that to your head. You don't have a concussion, do you?"

"Yes to the concussion, water, and Advil." Over the years, I had convinced myself not to turn down any help. Even if it did make me feel slightly pathetic. For a while, I'd pretended I could take care of myself and ended up taking showers in the school locker room for three weeks. I stood and dragged myself back into the kid's room.

"I have that right here." He turned around and got a cold water bottle out of his minifridge and handed me two red pills.

"I didn't make you almost pass out and throw up, did I?"

"I didn't exactly feel great before." I moved away from him.

The guy furrowed his eyebrows. "I'm not going to hurt you again. Relax." He stepped farther away from me and put his hands up. "See?"

For a second, I didn't know why he had said that. Then I realized I'd done what I always do when I felt slightly threatened. I'd taken a step back, and he'd noticed. I didn't even mean to do it anymore. It had become a habit over the years. A habit that made me seem like an inferior scaredy-cat. "That's what the last guy said," I muttered. Images of a bad foster home flashed through my mind, and my stomach felt hot. I could almost feel the scar on my back.

"What did you say?" he asked.

"Nothing."

"Yeah, you said something. What about the last guy? What did the last guy do? Are you talking about the kidnappers?"

"Yeah. Listen, I really need some sleep." He made a classic mistake. Never give anyone an easy way out if you are ever trying to get information. I slowly started to make my way out of his room. But I couldn't leave quite yet. I had some questions. "What are you doing here?"

"Training," he said.

"To become an agent? The CIA does that? I had no idea." I wondered if he knew about the Applied Research Group.

"It had better stay that way. If anyone ever found out what really went on inside these walls, they might get a nice long stay on a deserted island. Or die. No worries about you though, right?"

I nodded my head. That explained why the kid was such a good fighter. He had been trained by some of the best. There was no telling what he was capable of, and I had no intention of finding out.

"What do your parents say after you come home? Do you ever act different?" I asked.

"Nothing much, really. My dad commented on how long I could hold my breath and that my reflexes were a lot faster, but he just thought it was because I was getting older. Do you need help getting back to your room? I don't want you falling out on me again."

"Yeah, let's not ever bring that up again," I told him. I stood up and slowly walked out of the room. Then I remembered Macey. I didn't want her to meet this kid and have the same experience.

"Oh, and there's this girl. She's staying in the room down the hall. I actually think she's sleeping right now, so don't go barging in there. She'll take you down," I warned.

"And Sleeping Beauty's name is?" he asked.

"Macey Mallory."

"I think I can take anyone named Macey Mallory, but thanks for the warning."

I turned around and took a few steps, when he started talking again. "Hey, Chase?"

"What?"

"Sorry. About the black-eye-and-busted-lip thing. Won't happen again. Do me a favor, and don't tell anyone I did that."

"That's what the last guy said too."

CHAPTER 13

I fell asleep the second my head hit the pillow and didn't wake up until about nine the next morning. I would have slept longer, but Macey banged on my door and called my name. Half asleep, I trudged to the door and opened it.

"What happened?" she asked me the second she saw my face.

"What?"

"Your face. That wasn't there yesterday. What happened?" Macey asked me. She ran her fingers lightly over my eye, and chills ran up my back.

"Oh, there's a guy next door."

"A guy next door? What did you do?"

"I didn't do *anything*. He attacked me."

"Where is he?" Macey asked and peered into the room behind me.

"In the room next to me," I told her.

"I want to meet him," she said.

"Just be sure to knock," I warned her. She walked behind me and went through the bathroom that connected the two rooms. She paused outside of his door, looked back at me, and frowned at the bruises on my face. She turned back around and knocked on the door.

A few seconds later, the guy opened the door. He wasn't wearing a shirt, and I saw Macey's composure shift.

He looked at me. "So, this is Macey?"

"This is Macey," I answered.

"You better have a good reason for punching my friend."

"I thought he was an intruder," he answered and messed with his dark hair.

"And why are you here?" Macey questioned.

"I'm training to be a secret agent."

"A secret agent? That's a little cliché," Macey told him.

He didn't miss a beat. "Well, so is the girl acting like she's tougher than she is to impress the hot guy."

Macey completely ignored what he had said. "How did the CIA possibly manage to pick *you* for the training?"

"The CIA gave everyone in the seventh grade a standardized test in my county. But no one knew it was from the CIA, and it really wasn't a standardized test."

"And all your test answers added up to something?"

"Guess so. Anyway, about three months later—about a month before school let out—an agent came over to my baseball practice and talked to me about the opportunity at hand. Of course, I said yes. I was a kid. Kids love spies. I agreed to the training without giving it a second thought. That following summer, I spent six weeks training here. Mostly building up muscle and stuff like that. The year after, the agents taught me how to use all the technology, how to shoot guns, and some stuff I can't exactly talk about."

"So your job is decided for you, isn't it?" Macey asked.

"Yup." He smiled at her. "Actually, now I kind of want to be a florist. The only thing I would have to worry about is what kind of fertilizer to use and not which guy is holding a gun to my head."

"Someone has held a gun on you before?" I asked, but he ignored me, which meant no, no one had ever held a gun to him. He was trying to impress Macey, and it was disgusting.

"True. What's your name?" Macey asked.

"Crush Daysort."

"Your parents named you Crush?" I asked. "Like the knock-off brand of Fanta?"

Crush narrowed his eyes at me.

"So," I said. "Where's the food?"

"The cafeteria. Where else? Follow me." Crush tugged on a shirt and walked out the door. Macey and I followed him.

"He's full of himself, don't you think?" I whispered to Macey as Crush led us to where the elevator was. I could have figured that out.

"You're just jealous," Macey observed. "Give him a break. He can't exactly brag to the kids at school about what he does during the summer. He's obviously going to brag to us. We're probably the first people he's ever told."

"I am not jealous," I defended.

"Whatever, Chase."

Crush turned around and looked at the both of us. "You know what? How about we take the back way?"

I turned around and looked down the hallway. "There's no door."

"To you, yeah, there's no door. You just have to be smarter than that to find it." Crush winked at Macey, and I felt like I needed to throw up.

Crush walked to the end of the hallway, pulled a small latch that was built into the wall, and a door swung open. It was only about three feet tall and three feet wide. Okay. That was even more cliché than a teenage spy, but it did seem like a pretty good safety measure. Without hesitating, Macey went inside.

"This is awesome." Her voice echoed through the passageway.

Crush smiled at me. "Aren't you going to follow her?"

I walked over to the secret passage and crawled inside. Sure, I wasn't big on small spaces, but there wasn't any way I would let Crush know that. The crawlspace was awfully small for about ten feet, then it opened up enough to where I could easily stand up. The ceilings were about ten feet high, and the corridor itself was about four feet wide. Electrical lights on the sides of the walls flickered.

"Where does this lead?" Macey asked Crush as he filed in behind us. We began to walk.

"Um, I think to the main floor. I'm actually not supposed to be in these tunnels."

Macey stopped dead in her tracks and turned around to face us. "Great, so if we get caught, we have to answer to people that work for the CIA? The elevator would have worked just fine," Macey said.

"We won't get caught," Crush assured us, but I could hear the worry in his voice. This guy wasn't a convincing liar. He had tried to impress Macey, and it deliciously backfired.

We walked a bit farther until we came to stairs that went almost straight up. After going up a few flights, I could see the end of the tunnel.

"Now what?" I asked.

"I think you just push on the wall, and it opens up to the hallway."

Macey turned around and stared Crush down. "You think? You don't know for sure?"

Crush brushed around Macey and pushed on the wall a little harder than he should have. The hidden door opened easily, and Crush fell three feet to the ground. I choked back a laugh.

Sadly, Crush landed right at the feet of someone who worked here.

I was actually pretty surprised about how fast Crush got to his feet, but I was even more surprised when the woman pulled a gun on him.

"Hands up!" she screamed at him and backed him up against the wall. She trained the gun on his chest and then spotted us in the passageway. "Hands up, and get on floor. All three of you. Now."

Macey and I both got out of the passageway and put our hands up, but neither of us got on the floor. No one made a move to explain to the woman that we weren't brainwashed kids about to blow up the building.

"Put the gun down," I coaxed.

The woman screamed at us. "Get down on the floor—now."

"We'll talk if you put the gun down," I said as calmly as possible.

"Talk, and I'll put the gun down," she fired back.

"That's Crush, and he's here for training. I'm Chase Miners, and this is Macey Mallory. We're here on a protection deal with Agent Dotson. The elevator was making weird noises, so Crush thought it would be best if we took the tunnel up here. We didn't want to get stuck in the elevator and cause any trouble. You guys are so busy, and your work is so important.

We didn't want to bother you guys if it did break. We were coming up to tell someone."

"Crush?" She looked at me and back at Crush, who was still on the floor. "No, his name is Sydney Daysort." She put her gun down and told Crush to sit up. "All right, *Crush*. Talk."

"Well, I—I didn't think that it would—I wanted to—they needed to get up here and..." Crush seemed to be scared out of his wits. I had assumed he would have been calm under pressure.

"He wanted to help us out because we were both hungry, and he thought that the tunnel led to the cafeteria. He was going to leave us there and tell someone about the elevator."

"Is that true, Sydney?" The woman asked Crush as he stood up. She told us to put our hands down.

"Yeah, it's true."

The woman regained her posture. "Sydney, you know those tunnels are off limits and are only to be used during an emergency. I can't believe they give this much clearance to a teenager. I'll be informing your trainer of this." She turned her attention to Macey and me. She didn't look too happy. "Dotson should have known better than to bring you two here. I don't want to hear of you three again, understand?"

The three of us both nodded quickly. I couldn't believe our luck. But I assumed she had more important things to do.

"Smooth," Macey said and punched Crush in the shoulder when the woman disappeared.

"Funny," I said, "I thought secret agents were supposed to be great liars. Or at least decent ones. It was really great to hear you stutter, *Sydney*."

"Don't make me give you another black eye, Chase," he said seriously.

"You wouldn't dare."

Macey stepped in between us. "Chill, or I'll make the lady with the gun come back and finish you both off. Crush, you shouldn't have broken a rule in the CIA headquarters. That reeks of failure, and no one likes failure. Chase, chill out. We all have our faults."

"At least mine don't include lying about my name," I muttered and stared at Crush.

"Hey, Crush is my nickname. I'm not going to go around telling people that my real name is Sydney. And *you* want to talk about lying? You just lied not thirty seconds ago."

"I lied so we wouldn't have to spend the rest of our natural lives in a prison in the mountains somewhere," I fired back. "And at least I knew that we would get caught. I was thinking of a way to get out of it the whole way up those stairs. As an agent, that's a trait you need to pick up. I think it will be very useful, seeing as how your plan failed miserably."

"All right, that's enough! Both of you just shut up," Macey told us sternly. "Let's just forget the last three minutes of our lives and go get something to eat." She grabbed both of us by the shoulder and dragged us down the hallway.

"Food is the other way."

Macey turned us around.

"If you don't mind me asking," Macey said to Crush. "How do you get Crush out of Sydney?"

"Both of you are going to laugh," Crush said.

"*I* won't." Macey eyed me, and I threw up my hands.

"I pinky promise I won't laugh," I assured them.

"Whatever. You've seen the movie *Finding Nemo*, right? You know that turtle named Crush that tells Dory and Marlin to follow the current? I was obsessed with that turtle when I was little. I wouldn't answer to Sydney, and it just sort of stuck."

"Creative," Macey said.

"At least you weren't obsessed with Dory."

"It's dumb. I know. But it was a long time ago, and it's better than Sydney."

We'd arrived at the cafeteria and it was completely empty, which was good. It had eight TVs tuned to news channels from all over the world. There were a couple boxes of dry cereal, a couple pieces of rotten fruit, and a few vending machines. Dotson hadn't bothered to give us any food.

Macey and I crammed the dry cereal down.

"Best breakfast ever," Macey said and leaned back in her chair.

Then Agent Dotson walked in the cafeteria and sat down across from Crush, who sat alone on the other side of the table.

"I see you guys met. I meant to warn you about one another. Chase, what happened to your face?"

"I learned yesterday that you should always knock before entering a room." I looked over at Crush.

"Wasn't my fault," he defended again. "He surprised me."

"No, I scared him."

"You did not *scare* me."

"Chill it." Macey kicked me lightly in the leg, and I held my tongue.

Agent Dotson seemed to sense the tension as well. "Crush, I suspect you'll be showing these two around?"

"He showed us the tunnels."

Crush glared at me, but Dotson didn't seem to mind.

"Pretty neat, huh? You know, Crush, I'm the one that suggested you needed to be informed about the emergency exits. Knowledge of those tunnels might come in handy one day. It's good that you showed them."

I rolled my eyes as Crush smiled.

"Macey," Agent Dotson said. "Sorry to pull you away from your breakfast, but you have to come with me for a few minutes. There are a few papers you have to sign."

"I'm not signing my life away, am I?" she asked in an attempt to lighten the heavy mood that lingered in the air.

"Of course not." Agent Dotson managed a smile.

The two of them got up and left the cafeteria. That left me with Crush. I knew I couldn't get up and leave. I had no idea where I was going.

"We got off on the wrong foot yesterday. So, let's just try and make this work because we're stuck being suite mates for however long you're here. And you can't keep making me look bad in front of these CIA people. That lady is already going to tell my trainer. So, I'll start. Where do you live?"

"Florida," I said, dryly.

"That's cool. I love it down there. We don't get much hurricane action here." He paused. "Hey, if you live in one of the biggest tourist attractions in America, then where do you and your family go for vacation?"

"It depends."

"Depends on what?"

"You know how families are."

He nodded. "So, you just found that you have a brother and that your dad isn't dead? That must have come as a shock."

"What? How did you know about that?" I asked.

He raised his eyebrows. "You told me about it. Yesterday. Do you remember?"

"Not really. Yesterday is a huge blur," I told him, slightly concerned. I put another handful of cereal in my mouth.

"I don't think that's a good sign. What all happened to you? It looks like a big spider web latched onto your leg and hands and burned you. Your wrists are all scratched up, and you clearly hit your head."

"My head?" I decided not to lie about this one. I didn't really see the need to. "I fell off a fence and hit it. My leg and my hands were stung by a Portuguese man-of-war, which I'm allergic to. The cuts on my wrists are from handcuffs that the kidnappers put on me."

Crush stared at me. "Dude, just tell me the truth."

"I'm not lying. I would be lying if I said I got all the injuries from fighting hybrid aliens, but I didn't say that."

"Why were you climbing a fence?"

"You want the truth?" I actually wanted Crush to know the truth. It would be fun to see his reaction.

"Yeah."

"I was climbing a fence to get away from the police because I was wanted for an attempt at murder. I lost my balance at the top and fell," I said.

Crush's jaw dropped and his eyes widened. "Murder?"

"Shocker, right? An attempt at murder! Don't worry. I'm innocent and the charges were dropped."

"Wait. Back up. Who did you try to murder? When? Why?" I watched Crush's arm muscles tense as he braced them against the table.

"No, I didn't try and murder anyone. They just thought I did. I was the orphaned kid who took sweet revenge on his best friend for having a good life. It was a perfect plot, really. Except it wasn't true, and they have video proof of that. It was my best friend, a kid named Justin Patterson. He fell off a bridge, and I was in the wrong place at the wrong time. And here's the plot twist. Brandon, my biological brother, was adopted into Justin's family, so I actually knew my brother for most of my life, but neither of us knew it. About a week ago, a man that works for Ares pretended to work for the CIA and came to Brandon's house and told him that our father worked for the CIA, knew a bunch of secrets, and that we were in trouble. He also dropped the bomb that we were brothers. Then he convinced Brandon to tell me I was supposed to go to the pier so I can have all this explained to me."

"But that guy didn't work for the CIA, and when you went to the pier, he kidnapped you," Crush speculated.

"Exactly. And as the boat was driving away, Brandon screamed that they would have killed Justin if he didn't convince me to go to the pier."

"Wait. Ares? Who is that?"

"The group that has my dad."

"Give me a second to process all of this."

"Take your time," I told him. I couldn't believe that I'd shared all of that. Once I started to talk, I hadn't been able to quit.

After a few questions about how Macey had managed to get mixed up in all of this, Crush got up to leave. He said he was going to be late for training if he didn't leave now. I couldn't help but laugh as he walked away with a confused expression on his face. Maybe this place wouldn't be too terrible.

CHAPTER 14

The director of Ares stared at the two remaining men in front of him. Both of them were in bad shape. They were covered in bruises and scrapes. One had three breaks in his right arm, and the other man's face was so swollen that he could barely see. They supported themselves with crutches. They were the two that had attempted to capture the younger boy. The director knew it really wasn't their fault that they failed. He'd known the third man on the boat was a fraud. The CIA knew him as Agent Dotson, but the director knew him as Crenshaw. He was his most valuable friend and coworker. The director and Crenshaw had planned it all out, and it had gone perfectly. Except for the girl. She hadn't been a part of the plan, but she would be taken care of in time. The director wondered why Crenshaw brought her along, but he knew that he had his reasons. Perhaps it was to provide leverage over Chase. Threatening to hurt someone your victim loved was just as effective as threatening to hurt the victim. After all, Crenshaw was only loyal to Ares.

The director could tell the two injured men yearned to say something in their defense, but they kept their mouths shut. The director had a short temper and tolerated nothing. He was a man who would kill a child to get information, and he had done it more than once.

"I'm going to send in a man named Ivan Spivakovsky. If he can't catch Chase Miners, I will spare both of your lives. If he can catch him, consider both yourselves dead. Now leave."

The two men left the director's office, limped down the hallway, and stepped into an elevator that fell the next few floors. The fall killed them both. Their deaths were bittersweet to the director. The two men had been resourceful, but they might have figured something about Crenshaw. He couldn't have that. It would ruin years and years of work. Anyway, he was sure Spivakovsky could capture Chase. He would just need Crenshaw's help with disabling the CIA's security system.

Ivan Spivakovsky came in the door a few minutes later.

"Ah, Mr. Spivakovsky, I didn't think I would see you in person so soon. Please, have a seat."

"My people wanted to make sure everything was going as planned. You might have a problem with your elevator. It didn't work. I had to take the stairs," he said. The man spoke with a Russian accent that the director didn't like.

"Ah, yes. The repairman should be here shortly. Why would your people think anything was wrong? I'm the head of the operation, aren't I?"

Ivan Spivakovsky sat down. "May I remind you that you let a secret agent into your operation, director?"

"Never mind that. The plan is in motion. Your men will be there tonight at twelve forty five, ready to create the diversion. You and three other men will go and get the three children. They are staying right next to each other, so it will be fairly simple. We've been over this, if I'm not mistaken. Would you like to see a picture of the targets?"

Ivan shook his head. "How can you be sure that all of the security at the headquarters will be shut off?"

"I have a man in a high position in the headquarters. He will make sure the security system is off," The director of Ares said with a smile.

"I don't understand why you are kidnapping the other two children."

"Sydney Daysort has been training with the CIA for some time now. If we have him, we could end the CIA. Think about how outraged the public would be if they found out the CIA forced a minor to train with them. The girl, Macey Mallory, seems to like Chase, and no doubt the boy likes her as well. We can get Chase to cooperate with us using her."

"Why can't your man in the CIA just bring them to us?"

"That option was considered."

"Why was it discarded?"

"Crush Daysort isn't allowed to leave the headquarters. No doubt, if the three were eventually allowed to leave the complex, someone would chaperone the children. My agent might not chaperone the children at all. It would look strange if a man of his stature requested to escort them. Anyhow, he had no problem assisting us."

Ivan Spivakovsky seemed to be pleased and left without any more questions. He took the stairs again.

———

Later, the director got a call.

"Is everything going according to plan?" the voice on the other end asked. The director recognized the voice as his double agent, Crenshaw.

"Of course it is. The plan went *perfectly* last time we attempted to catch Chase. It's too bad my two didn't die on impact after the car flipped. Ivan Spivakovsky thinks that our plan failed. Ha. That idiot. After he completes this mission, I probably should kill him," the director said.

"No. You will make a lot of enemies that way. Killing a successful contract killer would be suicidal," the double agent advised.

"I suppose you are correct. I still am unable to believe that he agreed to work with us. Does anyone suspect anything of you yet?"

"I'm acting as if I'm one of them. As I always have," the man said, impassive.

"Good. Everything is going perfectly. Once we have Chase and his friends at the main headquarters, everything will fall into place. It is only a matter of time before we have the information."

CHAPTER 15

I found my way back to our floor without much trouble. I walked down to Macey's door and knocked on it. There was no answer, and I assumed that she still wasn't back from whatever Dotson wanted with her.

That meant I was alone with nothing to do.

What Dotson was still doing with her, I didn't know. I wasn't looking forward to my turn. But I did have a lot of questions that needed answering. For example, where was Brandon?

I crawled back into the bed and slept for what felt like a few hours. I hoped the sleep would make my headache lessen. When I woke up, it had all but gone away. I decided that another painkiller wouldn't hurt. Besides, my bruised eye hurt.

I decided I would go talk to Crush.

"You didn't knock," he said to me when I walked in. He was face down on his bed and didn't even bother to look who it was, but I supposed there weren't many people it could have been.

"Are we still on that?"

"Yeah."

"Where have you been? Macey isn't back yet, and I've been sitting alone for hours," I told him.

Crush shook his head. "Welcome to my life."

"What do you mean?"

"Spending hours and hours alone with no one to talk to. That's how my summers are."

"Then why do it?"

Crush lifted his head off the bed. "Do what?"

"Train with the CIA."

"Am I supposed to tell them no?"

I shrugged my shoulders.

"Yeah, I'm going to tell my trainer no. That'll happen."

"Come on, what is he going to do?" I asked. "Fire you?"

Crush stood up and didn't bother to put on a shirt. "He'd make me run, lift, sweat, and cry. Even if I did get out of the training, they would never leave me alone. You never truly leave the CIA."

"Yeah, these people seem to know everything about you and your family before you do. What do you do in training?"

"Don't think I'm allowed to say."

"Of course you're not."

He frowned. "I'm not allowed to tell anyone anything."

"So," I said, "on the first day of school when your friends want to know what you did over the summer, what do you say?"

"Usually, I say I went to some football camp or church camp. I'll say I went to the beach or the mountains for a few weeks. Regular summer stuff. Except once, I said I went to Alaska, and everyone wanted to know about the trip. I didn't know one thing about Alaska."

"I need to show you how to lie and get out of stuff. I think you might need it."

"I can lie," he protested.

"Really? Fine. Tell me two lies and one truth, and I'll know the truth." I was determined to show this guy that I was better than he was when it came to lying.

"I have three brothers and two sisters. I didn't like chocolate till I was ten. This isn't my natural hair," he told me.

I studied his face, and instantly I knew which one was the truth. "You dye your hair? Really?"

"How did you guess?"

"What's your natural color?" I couldn't believe he dyed his hair. Macey was going to love this.

"An ugly light brown."

"You need practice. Eye contact is important."

He rolled his eyes. "I don't care. I'll get better at some point."

"Sure you will," I told him sarcastically. "Now, give me more painkillers."

As I swallowed three pills, I heard the elevator, and I knew that it had to be Macey. I was curious about what she'd been forced to do all day.

Macey, without knocking, threw open Crush's door and plopped down on the floor with hair in her face. She had a box of pizza.

"I have just lived through death," she said and tore through the pizza.

"Where have you been?" I asked her.

"Where have I been? Where have I been? I'll tell you where I've been! I've been stuck inside a stupid room for hours with some stupid lady asking me all about what happened. For the last hour, she explained how I couldn't tell a living soul about anything I'm seeing. I know that. That was a complete waste of my life. Oh, and Chase? You have to do that tomorrow. Just thought you might want to mentally prepare yourself for the most mind-numbing and dull hours of your entire life."

"I'll live. Where did you get the pizza?" I asked.

"At the end of the lady's speech, she asked me if I needed anything."

"So you asked for pizza? Not for a ride back home?" I asked jokingly. I reached down and grabbed a slice and then handed the box to Crush, who took three pieces. His trainer probably regulated his diet.

"I remember listening to that speech. Not fun," Crush informed us.

"So what do we do now? My mind needs some entertaining," Macey asked Crush.

"I don't know. You guys figure that out. All I do is sleep, eat, and train when I'm here. Right now, I need sleep. My body feels like it's about to fall off." He ordered us out of his room and slammed the door behind us.

"That guy's just a bucket of cool, isn't he?" Macey said.

"So you don't like him?" I said. "You know he dyes his hair."

"Don't twist my words, kid," she answered back smartly but then frowned. "I wish I could talk to my parents again. I really hope they aren't worried about me. I mean, I know they are and everything, but I don't want them to be. I'm in one of the most secure buildings in the world, right? And this room isn't even supposed to exist. The lady told me she would call them and offer a plausible explanation."

I managed a laugh. "Sorry I dragged you into this."

"It's not your fault," she told me.

"It is my fault. I knew that someone was going to be at the pier. I should have gone by myself or not have gone at all. I put you in danger."

"I could have gone home another way." Macey said.

"You just moved there. How did you even know that way home?"

"My phone." she said.

"Where is your phone now?" I asked her. We had moved to the end of the hallway so Crush wouldn't hear us. We could listen to music if she had her phone. Anything to keep us from being driven insane from boredom, but I suppose that boredom was a safe thing.

"No clue. Now, did anyone answer any of your questions? Did they tell you anything about Brandon?" she asked.

"I know just about as much as you do. They haven't told me anything about Brandon. I'm sure they think it's safer that we don't know anything. Heck, they might even wipe our memories after this. But you know what's really weird?" she asked me, looking up at the ceiling.

"What?"

"On the car ride to Florida, I wished something crazy or fun would happen to me when I got here."

"When I got back to Florida, I wished that everything would just slow down and turn normal. At least you got you wish," I told her.

"I would have been perfectly fine living a completely boring life."

I slumped against the wall. "Wouldn't we all?"

CHAPTER 16

I fell asleep around ten that night, and I could tell that it was still the middle of the night when I woke up, even without windows. I wasn't sure why I had woken up. Then I heard a door slam. It sounded like Crush's. There were probably a thousand and one reasons as to why he was up in the middle of the night, but I didn't like about nine hundred and ninety-nine of them.

Then I heard someone's foot collide with a door and shouting.

I got out of bed, pulled on the shirt that I had been wearing the day before, walked to my door, and pressed my ear against it. Not two seconds later, the door flew open, and I was shoved to the ground with surprising force. The breath was knocked out of me, and I felt gloved hands pull me to my feet. I didn't even think to scream.

There were four men in dark suits in the hallway. One had Macey, and the other had Crush. The third had me. The last guy pointed a gun in our general direction.

Crush tried his best to get away from the man who held him captive, but every time he tried to make a move, the man would hit a nerve in his neck, and Crush's arms would go limp. After a few tries, he stopped trying to get away.

"The three of you are going to walk to the elevator and wait until one of us opens it. If either of you make a move, I'll knock the girl's brain on the wall. Understood?" the man with the gun told us. No one said a word, and I tried to lock eyes with Macey or Crush. I didn't want Crush to try anything and get the three of us killed. He probably thought he could take these guys. But we were outnumbered and unarmed.

The men held us by our shoulders and directed us to the elevator. The three of us were shoved to the ground. Crush attempted to stand and fight, but one of the men kicked him in his stomach and held a foot on his chest. Crush fought to catch his breath under the man. The elevator came to a stop, and I stood before someone could force me to my feet. The men still managed to get hold of the three of us, and we were directed to the nearest exit.

"Where is everybody? What about the alarms?" I heard Macey whisper to Crush.

"Don't know. This was planned carefully. Security was probably shut off," Crush whispered back to Macey.

"Shut up," one of the men yelled at them and hit the back of their heads. He didn't seem to care if he was heard.

I couldn't believe what was happening. Where was everyone?

"You mind telling us who you guys are?" Crush asked. He forced his voice to sound strong.

The men didn't say a word. They struck me as the strong, silent types. Then someone came through a door off to the side of the lobby. We were about thirty feet from the door that led outside. I saw a helicopter that was landing not sixty yards away from the building. How could that not have been heard? What was going on? Who were these men?

I had one guess.

"Hands up in the air. I've got a gun!"

I didn't dare turn around, but I knew the voice belonged to a woman. My whole body felt paralyzed. I probably wouldn't have been able to make it through the lobby if a gun hadn't been pressed to my back the whole time. The man holding Macey by her shoulders turned to face the woman. He raised his gun with both hands, and a bullet flew through the air and lodged itself in the woman's left thigh. A piercing scream shot through the air. If that didn't draw some attention to the situation we were in, the piercing wail of the fire alarm sure did. I looked over to Macey. She still had her hand on the fire alarm, and I could tell by her expression that she couldn't quite believe what she had just done.

Crush and I tried to make a break for it, but the two men holding us captive wrapped their arms around our necks and dragged us toward the door. The man that shot the woman came and grabbed Macey again, and they quickly joined us. People started to file into the lobby now, but it was already too late. Some went to see how the lady on the floor was. A few pulled out their phones. A couple pulled out their guns, but they couldn't risk firing. They could have hit us. It was a chaotic mess filled with screaming and the whirl of the helicopter.

We were thrown out the door, and three of the men followed us. The fourth man stayed back a few seconds and fired in random directions.

"Faster!" one of the men screamed. I felt the gun probe my back, and I increased my pace.

The three of us didn't want to get in the helicopter, but that gun was an effective persuasive device. There were about seven people sprinting to the helicopter, but they were too far off to help us. The doors to the helicopter closed, and the blades began to spin. I looked out the window and saw that the third and fourth men were making their getaway in a car. The helicopter rose into the air, and the agents on the ground quickly faded away, as did our only chance of escaping.

We were instructed to sit. I could feel my heart rate increasing as one of the men made his way toward us. He had rope in his hand and began to tie my feet to a shelf connected to the interior of the helicopter. I'd learned from my experience on the boat not to fight back when you clearly had no chance of winning. But Crush hadn't.

He stood and dove for the controls. He hit something on the control panel, and the helicopter veered sharply to the left. Macey crashed into me, and I slammed against the door of the helicopter. The rope pulled painfully on my feet. Crush still tried to gain control of the helicopter. I had no idea how he thought he could defeat two grown men with guns while he fought in his pajamas.

Crush yelled. All I could see were limbs striking and flying, and I wondered if he'd been hit. I wanted to stand up and help him, but I couldn't get the knot around my ankles untied. I watched as one of the men pushed Crush into the back of the helicopter. His head landed before his body did. He moaned and barely managed to sit up. His face was white. The only color was from blood that came from his lip and a cut above his eyebrow. He wiped at it and it smeared across his face like war paint. The kidnapper that wasn't piloting the helicopter turned around so that he was looking at us.

I brought my knees up to my chest and put my chin on my knees. Macey interlocked her fingers in mine, and I squeezed her hand.

"I told you we should have sedated them earlier. He could have been killed," the man in the passenger seat said to the other man. He reached inside of a bag and pulled out three syringes. Each contained a clear liquid. The man kneeled down to Crush's level, grabbed his neck, and pushed him against the wall. Crush tried to pry the man's hands off, but it made no difference.

"You're not going to throw another punch? Has the tough guy lost his touch?"

The man raised Crush's sleeve and Crush fought even harder. Still, the man jammed the needle in his arm. Crush winced as the liquid was pushed into his bloodstream. A small trickle of blood exited the wound and snaked down his arm. It didn't take long for Crush to pass out.

The man talked with a disgusting Russian accent that chilled me to my bones. I could hardly understand it.

"You're next," the man said to Macey. "The poor little girl. You didn't mean to get involved in all of this, did you?"

Macey closed her blue eyes as the liquid was injected into her.

I sucked in a breath and tried to settle my breathing. I didn't care that this man knew I was terrified.

The CIA knew that we were gone. That much I knew. They would be able to spot this helicopter and save us in the next few minutes. That was their job, and they would do it. Right?

I felt Macey's fingers go slack in my hand. Her eyes were all the way closed.

The man took the last syringe and thumped it with his pointer finger. "Then there's Chase. The main target. It was just an inconvenience that you dragged your little friends along. It's your fault that they are here. When they die, it's all because of you. There's no double agent to save you now, kid." He smiled at me. "I should have introduced myself earlier. My name is Ivan Spivakovsky. I'm a contract killer. Although business is slow, so I do the occasional kidnapping here and there. Never ceases to humor me. I've heard about the plans that the director has in store for the three of you. The man should write a book. I've seen his torture techniques in action. Brilliant, really. But I don't want to bore you with details. I want it to be a surprise, and you need to have a restful sleep. Sweet dreams."

I felt the icy liquid enter my bloodstream. As my eyes drooped, I knew that there had to be a double agent in the CIA that worked for Ares.

———

When I woke up, my hands and feet were tied, and there was duct tape over my mouth. I was vaguely aware that I was in the back of a semitruck. Then I saw a stream of light coming from the space under the latch of the truck. Besides that, it was completely dark.

I needed to see if Crush and Macey were in the truck too, but I couldn't exactly call out their names. I lifted both of my legs off the floor and slammed them back down. The noise echoed through the back of the truck. A few seconds passed before the noise was returned, and then returned again at a lower pitch. Good. We hadn't been separated. My stomach muscles relaxed. I started to scoot toward the noise, but when I'd gone a few feet, a chain that was connected to the rope around my legs was pulled taut, and I couldn't move anymore.

I felt the truck slow down and come to a stop about fifteen minutes later. I was already as far away as I could be from the hatch of the truck, but I tried to pull the chain and rope loose anyway. The hatch was pulled up, and because my chains were connected to the door itself, I was pulled up with it. My legs were straight up in the air, and just the lower part of my back touched the floor. I groaned in pain as the rope rubbed my raw skin.

I didn't recognize the man who looked down at me. I almost wished I were blindfolded. Or blind. Half of the man's face was discolored, and his lip was permanently swollen. It looked like a burn mark. He only had half a head of hair. If zombies were real, he would be their leader.

He came toward me, and I thought he was going to stick me with another syringe, but he unlocked the chain that connected me to the inside of the truck and the rope. My legs slammed down to the floor, and my ankles knocked into each other. A surge of hope filled me. Was he on our side? Were we about to be free? But my hopes were quickly dashed when he didn't make a move to untie the ropes. It killed me that I couldn't stand up and run. The hatch was wide open. Freedom was three feet away. We were on a dirt road, and bright green trees surrounded us from both sides, almost like being in between two walls. I wanted nothing more than to escape into those woods.

The scarred man walked further back into the truck, and I presumed he was unlocking Macey's and Crush's chains. He came back about a minute later with Macey and Crush on either side of him. The ropes were off their ankles but had been replaced by shackles, and their hands were cuffed. The man bent down and took out a knife. I sucked in a breath, and he laughed.

He started to work on the rope that was tied around my ankles, and once he broke through that, he put shackles on my ankles. He replaced the rope on my wrists with handcuffs. He tore the tape off my mouth, taking a few layers of skin with it. I remained silent. The three of us were able to take small steps down the ramp on our own. There, we were instructed to stand still or die.

The harsh sunlight hurt my eyes, and I had to keep them squinted. Crush and Macey seemed to have the same problem. My limbs felt heavy, and I was exhausted. I wondered what had been in that drug they had given us.

As the truck drove away, I saw a picture of a cereal box with a smiling girl on the front. The cereal was called Pluto's Swirls, and I was suddenly hungry. We were instructed to walk toward a pickup truck about a hundred feet away.

As I was shoved into the truck, I felt a needle pierce my skin. I was being sedated again. These men either thought we were going to escape or didn't want to listen to our complaints. A few seconds later, I felt the drug take effect. My limbs got heavy, and my eyes shut.

I woke up just as the truck lurched to a stop. The door opened, and I was thrown to the ground and blindfolded. My shoulders cracked when I landed. I heard cries of protest from Crush and Macey. I was grabbed again and jerked to my feet, and the shackles dug into my ankles.

"Not a rag doll," I protested. I tried to shake off the hands, but they held tight.

"We'll see about that," a man's voice said as he shoved me along.

We walked about a hundred feet before I was pushed through a door, and I felt the icy blast of air conditioning hit my body. I hoped that the footsteps behind me were Macey's and Crush's. The last thing I wanted was to be separated. I was pushed into a room and hands pressed down on my shoulders, and I fell back into a chair. The blindfold was removed from my face, and there was a man in front of me. He had dark hair and skin so pale it looked like he'd never seen the light of day. I heard the door behind me slam. All of a sudden, the fear left my body and was replaced by anger. Pure anger.

"I'm going to take a guess and say you're the famous director I've been hearing about?"

"Smart boy."

"Why am I here?" I asked.

"I think you know why. I am aware that some of my men told you about your father when you were kidnapped in Florida."

"Oh, yeah. I guess it didn't go over so well to find out that you had a traitor in your little posse of legally insane henchmen. And what kind of name is Ares? That name doesn't exactly put fear into my heart."

The man grimaced at the insult but otherwise ignored the jab. "The traitor has been taken care of."

"You killed him?" I asked. I didn't believe a word the man said. I'd just seen Dotson.

"No more questions, or I'll tell one of my men to deal with your charming little girlfriend. What's her name? Macey Mallory? I suggest you don't speak unless spoken to. I wouldn't want anything to happen to her."

I shut up.

"I assume my men told you about my means to get your father to talk?"

I didn't say anything. My insides were churning.

"I've tortured many adults before. Including your father. I've never tortured a child as long as I plan to torture you. The other kids broke and revealed the information that I wanted within a short amount of time. But you have no information that I want. I'm excited to see what the results will be. Adults and children take pain differently, and I look forward to documenting it. I can't wait for your father to reveal the information."

At this point, I was no longer breathing.

"When?"

"When what?" The director asked me mockingly.

"When will it all start?" I wanted to know how long it would be before I was dead. Or at least wishing I was dead.

"The sooner it begins, the better, I suppose. Your father is eager to see you."

The director led me out of the room and down a corridor. As I walked, I tried to look in the small windows of the doors to see if Macey or Crush were in one of the rooms, but the man saw and clamped his icy fingers around my neck and pushed me along.

We stood in front of a metal door, and I had a feeling that my dad was on the other side. The man pulled out a set of keys, unlocked the door, and pushed me inside. The room was fairly small. Maybe three times as big as an average jail cell. There was a table and a chair with a few papers and a couple pencils on top of it. A toilet was in the far corner, and a bed was on the opposite side. A man in his forties sat on the bed. He stood when I was shoved in the room. The door slammed behind me, and I was oddly aware of my heartbeat.

"Hey," I managed and got to my knees.

"Brandon?"

"Chase, actually."

He got off the bed and helped me stand up.

Scars ran up and down his arms. He had another scar on the side of his head. He was in cargo shorts and a dingy white T-shirt. His hair color was faded, but I had his eyes. An intense blue. He didn't look as unhealthy as I imagined after however long he'd been held captive, but in the corner, I could see a blood stain on the wall.

"I'm so sorry. This is my fault. I've put you and your brother in danger." He looked down at my hands. "They didn't take the handcuffs off?"

I shook my head.

"Where have you been living? Who have you been living with? I was so worried after your mom..."

"I live in Florida, on the coast."

"With who?" he asked, and anxiety rose in his voice.

"Um, you know. I live around. Foster care system."

"What? The agency was meant to see that both of you were adopted and kept together."

I raised my eyebrows at that. "Brandon was adopted."

My dad went to the chair and sat down. "Is Brandon here?"

"No, the CIA wouldn't tell me where he is," I told him.

"Is there anyone else here?" he asked.

"Yeah, two others. One of them is with the CIA, but he's only like sixteen or seventeen."

My father walked up to me and put an arm around me. "You have to get out of here. At all costs. Do you understand me? You're the bartering chip, and that's the only thing they have over me right now. If you can get the others out of here, then that's even better. You have to understand I can't tell them anything."

"What about you?" I asked. I was tempted to ask what the information concerned and why it was so important, but I knew he couldn't answer.

"I'll be fine. Get back to the headquarters and tell them where I am. You have to tell them in person. It's too dangerous to use the phone or the Internet. Ares is everywhere. Don't tell them anything else. No matter what they do, you can't tell them anything. Not that you know much. At least, I hope you don't. Knowledge is dangerous."

My dad was about to tell me more, but the door swung open, and a man I'd never seen before busted in, grabbed me by the shoulders, and wrenched me out of the room. Before I was completely out of the room, I heard my dad yell that everything was going to be all right. I found that a little hard to believe.

CHAPTER 17

I don't even remember being put to sleep.

When I woke, I immediately tried to sit up, but there was something that held down my wrists, arms, head, and torso. I could hardly move, and my shoulder was killing me. I was on a wooden table, but there were no legs. It was suspended in the air by ropes. The ceiling was perfectly white, and the room smelled like medicine and bleach.

There was a woman in the room with me.

"Have you ever heard of waterboarding, Chase?"

"No."

"It's an old and effective form of torture. Or interrogation method, as politicians and government agents refer to it."

I sucked in a breath of air. I had a feeling my dad was being forced to watch this. He had already told me that he couldn't tell them anything. That meant Ares was going to torture me to death. The man didn't even know me. He had thought I was Brandon. He probably wouldn't care that I was being tortured. The lady pushed hair out of my face, and her bony fingers stroked my cheek. I shuddered, but there was nothing else I could do. I was strapped down and completely at this woman's mercy.

"Such a pretty boy. Lovely bone structure and beautiful skin and hair. It's a shame, really. The director will probably end up killing you. I'll have to talk to him. I could *definitely* make money off of you if he let me. I know people that would pay a lot for just an hour with you," the woman said as she ran her bony fingers along my stomach. Her fingers stopped at the top of my shorts.

The table that I was on was tilted so that my feet were slightly above my head. The woman placed a towel on my face and tucked the corners under my neck. I tried to shake the towel off, but the restraints were too tight. I could feel it press down on my windpipe. The woman poured water on my face, and for the first half second, I couldn't tell what was happening because the water hadn't soaked all the way through. For another half a second, I thought it wasn't so bad.

Then the water hit my face.

Immediately, it got into my nose, and I started to cough as the water traveled down my throat. The water entered my mouth, and the drowning sensation grew worse. Panic surged in me like a living and breathing beast. There was no way I could get the water out. Gravity was working against me.

The water flow stopped, and I erupted into a coughing fit. The water in my lungs burned, and I could feel blood rushing to my head. As the towel was lifted, I opened my eyes and saw the lady above me. My vision was blurred, so I couldn't see her expression.

"How was it?"

I didn't answer. I didn't think I could. I was too busy coughing and wheezing. I pulled against the restraints.

"I suppose it didn't feel too good?" she asked sweetly.

It took everything I had not to cuss her out, but I imagined that would only bring a slap in the face. She waited two minutes before she spoke again. By this time, I'd more or less calmed down. I'd only been under around ten seconds, but it had felt like ten years.

"I've never been waterboarded before," she said.

"You're a lucky one, aren't you?" I spit more water out of my mouth. "Lucky and ugly."

She poured water on my face again.

CHAPTER 18

I was thrown in a white room with my limbs completely free. I fell to my knees, caught my breath, and fought to keep my eyes open. Tears brimmed my eyes, and all I wanted to do was melt into the walls to escape this mess. I lay down, covered my face with my hands, and tried to go to sleep.

I woke up when someone fell next to me. I immediately dove backward, but I saw that it was only Crush. He groaned and smiled weakly.

"What's up, Pretty Boy?"

"Nothing much. Hanging out in this white room. What about you?"

"Oh, I'm just catching my breath for a second. The usual," he said with labored breathing.

"Cool. Cool."

He sat up and looked at me. "What happened to you?"

"They waterboarded me," I said weakly.

"They dunked me in water and kept me there. A lot." As if to prove his point, he shook out his dark hair and sent water everywhere. His shirt was soaked, and he took it off. I didn't blame him. The room was chilly.

"Macey's not here?" he asked.

"No. Not yet. She's not...right?" I asked.

"No. Why would they kill her and not us? She's fine—or as fine as she can be."

I nodded.

"What was it like?" Crush asked.

"To be waterboarded? You could get anyone to say anything. I could get you to admit that you are a weak and spineless individual. It feels like you're drowning. There's water in your lungs and nose, and there's nothing you can do about it," I muttered. I didn't feel like talking about all the woman had said to me. It was way too creepy to be repeated. "And you?"

"Being dunked wasn't much better. I can hold my breath for pretty long, but I panicked. It was like something my brother would do, except these people were set on seriously hurting me."

"You have a brother?" I asked to change the subject.

"Yeah. His name is Michael, but people call him Mic."

"Does he know that you work with the CIA?"

"I think he knows that I'm lying when I say that I go to camp. I don't know how. Maybe I talk in my sleep or something. He asks me tons questions when I get home, like he wants me to mess up and admit that I really don't go to camp. I always catch him looking through my stuff and staring at me. He goes through my laptop too." Crush was down on the ground and rubbed his eyes.

I thought about asking him if he knew anything about the Applied Research Group. It'd been on my mind recently. Were they good guys? How corrupt were they? Was Crush training to help them? Were they the ones that turned off the CIA's security system? I decided not to bring it up because there was a strong chance that we were being monitored, and I didn't want to be the guy who blew a national secret.

Suddenly, Macey stumbled in and fell to her knees. Her face was distraught, and she bit her lip.

"Macey. What happened?" I put a hand on her shoulder.

"Water hit my forehead for—for hours! Drip, drip, drip. For hours! I couldn't stand it anymore! I freaked and screamed until they let me out." Her hands shook, and she rubbed furiously at her forehead, like the water was still there.

"You're fine now. It's okay," I said. I tried to comfort her even though I knew that the phrase "it's okay" was the last thing she wanted to hear.

"I know. I know. It was just so nerve-racking. It didn't hurt or anything, but the water would get in my eyes or mouth, and I couldn't get it off."

Macey looked from Crush to me. "What happened to you guys?" she asked.

"I was dunked in water. Repeatedly."

"I was waterboarded. Basically, they made me feel like I was drowning," I told her. "And it sucked."

"We have got to get out of here," Macey said anxiously.

"I'll get us out of here. We'll live," Crush said, as if he already had a genius plan of getting us out of here in one piece.

Macey shook her head. "What if we don't live? People don't get out of things like this. What if we die here? They'll kill us, and no one will ever know the truth about what happened."

"We'll get out of here. We have to, right? I always get out of things," I said hopefully. I thought back to what my dad told me. I didn't see how I could possibly get out of this, much less get back to the CIA headquarters and tell them what was happening.

No one said anything for a few moments.

"So, does anyone want to hear what I have to say?" Crush asked sheepishly.

Macey threw her hands up in the air and looked at the ceiling. "Let's hear it."

"Think about it. Water can kill and burn you, but it can't exactly give you bruises. So they don't want us to have any signs of physical abuse. But why?"

"Um, because they're sick in the head?" I asked and thought back to what the woman had told me before she waterboarded me.

"Maybe they need us for something, and we can't look like we've just walked through the gauntlet."

"So they're going to sell us or something?" I asked without any emotion.

"Who knows?"

"They might think we know something, so let's keep it that way. Once they know that we're clueless as a bunch of hamsters, then it's off with our heads," Macey said and made a cutting motion across her neck.

I noticed Crush looked away as Macey said that. I wondered how much he knew about the CIA, and if he was willing to protect the secrets.

"Do you think your dad told them what they wanted to know and that's why they stopped torturing us?" Crush asked.

"No."

Boredom set in as the conversation lagged.

At first, it was like being bored in school. Then it was the lazy Saturday boredom. Then, it progressed to a boring break. Then it was boring like a boring summer vacation (I longed to have one of those). Then, it was the boredom in juvie kind of feeling. Finally, it was the "being locked in a completely white room and feeling like you were going insane" kind of boredom.

"Please, someone make a joke or do something," I pleaded. "I'm dying over here."

"What are we supposed to do? Laugh about this?" Macey asked.

"No," I said. "But you guys act like we're already dead. We'll get out of this."

"Is anyone else starving? Because I am," Crush said. He got up and started to walk around the room. We would have tried opening the door, but there wasn't one. We only had a rough idea of where the exit was because we'd been thrown through it.

"I don't see any cameras or microphones, but that doesn't mean that there aren't any," Crush observed. "They'd have to be stupider than a pile of rocks not to monitor us. What kind of operation are they running here?"

"An inhumane one," Macey said.

"A sick one," I added.

Then I heard two voices outside. They were faint, but I could still make out the words and the voices. One of the voices sounded extremely familiar. The three of us crept to the wall, and the voice I recognized spoke.

"He hasn't talked yet? You did make him watch Chase being waterboarded, right?"

"Of course."

"Did he do anything?"

"You were sent the video."

"Then why did you stop me?" the voice I recognized asked angrily.

"The director said that phase two should be commenced as soon as possible."

"Did he really? That's great. Go and get someone to unlock the cell and then make sure the kids are brought to room nineteen."

The conversation ended there, and the footsteps faded down the hallway.

"Was that who I think it was?" I asked.

"Yeah," Crush answered. "It was exactly who you thought it was. This is terrible. When they come to get us, we have to get out of here. And fast. We have to warn the CIA about the traitor. National security is at risk." Crush put back on his shirt.

"Wait," Macey said. "I thought his work for Ares wasn't real. What if he's just playing along?"

"Then he wouldn't have been so happy about phase two. Whatever that is."

It all clicked in place. The director hadn't killed Agent Dotson. They had been working together all along. Only the two of them really knew what was going on. The rest of the Ares members didn't know that Agent Dotson secretly worked for the CIA. The CIA knew that Agent Dotson worked for Ares, but they thought he worked for them in their favor. They thought it had only been to make sure that I got off that boat in one piece. Agent Dotson's loyalty was with Ares. Not the CIA. He'd been a triple agent, if such a thing existed.

"That traitor," Macey whispered under her breath.

I sunk to the floor. This was all so confusing. My head and shoulder ached.

I managed a few more words. "Don't let them find out that we know."

The door slowly opened, and three men stood in the doorway. They told us to follow them. Seeing as we really didn't have much of a choice, we all trudged into the hallway, heads down. The one man we thought we could trust turned out to be just as evil as the rest of these people. I wondered if we would be tortured with water again. I cringed at the thought.

One of the men walked in front of us, and the other two walked behind us. As if we would have a chance against the guns they carried. We walked until we came to an elevator; the three of us were pushed inside, and the doors immediately closed. I felt the elevator ascend.

"We don't know anything, remember?" Crush told us.

"We *don't* know anything," Macey said.

She and I didn't know anything; she was no help to Ares, information-wise. But she was helpful in other ways. Ares already knew that if they threatened me with hurting her, they could get anything they wanted. The doors opened, and there stood the director. He was oddly short, but he had huge arms. He was probably about five seven, and Crush and I were easily taller than he was. I could see the gun strapped to his waist, accompanied by a five-inch knife, which made up for his lack of height. He also had two more huge men standing behind him. "Follow me."

"What are you going to do now?" Macey asked.

No answer.

"Did my dad tell you anything?" I asked. I was sure he didn't. I just wanted to annoy the man.

"No. He didn't. And the three of you are going to suffer because of it." The three of us exchanged nervous glances.

"How could you expect him to? He doesn't love Chase! He barely knows him!" Crush yelled at the director.

My eyes widened. Was Crush trying to get himself killed? The director turned around and slammed Crush up against the wall. He grabbed him by the neck and pulled him up off the ground until his feet didn't touch the ground. Macey made a noise in her throat.

"I could kill you right now. I am in complete control of your life. Didn't your parents tell you to respect authority?" He let go of Crush, who sank to the ground and gasped for air. The director kicked him in the stomach, and Crush groaned. It was kind of ironic, as that was exactly what Crush had done to me.

"Get up," the director told Crush. He kicked him again.

After a few seconds, Crush climbed to his knees and slowly stood. One of the men grabbed him by the arm, and we started to walk again. We were led to a room, where the door was unlocked and we were pushed inside, and no one followed us in. My father was inside the room. His feet were shackled to the floor, but his hands were free. I noticed that he had a black eye that looked pretty fresh.

"What happened?" I asked.

"I tried to get into the room, the one you were being waterboarded in, and things got ugly." He paused. "Listen, I'm so sorry about what you three had to go through, but it won't stop unless you get out of here. They'll keep hurting you unless I tell them the information. I can't do that without risking the lives of a lot of people. That's why you three have to leave. If what Chase told me is true, and you're an agent-in-training," he said looking at Crush, "things are going to get messy if that information is leaked to the press."

"How are we supposed to get out of here? And why did they leave us alone with you?" Crush asked.

"They probably want you three to guilt-trip me into telling them what they want to know. There's no doubt that we're being monitored right now, so be careful what you say."

"Where's the information? Maybe we can get there before them and destroy it," I asked.

"Now, Chase. You know I can't exactly whisper in your ear where it is. All three of you probably have listening devices on your bodies. And it would be really dangerous for me to tell *you*."

"Then how exactly are we supposed to help you?" Crush asked.

"Just get out of here. There's a secret passage down the hall. It's to your right. These people are too idiotic to blindfold me in the corridors," my father said loudly. I didn't understand. What was going on? He'd said it himself. They were probably monitoring us, and he'd just revealed his plan to them. How in the world had he kept the information a secret for so long? He was crazy.

"You'll know what to do. Just run," he finished. I held up my finger to indicate for him to shut up, but it was too late. Who did he think we were? We had no clue what to do.

The men came back into the room and looked annoyed. Crush screamed and leaped into action while Macey slipped out the door. He kicked the man closest to him in between his legs and then delivered another swift kick to the head and sent the man sprawling on the ground. Mimicking Crush's moves, I kicked one of the other man's knees and then kicked him in the head. We had the element of surprise, but the two other men had everything else. Like strength and weapons. Crush and I ran out of the room and shut the door behind us and wasted precious seconds bolting the door shut.

Macey was halfway down the hallway and running her hands frantically over the walls. Crush and I ran down the hallway. We both knew we couldn't have seriously hurt either of those men. They would be out the door and on us in no time. Macey let out a shriek of excitement as she bent down, her hands clasped on something. She pushed wet hair out of her face and pulled on a latch, and the door started to give a little. Crush grabbed the handle, and they both pulled. The opening led into a tunnel, exactly like the one in the CIA, almost like it had been designed using the same blueprints. We threw ourselves in and slammed the door as the men came out of the room.

"Where did they go?" one of them yelled.

"Go to the control room and sound the alarm. I'll stop the elevator."

We held our breath as we heard one of the men pass us.

"Where do we go?" Macey asked once it had been quiet for a few seconds.

There were two staircases built into the walls. One went up and the other went down.

"Down," Crush said.

The secret tunnel was moldy and probably hadn't been used in a long time. Most people might have forgotten about it, which explained why the guards didn't bother to check here. But if that was true, how did my father know about it? But I had other concerns right now. What if we went down too far and ended up underground? We ran down about thirty stairs before we saw another hatch.

We stopped running and listened. The silence was eerie, but all the same, it was silence. Crush was the first one to get to the hatch and pushed on it, but it didn't budge. Fear coursed through me. What if we couldn't get it opened? What would happen then? Would the men find us? Would they leave us here to die? I shook my head. I had to stop thinking about these "what if" questions. I had to shut my imagination off. Imagination was a dangerous thing, and I had to avoid it. The most important thing right now was to get out of here.

Macey and I joined him, and I hoped that it wouldn't end up like the last time we used a hatch door. Thankfully, this hatch door was old and in need of oil, so when the hatch started to give, no one ended up on the ground. Light streamed into the small room. Crush looked out the small opening and whispered that he thought it was clear. That didn't reassure me.

Crush opened the hatch door until it was wide enough for us to slip through, and we landed in a dimly lit hallway. I noticed a window that had light streaming through it down the hallway. I pointed to it, and as soon as the others looked at it, the alarms started to blare. It was like a fire drill at school, only ten times louder and one hundred times scarier. I knew that we wouldn't be able to hear if anyone was coming up on us, and there was no doubt every security camera in the whole building was searching for us. How did we think we could do this? We started to panic; Macey took off in one direction, and Crush took off in the other, but I was able to grab both of their shirts and pull them back toward me. We couldn't be separated.

Then the lights flickered off.

"Guys?" Macey whispered. I could feel her shaking. Or that might have been me.

"Here," I said.

"Right here," Crush said.

"What do we do now?" she asked. I could hear panic in her voice. Heck, I heard panic in all of our voices.

"The window," I said, and even though I knew they couldn't see me pointing at it, we could all see the steady stream of light coming in. I heard a chorus of barks over the siren. And it didn't exactly sound like a dog that you might find in the purse of a celebrity.

More "what if" questions scattered across my mind.

The window didn't have a latch to open it, and we didn't have anything to smash it with. There was no way Crush could break glass with his bare hands, no matter how strong he thought he was. If we couldn't find a way to break the glass, that meant we would have backed ourselves into a corner with angry dogs on our trail.

"We'll never break the window and make it out in time. Those dogs are getting closer," I said.

"Do you have a better plan?" Crush asked.

"No. I was hoping you did," I told him.

"Macey?" Crush called out. We almost had to yell to be heard over the scream of the siren. "Where are you?"

"Right here!" she screamed and stepped back into the light. She had a fire extinguisher in her hand.

"Nice," I said.

She swung the extinguisher like a baseball bat, and the glass cracked. She swung it again, and it shattered at our feet. I turned my face away. She set down the extinguisher just as the dogs sounded like they were a few dozen feet away. I had a feeling that people with guns weren't far behind.

"Move!" Crush yelled at us.

I didn't need to be told once. I was halfway out of the window before the words even left his mouth, and Macey was right behind me. The window had some kind of railing underneath, but there was barely enough room for Macey and me to stand on. The ground was roughly fifteen feet below us, but it might as well have been five hundred feet. We couldn't afford any broken bones now. It was time to tuck and roll.

"Crush! Hurry up!" I called.

Then I heard a scream, and the extinguisher extinguishing whatever it was meant to extinguish. The barking stopped and Crush came out onto the ledge. He had been bitten on his arm, and it was bleeding badly. There was no time to fix it.

"Jump!" he screamed.

So we jumped.

I will never understand how people can possibly hit the ground running. It's impossible. I landed on my feet at first, but then somehow ended up on my back, and my wrists took most of the blow. A shock of pain went up my arm and my shoulder tingled. I looked back and saw the barrel of a gun sticking out of the window. A bullet whizzed right by my leg, and my heart leaped. Two more shots followed that came so close I felt the air ripple. We were close to the edge of the building, so we stood up and rounded the side of the structure, away from the gunmen. I peeked back around the corner and saw that they were about ready to jump too.

"Go! They're coming."

Macey, Crush, and I dashed toward a line of eight black trucks parked about twenty yards away from us. We hid behind them and stopped for a few precious seconds to catch our breath.

"How do we get away?" Macey asked, breathless.

"We start one of these puppies up and hope it doesn't run out of gas," I said. I quickly looked to see if the gunmen were near us. They were barely fifty feet away, but they hadn't spotted us yet. We ran to that last truck to get as far away from the men as possible. I crept to the front of the truck to see if the keys were somehow in there, or better yet, in the ignition.

There was a set of keys on the dashboard.

I blinked a few times to make sure I wasn't seeing things, but there was a key ring with a few keys on them. I motioned to Macey and Crush, and I slipped inside the unlocked truck. I only had about five seconds to pick out the correct key, start the truck, put it into gear, and make sure I didn't run over anybody.

Macey and Crush climbed in the backseat and got down low. I stuck a random key into the ignition and turned it. The engine fired up, and smoked poured out of the back. I glanced at the gas gauge. We barely had half a tank left, but that was plenty. I threw the truck in reverse and floored the gas pedal.

"Get down!" Macey yelled.

I ducked, and a shower of bullets came through the windshield, and a hole appeared in the headrest directly behind me. I spun the wheel so the truck faced the way I wanted to go. I put the truck into drive and floored it again. I was at ninety miles per hour in a matter of seconds. Why were they trying to kill us? I thought they needed us.

Then I looked down at the floor. They weren't bullets. Were those darts? Were they shooting darts at us? I bent down and tossed one back to Crush.

"What is that?"

"How am I supposed to know?" Crush yelled back and tossed the dart to the floor.

"They're right behind us," Macey yelled from the backseat. "They're going for the tires! With possible real bullets."

I started to zigzag across the rough terrain. I'd seen what could happen if one of the tires on a truck blew, especially if you were going this fast. I was determined not to let that happen.

"Go faster!" Crush yelled.

I knew that there was no way we could get away from these guys. They knew the area, and we didn't even know what state we were in. Then a fence came into view.

"Chase," Macey warned.

"I see it."

"And what do you plan to do about it?"

"Ram it."

The fence gave way immediately. We hit a bump, and the truck went airborne as the fence flew over to the side and crashed to the ground. I looked in the rearview mirror. They were gaining on us, and once they caught up, they would probably ram the back of the truck. I kept such a tight grip on the steering wheel that my knuckles turned white.

"Is there a gun? Anything?" I screamed.

"I don't see anything," Macey answered.

A dart came through the back window and nicked my ear. There was no way I was letting these guys put me under *again*. They'd already taken out the back window. It was only a matter of time before one of us actually got stuck with a dart.

"What do I do?" I asked.

"Keep driving!" Crush howled at me. "And keep your head down."

I lowered my head until I could barely see the road in front of me, and a rain of darts came around and in the car. I hoped that if one of them did end up hitting me, I would have enough time to stop the truck. I hit a huge rock and the truck went airborne again and crashed back on the ground with a thud. I lost time attempting to regain my composure and tried to find the gas pedal with my right foot. I floored it again, and we all slammed forward.

"Chase!" Macey screamed at me.

"Yeah?" I yelled back.

"The bag. Hand me the bag."

"What bag?"

"The one that's right beside you."

I took my eyes off the "road" for a few seconds, reached over with one hand, and pulled on the bag. I handed it back to Macey and straightened out the truck. I was going well over one hundred miles per hour.

I heard a gunshot go off and ducked before I realized it had come from our truck. I glanced backward and saw that Macey and Crush both had handguns and had leaned out of the window to shoot at the truck that followed us. It struck me odd that there was only one truck going after us. They'd gotten a helicopter to aid in our kidnapping, so why didn't they put more effort into making sure we didn't escape?

I went over a hill, and a forest came into sight. My hopes lifted. I'd always felt safer in the woods. There were no people, and that made it easy to disappear and forget. You could pretend there wasn't a world where the tree line began.

"I'm going to stop at the edge of the trees and then we're going to haul butt into the woods and run until we can't. Got it?" I said.

They might have heard me, or they might not have. I figured they would know what to do when I stepped on the brakes. We were only twenty yards away now. I slammed my foot on the brakes, and we all jutted forward. I threw open the driver's door and jumped out of the truck. I looked back and saw the truck that hurtled toward us with bloodthirsty men. We needed to get out of there. Now.

We all sprinted into the woods and almost immediately, a patch of thorns snagged my shorts, but I was able to pull them free and keep running. In the back of my mind, I tried to remember when I'd put on these shorts and couldn't. The clothes weren't mine. Actually, we all had on the same clothes. A white T-shirt and khaki shorts. I looked behind at the men. They had guns, but they weren't firing. Maybe it was because they couldn't get a direct shot. The woods were thick. Branches whipped my face and legs as I looked around for Macey and Crush. Macey was to my right, and Crush was to my left, and I knew we wouldn't be able to outrun these guys. No way.

I looked over at Macey. She had a gun in her hand and held it close as she ran. The men were faster than we were, and soon I felt hands brush my back. Pure fear and a shot of adrenaline coursed through my veins, and I ran a little harder. But it wasn't fast enough. The man was on top of me, his knees on my chest. I gasped and let out a cry.

"Good to have you back."

I whipped my body back and forth, but the man didn't budge. I brought up my knee and kneed him in the back. His upper body jerked forward.

"Get off me!"

The man reached for his dart gun and smiled at me.

We'd been so close.

"Get off him. Now."

It was Crush's voice.

I looked over at him. He had a gun, and it was trained in our direction. I could see his shaky hands.

The man jammed the dart into my skin. At first, I didn't feel too much. My breathing started to get slower, and my eyelids drooped. It was the same feeling I'd gotten on the helicopter and every freaking other time these people had sedated me.

Darkness.

CHAPTER 19

I woke up in a thicket of green bushes. I sat up slowly. My throat burned, and my stomach growled. My chest felt like a big bruise. I shut my eyes and felt hands on my shoulders. I was eased back down.

"What happened?" I asked as pain shot through me.

"We got away," Crush said after a few moments.

"How?"

"After the guy knocked you out, he got off of you and started to move toward Macey and me. By this time, his little buddy was there. I threatened to shoot them if they didn't turn around and leave. They kept coming, so—so I shot them."

I sat up.

"You what?"

"They're not going to die. I shot them both in the knees. Left a nice little blood trail. I took their dart guns and threatened to shoot them with that. They didn't get why that was a problem until I told them they would bleed to death if they fell asleep. They probably won't go back. They'll get killed there."

"So they're still out there?" I asked and took in my surroundings. We were in a hollow part of a thicket. We were all extremely close. The hollow was probably about three feet tall and five feet wide. Macey was on her stomach, eyes closed, and arms under her head.

"Maybe. But they're in no condition to mess with us. Besides, we're pretty far away."

"How did I get here?"

"I carried you."

I cussed under my breath.

"Is that a problem?" Crush asked.

"Yeah."

"Why?"

"'Cause now I have to be nice to you."

Crush laughed.

"Is she asleep?" I asked, referring to Macey.

"No," Macey grumbled. "She's just really tired."

"Join the club," I said.

"You just had an hour nap," Crush protested. He'd ripped the edge of his shirt and tied it around his arm. The white fabric was now red.

"Forced sleep doesn't count."

"Do you really think those men won't find us?" Macey asked, speaking into the ground.

"Um, maybe not those particular men. Chase's dad might have been right. They could have devices on us. Tracking devices. Anybody have anything like that?"

"Don't think so," I said.

"I'm good," Macey answered. "But I do have a whole bunch of bruises and no clue how they got there."

"Yeah, and my shoulder hurts. I don't remember hurting it."

"Look, we can talk about that later. Right now, we need to figure out what to do. We've stayed here too long," Crush said.

"We just walk that way," I said and motioned away from the headquarters.

"Then what? Where do we go?"

"My dad said we have to go back to the CIA headquarters and tell them where the headquarters is. We should probably add in the part about Dotson being a traitor."

"And how are we supposed to get there?" Macey asked.

"Macey has a point, Chase. We don't know where we are. I don't see how you think we can get to the headquarters. Besides, Dotson might go back to the CIA headquarters and mess things up for us or go to another country. We need to find someone we can trust from the CIA and tell them everything," Crush said.

"We thought we could trust Dotson," I said.

We got out of our hiding place and began to walk north, away from the headquarters and toward whatever was in these woods.

"Hey, Chase?" Crush asked.

"What?"

"Where *did* you learn to drive like that?"

"I don't know."

"What do you mean you don't know?"

"I just don't know."

"You're only fifteen, right?"

"Yeah."

"No offense or anything, but you don't exactly have any parents to teach you how to drive or anything. So where did you learn?"

"Friends. And if you have to say 'no offense or anything' before you say something, it's probably best not to say anything."

We walked about four miles before we came to a river. By this time, I was drenched in sweat, but the drowsiness from the drug had worn off. We walked down the steep bank and onto a sandbar that jutted out into the river. I bent down and splashed some of the water on my face. The cool water felt great, and I wanted to dive in. Maybe the water would soothe the pain in my shoulder.

"I don't know about the two of you, but I'm parched." I cupped my hands and drank some of the water from the river.

This worried Crush.

"Chase, stop it. The water has pollution and could make you sick. It's asking for trouble," Crush said as he pulled me back from the water. "Come on. You know they're still looking for us. They'll probably use that helicopter to look for us, and it will be easier for them to see us if we're not in the woods."

I could see Macey eyeing the water and knew she was just as thirsty as I was. Crush had to be as well. I knew that dehydration could kill you as easily as a bullet could.

"Crush, you're being ridiculous. Both of you need to drink water."

Maccy didn't need to be told twice, but Crush still wasn't convinced it was a good idea.

"It's not like you're going to die from the water, Crush," I told him. In a few hours or so, he would be feeling the effects of dehydration, and I knew from experience that that could slow you down as much as having five broken toes would.

"Oh, and you have so much experience drinking out of rivers?" he asked me.

Macey shifted uncomfortably and I raised my eyebrows. "Actually, yeah. I do."

"And how is that?"

"When I escaped from juvie and when I ran from foster homes, that's what I drank. River water. So get off your high horse and just drink it." I didn't think it was necessary to mention that if you consumed unfiltered water in bulk, it would leave you with a stomachache.

Crush threw his hands up in the air. "Fine. But if I get sick, I'm blaming you." He bent down to drink some of the water. He got his hand wet, and I saw him wipe the blood off the surrounding skin of his dog bite. He grimaced. Thankfully, the bleeding had stopped, but I knew it must be painful. That might take him out before Ares was able to. I looked over to Macey and noticed the cuts around her wrists and ankles. I thought it would be best not to ask about that now.

We got back in the cover of the woods and started to follow the current of the river. We hoped that it would lead us to a town—a house—something. I trailed behind Macey and Crush. I couldn't shake the image of my dad out of my head. I knew that I would probably never see him again. He was probably dead by now. I'd barely seen him for ten minutes. My heart leaped into my chest, and I fought back tears. I hadn't had time to think about feeling any emotion, everything happened so fast. Macey dropped back and walked beside me, like she sensed that I wasn't exactly having a great day.

"How are you?"

"There have been better days," I answered.

"I bet. You just met your dad after—what? Fifteen years? I can't even fathom what you must be feeling right now."

"What about you? I dragged you into some crazy world with a bunch of killers and psychopaths. You were tortured with water." I didn't feel like talking about myself.

"Stop it. I don't blame you at all for anything. This is the craziest thing that's ever happened to me. Chase, we're involved with something that has cost people their lives and kept the CIA on their toes for who knows how long. And we found one of the best-kept secrets of this nation." She looked at Crush, who walked about twenty feet in front of us. "The CIA recruits teenagers."

"Yeah, my mind stopped processing all this stuff a long time ago. I think it has something to do with the lack of the necessities. Coke and cheeseburgers."

"Amen," she said and then paused. "Do you seriously think we can make it to the CIA without being—you know…?"

"Maybe. I really don't know. I guess we can worry about that later. We have no money and no means of transportation. We're getting ahead of ourselves. First, I guess we need to get out of these woods and find somewhere to sleep, get out of these clothes, disguise ourselves, and get that cheeseburger. Our top priority is to get as far away from these people as possible. And decide if we can trust anyone at the CIA or Mr. I-Was-Trained-by-the CIA," I said.

"You don't trust him either?" she asked. "You would think all those summers locked up underground would mess with a person's mind."

That surprised me. I thought Macey would fall in love with Crush. He was a secret agent. Crush spent hours in the gym, and he showed it off. He was a spy, a patriot, and he was mysterious. How could she not be crushing on him? No pun intended.

"It's not like I don't trust him. He did save my life and all. I just don't like the way he acts sometimes. Like at the river."

"Hey, how 'bout you two lovebirds stop flirting?" Crush asked as he looked back at us.

"Crush, when do you think we'll get somewhere? I'm starving, and it's hot. Maccy and I think we just need to focus on getting away from here before we bother with getting to the headquarters."

"I know Ares wouldn't have their headquarters too far out—that would only draw attention," he said. "But they don't want to be too close to civilization, or that would draw attention to them. They would want a happy medium. But I don't see how they eluded the CIA for so long. They assumed that the headquarters was in another country or near the border."

"And how do you know all this?" I asked.

"I picked up on a few access codes," he boasted.

"That's nice," I said and eyed Macey, who smiled. "And I assumed you were caught and failed to lie your way out of it?"

"Hey. I'm an excellent liar," Crush defended.

"That's a lie right there," I said. "You know how I and everyone else can tell? Your voice went higher. If you fix that, then you might be able to convince your teacher whatever lame excuse you tell her about not having your homework."

"Wait," Macey said. "How do we know we're not in another country? We could be in Canada for all we know."

"That's a brilliant question," I said.

Macey and I both caught up to Crush and fell in line with him. "And how do we know we're not near the border? How do we know anything?"

"We don't. Let's just hope whoever lives here speaks English."

"What? You don't know another language?" I asked.

"Honestly, I was supposed to start to learn a language next week. That's not going to happen now. Although my Spanish isn't too bad."

"Oh? Really? Say something," I told him.

"Fine. Eres feo y diminuto."

"What did you say?" Macey asked as she climbed over a log.

"Tell you what. If we get out of this alive, I'll tell you."

We walked in more silence. I don't know how much time passed. It was almost impossible to tell. When the sun started to set, it occurred to all three of us that we would have to sleep on the hard ground that night.

We walked until it was hard to see and finally chose a place about twenty-five yards from the edge of the river and sat down. I cleared away all the pinecones and tried to make it as soft as possible.

"Well," Macey said, "at least we avoided being shot for a few hours."

I yawned. As tired as I was, I didn't want to go to sleep. This was the kind of stuff that you had dreams about, and I wasn't looking forward to it. The sound of the river made me think of being waterboarded, and I shuddered. I rolled over on my side and wondered if it would be okay if I went to the river to get another sip of water. So far, the water hadn't made any of us sick, but with my luck, I'd probably fall in the river and hit my head on a rock. But I was so thirsty. The hunger pains had set in two hours ago. I was a little concerned about why they hadn't set in earlier. We'd gone a very long time without food. I knew I would wake up with a familiar headache.

A bat flew over my head, and I realized I wasn't that worried about snakes or any another animal coming up to me in the middle of the night. I'd gotten over that fear a long time ago. I was worried about the whirl of a helicopter or someone with a machine gun. But Macey was right; we'd avoided Ares for a few hours, and hopefully, we would be able to have a few more hours without being caught.

I swatted the swarm of mosquitoes over my head and groaned. Not only was I going to be eaten alive, but I was also going to be driven into insanity by the buzzing sound they made. But this wasn't the first time I'd slept on the ground in the woods. I'd made it through nights in the woods before. The situation was just a bit different. I wasn't alone.

"Guys?" I whispered.

"What?" Crush asked.

"There are a thousand and one mosquitoes over my head," I said.

"What do you want us to do?" Macey asked, groggily.

"I don't know. But these things are about to make a meal out of my blood," I complained.

"Just bring your arms in your shirt and shut up so we can go to sleep," Macey grumbled.

———

I think it was around two in the morning when I woke. The light from the moon streamed through the treetops and gave the ground a ghostly look. It reminded me of the Haneys' house. I could look out of the window in my room and see the splats of moonlight on the ground. I'd never seen that. It was the first time I'd slept somewhere that was on the second floor and had time to appreciate the view.

I heard the noise that woke me up for a second time, and my worst fears were confirmed. Ares had found us. I could hear dogs barking and the whirl of a helicopter. Man, they were really using their resources to find us. I started to think they'd let us go, but escape wasn't meant to be easy. I stood up and shook Macey and Crush until they were awake.

"Guys, we got trouble in paradise."

Macey and Crush slowly got to their feet.

"Is that a helicopter?"

"Yes, sir, it is. We need to get moving."

We ran toward the river. The plan was something we should have done hours ago. We would cross the river and hope the dogs were thrown off our scent. The water was chilly, but not dangerously cold. I carefully got in the water and walked out until I couldn't touch anymore. I started to swim across the water. I briefly thought of Crush. How would he handle being in the water again? The dogs couldn't smell us in the water, but the helicopter could easily put a spotlight on us—and that's just what they did.

"Dive!" I yelled.

I blew out air so I could sink and started to cautiously swim the way I had been going. I could feel myself being pulled back, so I put my foot on the bottom as often as I could to give myself a push. The last thing I needed was to bang my head against one of the rocks. I kept one of my hands out as I swam.

I came up for air. The spotlight from the helicopter streamed back and forth, and as soon as it neared me, I dove back under the water. I came back up and scrambled over a rock that stuck up out of the water. The bank was just ten feet away. I crawled up the bank and ran under the cover of the trees.

"Macey? Crush?"

"Right here," I heard Macey call out. She came out from behind a tree.

"I'm coming." Crush said as he scrambled up the gently sloping bank.

"All right, then. Let's go. The dogs might be here soon." I could hear the barks not too far off.

We ran alongside the bank until my heart felt like it might explode. I could still hear the whirl of the helicopter, but the barks of the dogs were gone. Perhaps we'd lost them. For the time being, anyway.

"Can we stop?" Macey asked.

"You think they're going to find us again?" I asked once we all had our breath back.

"Probably. Just not right now," Crush responded.

We walked away from the edge of the river and stopped in the thickest part of the forest.

"We need to keep moving," Crush said. He'd taken off his shirt and was in the process of removing the water. He didn't bother to put it back on. He really needed to tie it around the bite.

We walked and walked. It reminded me so much of my walk back to Florida. Except this time I wasn't barefoot, and I wasn't alone. The sun started to rise, and I fought to keep my eyes open. The headache was definitely here.

"Who wants to stop and take a rest?" I asked and yawned. I didn't wait for an answer. I was exhausted, wet, and a bit chilled. Not to mention my shoulder hurt, for reasons still unknown. I sat down, leaned up against a tree, and closed my eyes.

"Chase?" Macey asked.

"Hmm?" I asked, sleepily.

"Crush thinks we should keep moving."

"Crush thinks a lot of things. Come on, guys. We need sleep if we want to stand a chance," I said and closed my eyes again.

"Come on, Crush. Chase is right. I'm exhausted. There's no way we can keep going," Macey coaxed.

"Fine. I guess you're right. But not for a long time, okay? Maybe half an hour."

CHAPTER 20

Unfortunately, Crush stayed true to his words. As soon as I had closed my eyes, Crush shook my shoulder.

"Guys, wake up. We need to keep moving. We don't want Ares finding us again," Crush said.

I cracked opened one eye. The only reason I sat up was to remove the acorn that had lodged itself into my neck. I was so hot I could have taken a bath in my own sweat. We couldn't have been in Canada. Macey sat up to massage her left shoulder and glance at a cut on her shin. She regarded her wrists and ankles and sighed. The cuts must have been from the bindings Ares put on her during the water torture. I looked over at Crush. He checked the dog bite, which was swollen and a bright red. That wasn't good.

"How's your arm?" I asked and stood up.

"It's infected, or it's going to get infected. Stupid dog. I should have killed it." He started to walk, and Macey and I followed.

"I need food," Macey said after a few moments. I was glad she was the first one to complain about the hunger. "That bark is starting to look good," she said and gestured to a pine tree.

If I had learned anything, it was that water took the edge off of hunger pains. I walked over to the river and had three handfuls of the water. I knew it was pushing it, but I didn't care. I picked my head up and saw two people in red kayaks easing down the river. I froze and gawked at our first sign of civilization. I ran back into the woods before they turned around and saw me. I had an idea.

"Guys," I screamed. "There were two guys going down the river. There's probably a put-in somewhere or a house. We might be getting close to a town."

"Then let's go," Macey said. We picked up our pace, but not by much.

I prayed that wherever they were headed wasn't that far away. I didn't think the three of us could walk too much longer.

"Where do you think we got these clothes? I don't remember putting them on."

Macey and Crush glanced down at their clothes and frowned. We were in the exact same thing, even down to the socks and shoes.

"They must have given them to us."

"I gathered that much. I don't remember putting them on," I said again.

"That's not really one of our main problems here, Chase," Crush told me. I don't think he meant to, but he glanced at his wounded arm.

About once every four minutes, one of us would walk down to the river to see if the kayakers were still in sight. Once, they stopped to eat, so we were able to get somewhat ahead of them. Another time, one of the kayakers flipped, and we got farther ahead. After two or so miles, we came upon a two-story log house that rested near the river. The deck was connected to the house, and it jutted until it was a few feet away from being directly over the river. There was a nice dock, and the put-in was concrete. I was thankful the house wasn't on the other side of the river. I didn't feel like crossing it again. Sleeping in wet clothes hadn't been fun, and they were still a little damp.

The two kayakers got out of their kayaks and sat down on a sandbar in the middle of the river, and I could see they were both guys in their midtwenties. I figured we had about ten minutes.

We crept around to the front of the house and climbed up the wooden steps that led onto the porch.

"Wait," Macey said. "We're going to break in?"

"Yeah, why did you think we followed them for miles?" I asked.

"I knew why," Macey defended. "I just didn't know we were going to break in. Or I thought that there was going to be a paved road that we could follow. I don't know what I thought, okay?"

I walked up to the front door, turned the doorknob, and gave it a push. The door opened with no problem. "Hey, it's not my fault these people don't lock their doors. Now come on, we don't have long, and I really don't feel like getting caught."

We walked into the kitchen. The house was clean apart from wet towels on the floor and two bowls of soggy cereal on the kitchen table. The kitchen had white countertops and a wooden table. The refrigerator was silver and fairly large. The walls were painted a pale green, and there were old bottles of wine on top of the wooden cabinets. The house was one big square, with the kitchen, the dining room, and the living room all in the same open space. There was a set of stairs off to the right of the living room that led to the upper story.

I ran to one of the cabinets and grabbed a glass. I filled it with ice and water and chugged it. I opened the fridge and began to rummage through it. There wasn't a whole lot of food, but I wasn't going to be picky. I grabbed a huge jar of pickles, set them on the counter, and popped the lid. Then I realized Crush and Macey were staring at me.

"What?" I asked as I ate a pickle. "Come on, stop standing around. Get something to eat and drink so we can get out of here."

"It looks like you've done this before," Crush said. He got a cup out of the cabinet and drank an entire glass of water in one gulp. Then he went to the counter and splashed some water on his bite. He started to rummage through the cabinets for medicine but came up short. He grimaced, and I knew that the bite really bothered him.

"I've never broken into someone's house to steal food," I admitted. "Now, anyone want a pickle?"

Macey found bread, and Crush found a bag of meat that didn't smell all that bad, so we threw together some sloppy sandwiches and ate them.

"They're coming," I said. I'd kept an eye on the door we'd come through. We'd only been inside for five minutes, but the two guys were already coming up the steps, laughing. They would be able to see us in a few seconds if we didn't do something.

Crush jumped up and hid in a closet. But I knew better than that. I'd learned to never back myself into a corner. Ever. But there was no time to get him out. So I grabbed Macey, and we flew halfway up the staircase. Then we were forced to stop. The guys had walked in. We sat down on the stairs and pressed up against the far wall. They wouldn't be able to see us unless they walked into the living room area. If they stayed in the kitchen area and didn't go in the closet where Crush was, we wouldn't be seen. But how would we get out?

"I can't believe you flipped," one of them said.

"I can't either. I thought the shorter kayak would be easier to maneuver, but I guess not."

The other guy started to say something, but he was interrupted. "Dude, what's with the pickles? I had a bowl of cereal this morning and you did too. Who took out the pickles?"

"Didn't your sister say something about coming?"

"Yeah, but she doesn't leave Colorado till tomorrow. Is there someone in the house? I didn't lock the door this morning."

"No way. How would anyone even know this house is back here? I've been here many times, and I still take wrong turns."

"Shut up. I think I hear something."

I heard the guy slowly walk around the house, and there was no doubt that he had a weapon in hand. I hoped he wouldn't find Crush. He was already hurt and probably didn't have much strength to defend. I looked over at Macey. Her face was white, and I probably looked the same. If we got caught, we were so dead. I heard a door creak open and then there was yelling. They'd found Crush. Macey and I poked our heads through the railing and saw Crush dash toward the door, but one of the guys stepped in front of him and grabbed his bad arm, and Crush yelled out. The guy dragged him deeper into the house. Crush let out another cry as he clenched his fist and swung. His fist collided with the guy's mouth. The guy stumbled back and released Crush. The other guy had a metal rod in his left hand, and it was raised, ready to strike. Crush was now backed up against a wall, his hands up in the air, surrendering. The two guys had their backs facing us, and the metal rod barely touched Crush's chest. It almost looked like a sword. He gripped his bad arm and glanced up at us.

"Who are you?" the guy with the metal rod screamed at Crush.

"Look, we can talk about this. Just put down the rod," Crush coaxed in a shaky voice.

"Tell me what you're doing before I call the cops and have you arrested for breaking and entering. And who takes pickles?"

"I didn't *take* the pickles. I just *ate* a few."

We had to do something, but I didn't know what. I knew that Crush was running out of things to say. He was an awful liar. Alone, the two guys couldn't corner all three of us. But they had a metal rod, which could kill someone. Crush needed to get the rod out of his hand. The guy without the rod advanced, and it looked like he was about to punch him. Crush took a defensive stance.

Macey screamed before the punch got to Crush. This made the friend stop for about a millisecond, and Crush fled. The other guy immediately swung the rod and it connected with Crush's back. He fell to the ground with a thud.

"Don't move," he warned Crush. Crush groaned, rolled onto his back, and grabbed his arm. The guy glanced up at us. "Come down the stairs right now with your hands up, or I'm going to hit your little partner in crime. Understand?"

Macey and I carefully walked down the stairs.

"All three of you, sit on the floor and don't move a single muscle."

We did as we were told. I helped Crush sit up, and he took in a sharp breath. I felt something sticky on my hand. It was his blood. I began to formulate a lie.

"You guys are just a bunch of kids. What were you three doing?" one of the guys yelled at us.

"Nothing much. What about you? Are the fish biting?" I asked him and tried to control my anger. The more I kept him talking, the longer I would have to come up with plausible lie. Anger burned inside of me as I saw blood seep down Crush's back. He had his eyes shut.

"Yeah, the fish were biting, but we threw them back in the water. I'm actually thinking of throwing the three of you in the river," he said and lowered the rod.

"You hit pretty hard," Crush said.

"I didn't realize you were a kid," he objected. "But you three broke and entered."

"Technically, we just entered. Nothing is broken," Macey said matter-of-factly.

"Look, you are the least of our problems right now. We were kayaking down the river with some of our friends, and things went bad. They started drinking. A lot. We stopped on some rocks to eat the peanut butter sandwiches I made, and things got heated. They got mad and took our kayaks. We tried to get them back, but the current was too fast, and we didn't feel like dealing with drunks armed with paddles. I remembered seeing this house when we went by, so we started to walk. Thought there might be a road nearby."

The one with the rod raised his eyebrows. "What was the fight about?"

I looked over to Macey. "She called her boyfriend out about his drinking problem. He'd promised his mom he would stop. Said boyfriend yelled some things that shouldn't be repeated at her, so the boy who has a bloody back and I took up for her. And things went bad."

"How far have you guys walked, exactly?" the one with the rod asked. He moved close to the phone, and I had a feeling he was going to dial three numbers if I didn't make this next part good.

"Not that far."

Oh, yeah. Good job.

"Maybe I should call your parents for you." He inched closer to the phone, and I started to panic. There was only so much I could make up. Crush bumped my shoulder and slipped something into my hand. It was a dart that Ares had used on us. Crush and I made eye contact, and he showed me the dart in his hand. If things got messy, we were going to use these.

"Look, if you guys could just point us to the road, that would be great," I said and beckoned Crush and Macey to follow me to the door. Macey tripped, but as I looked back to make sure she was okay, I saw that she had unplugged the cord for the house phone that was on the side of the wall. There was no way this place had cell phone service. Not this far out in the woods. Good. No police.

The two guys stepped in front of the door and blocked our exit. "Look, I can't let you guys leave."

"Why not?" Macey asked.

"I can't let a bunch of hungry kids leave my house after they got ditched by their friends. Anyway, I hit him pretty hard. I'm going to have to explain that to his parents. Why don't you sit down?"

The three of us didn't move.

"Sit," the guy said again. He reached toward me, and I immediately flinched back. His friend locked the doors. Crush nudged me, but I didn't want to attack just yet.

"You don't understand. We have to leave now. We are trying to beat them to our truck. They might mess with it."

They didn't let us by, and Crush nudged me one last time. I gripped the dart harder and flew at the guy that hit Crush and inserted the dart into his stomach before he even had a chance to move. Crush had done the same. The drug started to work almost immediately. The two friends leaned against the table and cussed at us, but there was nothing they could do. They sank to their knees, and within another minute, they were unconscious.

"All right, that will keep them out for about an hour. We have to cover a lot of ground within that time. But we need to eat and drink as much as we possibly can."

After scarfing down all of the food we could handle, we walked into the front yard. There was a truck in the driveway with a license plate that belonged to New Mexico.

"We should take it," Crush said. "I saw keys on the table."

"No," I said.

"And why not?"

"When they wake up and realize that their truck is missing, they'll definitely call the police."

"They're going to call the police anyway. You guys knocked them out," Macey said.

"Yeah. I say we take it," Crush prompted.

"Look, you guys have to trust me on this one. This is a situation where I have experience. We knocked the guys out with drugs taken from Ares members. But you never want the police mad at you for reasons you can avoid. Those guys can't prove we did anything to them without getting a blood test, which will take a long time to get back. The police won't look for three runaways, but they will look for thieves."

"So, you're saying we should keep walking?" Crush asked.

I could understand why he didn't want to walk anymore. He had a possibly infected arm and an injured back. I knew it hurt more than he let on, but he was just going to have to suck it up for the time being.

So we walked.

"Crush, is your back okay? That guy would have killed you if he had hit your head," Macey said after a few minutes.

"I know," Crush whispered, his personality doing a complete turn-around. He wasn't nearly as defensive as he had been a few minutes prior. He was almost vulnerable, if such a thing was possible for him. His head was down, and he stared at his shoes. He picked up his head and looked at me.

"How do you lie like that? How do you come up with those stories so quickly? I wanted to believe it. I stood there and explained how I ate pickles versus taking them. I almost got my head smashed. I *would* have gotten my head smashed if you hadn't come in."

"Don't be so hard on yourself. I've had a lot of practice. You had a near-death experience."

"Yeah, but I kept looking at you guys, so that's probably how they knew you were there. 'Cause of me."

"Oh, shut up," Macey said. "We would have come out sooner or later. Even if I hadn't yelled."

"You know, the CIA was thinking about sending me on a test mission. See how I handle stuff and everything. I thought I was ready for it. I'm obviously not." He paused. "Do you think they'll really call the police?" Crush asked.

"I would if three kids that were dressed exactly the same came into my house and knocked me out," Macey joked. "But don't worry too much. I unplugged the phone cord. That will delay them some."

"They'll call the police then."

"Exactly. Then they'll call the police," Crush said.

"I guess we'll just cross that bridge when we get there," Macey said and walked faster.

CHAPTER 21

When the dirt road finally met the other road, we were all relieved to see it was paved. That meant it led to somewhere important. Like food. We turned to the left, away from the headquarters, and walked about one hundred and twenty feet into the trees so a passing car wouldn't notice us. After about fifteen minutes, we stopped and sat down. Crush was walking slower than he had been.

"I swear if I don't see a Wendy's soon, I'm going to scream," Macey said.

"What? The one sandwich wasn't enough?" I asked sarcastically.

She narrowed her eyes at me and threw a pinecone, which hit me square in the chest. I didn't even bother to throw it back at her.

"Even if there is a fast-food place, we don't have any money," Crush said as he stood and signaled that we should walk again.

We walked a whole lot slower this time. I noticed Crush as he rubbed his arm. We needed help for him.

"I grabbed ten bucks off of the counter when we left," I told them. "Those people really need to start locking their doors and hiding their money." I bent down and took the money out of my shoe.

My two companions turned and stared at me.

"Maybe you're a son of Hermes," Macey said. She snatched the money from my hand and smiled.

"Hermes?" I asked. "Sounds like herpes. What is Hermes?"

We came to a creek, and I went down the steep bank first and then helped Macey down. Her hand felt warm in mine.

"Not a what, but a who," she answered. "Hermes is the Greek god of thieves.

"Why are you thinking about Greek stuff?" I asked.

"Ares is the Greek god of war. I wonder if they're like a cult or something."

"Maybe. But it's a stupid name."

"It fits them fairly well. I imagine Ares would have no problem picking a fight with a bunch of teenagers."

We jumped over the shallow creek (I wouldn't drink from that one) and climbed up the other side of the bank.

"Crush?" I said. He had been quiet for the last few minutes, and his face was white. "How are you holding up?"

"I'm fine," he answered unconvincingly.

"Come on, dude. We've already established that you're an awful liar." I stopped and turned around so I could face him. "Let me see it."

Crush frowned, but he reluctantly turned to show me the bite on his arm. It was still red and inflamed. I wasn't a doctor or anything, but it didn't take a genius to tell that it was infected and was in need of medical treatment. If it kept getting worse like it was, finding a fast-food restaurant was going to be the least of our problems.

"How badly does it hurt?" Macey asked him.

Crush shook his head. "Not at all."

"You wouldn't admit you were hurt even if your arm was cut off or your foot was twisted the opposite way," she said.

"I might admit I felt a slight pinch," Crush whispered.

"Let me see your back," Macey instructed him. I could tell she wanted to help him, but there was no way for her to. I remembered how she had insisted that I follow her home so she could tend to my infected foot.

Crush turned around and lifted up his shirt. There was a thick red line that went across his back where the rod hit him and the skin had been slightly broken. He would have a bad bruise in the morning. If we managed to live that long.

"Um, it doesn't look that bad," Macey tried to assure him.

"Oh, it will. Trust me. The bruise is going to turn purple and green," I said.

I couldn't help but notice that Macey and Crush glanced up at me. Crush wasn't the only one who had been hurt like that before.

We talked about normal things. Or at least we tried to. Somehow, the conversation always gravitated back to what was going on and what our plan was. Right now, the only thing on our mind was to get as far away from here as possible and find food. Finally, the woods started to thin out, and we came to the back of a neighborhood.

"I hate walking," Macey complained.

"My back hurts," Crush complained.

"I'm still hungry," I complained.

We were a cheerful bunch.

Crush leaned against a tree and sank down to the ground. "Can we just hang out here for a little bit? Then maybe we can head into the neighborhood and try to find our way to a town."

Our little rest turned into a full-blown nap. When I woke up, I had no idea where I was or what I was. I sat up and swatted the gnats on my face. The sun was setting, which was a good and bad thing. Now we wouldn't be burned to death by the sun, but it also meant we had less time to find somewhere to crash for the night.

Crush was asleep on his stomach. He probably wouldn't be able to sleep on his back for a week or two. He didn't look asleep. He looked unconscious.

Then I realized Macey wasn't there.

"Macey!" I yelled as I stood.

No answer.

My heart started to pound. Where was she? Ares couldn't have gotten her. They would have taken all three of us. I screamed her name, and I didn't care who heard me. About thirty seconds passed before I felt a tap on my shoulder. I jumped about two hundred feet in the air and whipped around.

"Macey! Where were you?"

"I was climbing a tree. I was trying to get a better look, but I think that only works in books and movies. All I saw was the back of that same house," she said as she pointed to the last house in the neighborhood.

Crush barely stirred when Macey shook his leg, which was slightly concerning. He seemed to be getting worse by the hour. Macey shook his leg harder. He told us that all he needed was five more minutes of rest. I told him we didn't have five more minutes and to get his lazy butt up. He opened his eyes and sat up. He looked at his arm, confused and frowning.

"Is my arm gone?" he mumbled and tried to lie back down, but I wouldn't let him.

"No. You're fine, Crush. We'll get you food and water, and we'll make it better, but we need to get out of here first," Macey told him.

I would have accused him of being a baby or acting like a drama queen, but I felt fairly lightheaded myself. And I didn't have a bruised back or a bitten arm. I kept my mouth shut.

Crush struggled to his feet, and we started to walk in the direction of the neighborhood. It would have been nice to walk on a paved road. I was sick of dodging trees and bushes. I'd tripped over a root at least five times. During the trek to front of the neighborhood, my headache came back, and I could feel my patience thinning. The small snack we'd had at the river house had eased the pain a little, but now it was back. I knew we needed food and water. Now.

There was a small but modest Baptist church not fifty yards from the beginning of the neighborhood, with a huge yellow poster above the doorway that said "Summer Kick Off." We watched kids walk into the church in casual clothes, and they waved as their parents drove off. I heard loud Christian rap coming from speakers inside.

"We're going in there, right?" Macey asked.

"Grandma wanted us to. We've been so bored the past few days, and we need to be around kids our own age. While she's out playing cards, she thought we should stop by. But that's the story we'll say only if someone asks us. Don't volunteer it."

Macey put her hand on my shoulder. "You sit up at night and come up with this stuff, don't you?" She paused. "Let's just hope they don't notice our fashion choices."

"Do you think you can act like you're not dying inside for a few minutes?" I turned to Crush. He'd hardly said anything this entire time, which was quite the accomplishment for him. He knew he was sick as much as he knew he was a human. He needed to go to the doctor, but there was no way we could get him to one unless he passed out in the church and someone insisted on helping us.

Actually, that didn't sound like that bad of an idea.

"Let's go," Crush said with a weak smile.

"We need to tell somebody what's going on," Macey said.

"Why would we do that?"

"Come on. It's not like we did anything wrong. We can't get in trouble." She glanced at Crush.

"Oh, but we can. I didn't do a thing the night Justin fell off the bridge, but we all know what happened. Juvie. Anyway, how would be explain ourselves? We can't tell them about Crush. I can't say anything about my family. No one would believe us. If we said anything about how there is information that could change everything, well, the people wouldn't take that lightly. We would end up in a crazy house."

We walked in the church and followed the kids in front of us down a hallway and took a few turns in the narrow corridors. We walked into a dimly lit room with a small stage in the front. I didn't notice anything else, but I did smell the food. All three of us were immediately drawn to the boxes of pizza that were on the table. There were bottles of sodas neatly lined up and cups stacked up off to the side. I couldn't have asked for anything better.

All three of us grabbed a plate and started off with two pieces. I knew if we took more than that at once, we might draw attention to ourselves.

"Best. Pizza. Ever," Macey muttered between bites.

"Agreed," I said as I finished off my first slice and started on the next one.

Now that I had food, I could focus on my surroundings. The youth room was cool. There was a huge TV mounted on the wall with a countdown. Five minutes until this thing started. I could easily eat two other pieces of pizza in that amount of time. We could always leave before the service started, but I needed a place to rest. Anyway, Ares would never think to look for us in a church. The room had red carpet and a stage that rose about a foot off the floor. On the stage were a few guitars, a keyboard, and a set of drums, along with a couple microphones. The light was dim, and the music blared, and that made it easy to blend in. I turned around to get another piece of pizza and caught two girls staring at me. They waved at me, and I managed to smile. They giggled and turned away. I caught Macey's eyes.

"What?" I asked and stuffed the pizza in my mouth.

"Nothing. But it looks like we're about to have some company."

I turned back around and saw a college-aged girl walking our way. Her smile was plastered on her face, and she wore a wooden cross around her neck.

"Hello," she said cheerfully.

All three of us waved slightly, and I looked back down at my plate. I was suddenly aware of how awful we smelled and how much we looked like we had just escaped an asylum.

"You guys enjoying the pizza?" she asked.

"It's the best thing ever," Crush said.

I wished he'd kept his mouth shut so this lady would leave. We didn't need any questions from anyone.

"It is? I told Samuel that it would be. He thought that a chain restaurant would be better, but I convinced him that it would be better if we bought from a small business."

"Samuel?" Crush asked.

"The other intern. He's the only tall one over there with black hair. These guys here haven't exactly hit puberty." She laughed at her own joke and continued. "I don't recognize you three. Is this your first time here?"

"Yeah," I answered. "Our grandmother lives in the other neighborhood down the road, and she's out playing cards, so she dropped us here."

"Cool. Come on, it's about to start, and the first-row seats are the always taken up the soonest."

The three of us shoved the rest of the pizza down our throats and chose three seats next to each other in the back row. I planned to take a nap, but that wasn't going to happen. The speaker that the preacher used was nestled right behind me. Great.

I didn't focus on whatever the preacher was saying, but Macey listened intently. My mind whirled and so did my stomach. I should have eaten that pizza slower. I closed my eyes, and for the first time in a couple of days, I let myself feel safe and relaxed.

It felt like my eyes hadn't been closed for five seconds before Macey shook me awake and scolded me for falling asleep. I opened my eyes and heard the preacher telling us to go to our regular small group. My immediate plan was to just get up and leave. Grandma's game ended early, and she was ready to take us back to her house. But the intern had already directed Macey to a separate room with the girls her age. The same happened with Crush. His face had some of its color back, but he still looked weak. I was surprised that no one said anything about him. There was no way anyone could miss that bite. Or how we all matched like a bunch of inmates.

The intern pointed to a group of guys my age and the other intern— the tall, black-headed one, Samuel. The group sat up against the wall opposite the TV and laughed about something. I walked over to them and sat down, and a few even nodded at me. One boy said something to me, but I didn't pay any attention to him. My instincts told me to get the others and get out of there.

"Well?" the boy asked again.

"What?" I asked.

"I asked about your friend's arm. It looks pretty bad."

All the boys, and even the intern, stared at me now. My stomach felt weird, and my face flushed a deep red, although I had no clue why. I didn't even have to lie.

"A dog got him."

"Is he okay?" the intern asked me.

"Yeah. He's on pills."

"Didn't the doctor say to wrap it up or something?" another guy asked.

"I wasn't in the doctor's office. I stayed home, okay?" I told him.

"So, what did you guys think of the sermon? Anything stick out to you?" the intern asked. He looked at me, and I shook my head.

"Yeah, sure. It was great," I answered.

"Learn anything?" he asked me.

"You should never sit in the back unless you like the speakers in your ear."

Everyone laughed, but I hadn't meant it as a joke.

"Not what I meant, but it's a start. Jackson? What about you?"

While they talked, I wondered how Macey and I were going to manage getting Crush to a doctor. People were bound to ask us questions, maybe even insist on taking Crush to the hospital. We couldn't handle him becoming weaker. If and when Ares did catch up to us, he needed to be on high alert.

"All right, guys," the intern, Samuel, started. "We got about five more minutes before we leave. Who wants to see the score to the Red Hawks game?"

The guys cheered, and one of the boys grabbed the remote for the mounted TV and started to flip through the channels. I'm not sure what caused me to look at the changing screen when I did, but I nearly fainted when I saw Crush's, Macey's, and my face on the screen. It was just for a second, but I was sure it was us.

"Wait," Jackson shouted out. "Go back."

My heat skipped a beat. I thought I might throw up on the carpet.

"Why? That was the news channel," the boy with the remote said, but he flipped back to the channel where I'd seen our picture. Thankfully, the news channel had moved onto the next segment.

"What did you want to see, Jackson?" one of them asked.

"I don't know. I thought I saw the new guy," he said and pointed to me. All the boys laughed. Except for me.

"That was the national news. Why would he be on there?"

They started to laugh again, and I felt my face burn redder than Crush's bite. Why did the news do a story on us? What was going on? Had the media found about our kidnapping? Were they trying to find us? I had to warn Macey and Crush. We needed to get away from here right now before someone figured something out. The intern's eyes lingered on me. He pulled out his phone.

The boys cheered. The Red Hawks were winning.

"All right, let's leave and beat the crowd. See you guys Sunday," Samuel said.

I immediately stood up and made my way to the door. I looked down the hall, but I didn't see Macey or Crush. I turned around, and a few of the other boys were on their way to walk out.

"Hey," I asked. "Do you guys know when the other groups will let out?" I started to wring my hands. This wasn't good.

"Not much longer."

"Okay, thanks," I told them.

I turned away, and the intern was standing there a few feet away from me. I gasped and took a step away.

"Sorry, did I scare you?" he asked, a fake smile on his face.

"Little bit. I'm just waiting for my, uh, brother and sister. I guess they're in some other small group."

"Why don't you come and get a T-shirt?"

"I don't have any money."

"It's okay. They're free if it's your first time."

I couldn't turn the guy down because I knew he would only get more suspicious. Anyway, the shirt I had on was on the verge of ripping. We walked back in the room, and he closed the door tightly. He grabbed a shirt from under a counter and handed it to me.

"That boy on the news sure did look like you, didn't he?"

"It's weird, right?" I laughed. So, this is why he wanted me to come back with him.

"See if this rings a bell." The intern raised his phone and started to read from it. "Three teens are wanted by authorities for armed robbery, murder, unlawful restraint, and arson. The three minors robbed a grocery store and took over thirty thousand dollars in cash, medicine, beer, and food. Security cameras caught the three smashing all the checkout registers, computers, and bottles of wine. It was reported that they stole all the movies out of the Redboxes. A fire was set in the bakery section, but firefighters were able to put it out before it caused any more damage. In all, the three caused roughly one hundred and fifty thousand dollars in damage. Authorities are still in dismay of how the three teenagers managed to make a clean getaway and where they are keeping the stolen items. There were two janitors working late that night. One was shot and killed while the other is in critical condition. The three restrained the injured man to a pole near the fire. It is obvious that the three teens had outside help. If anyone has any information, they are encouraged to go to authorities. The number for the hotline is located below."

My legs turned to a liquid. Samuel turned his phone to me, a slight look of disgust on his face. What I figured to be Macey's and Crush's yearbook pictures stared back at me. My picture was a mug shot. A video of three figures raiding a grocery store began to play.

I froze. This was bad.

How in the world could there be video footage? We hadn't done that. Who was responsible for this? Ares? The CIA? I felt like screaming and throwing the phone into the wall.

"No. No. That didn't happen. We were framed."

"Isn't that what all the fugitives say? Who should I call? The police? Let me look at that hotline really quickly..."

"No. You can't. It's all a lie. Please. I'm begging you. Please don't," I asked him. There was no point in denying or trying to lie. My main objective was to get away, not to convince him otherwise of something he knew was true. Or sort of true. Where were Crush and Macey? We didn't have any more time.

"Then you might want to start with the truth," he told me. He tapped the first number.

I knew I couldn't tell this guy the truth. I mean, I could, but he wouldn't believe me for a second, and he'd call the cops faster than I could stop him. It would take too long anyway. So, like any smart and reasonable person would do, I ran out of the room and back into the hallway. I yelled for Macey and Crush. They rounded a corner and looked relieved to see me.

"Chase? Where have you been?" Macey asked. "What's wrong?"

I eyed Crush, expecting him to yell at me for disappearing, but he remained silent. His face was a pasty white. Samuel came up behind me and grabbed my wrist. I tried to jerk away, but he wouldn't let me go.

"I've called the police. They'll be here in no time. The station is right down the road."

"Hey!" Macey screamed. "Let him go!"

The intern turned around to look at Macey and Crush, and his grip loosened just a little bit. I tore out of his grip and backed away. Macey and Crush were beside me, and it surprised me how much safer I felt with them around.

"What's going on?" Crush demanded and faked his strength.

"We made the news," I informed them. "Turns out we robbed a grocery store and took thousands of dollars and killed a guy. They also have video footage. I think we were in Ares's wonderful care longer than we thought. Amnesia, anyone?"

Both of their faces fell.

"I'm literally going to kill every one of those guys," Macey said between her teeth.

"You didn't tell this guy the truth, did you?" Crush inquired.

"I didn't tell him anything."

Crush nodded his head at the intern. "Seems to me like we're wasting our time here. Come on guys; let's hit the road. Grandma is waiting."

We were the last four in the church, and Samuel blocked the main exit, but we pushed past him and ran down the hallway. He pursued us and yelled at us to stop. Macey and I jumped down the steps that led out of the church and then ran behind the building. Crush joined us a few seconds later. We ran the length of the church, which was no wider than the parking lot. We planned to make a mad dash for the woods. I glanced back and saw that Crush was breathing heavily and holding his arm. I could hear sirens.

"Crush. Come on. Hurry up! We have to go."

I stopped running to let Crush catch up, but I peeked around the side of the building to see how many police cars were there and where Samuel was.

I couldn't see Samuel, but I saw his truck. So where was he? I was positive he had chased after us. Two police cars came into the parking lot and kicked up dirt as they screeched to a halt. I stopped breathing, and I heard Macey gasp. Did Samuel think there would be gunfire? Was that why he hid? We were kids. They wouldn't shoot at us, right?

"Samuel was right. That was fast," I muttered.

I had no idea what to do. If we ran, then they would just run after us, and Crush couldn't keep up. We couldn't leave him. No matter how annoying he got. I figured I had less than ten seconds to come up with a plan that didn't end with us in the back of the cop car, handcuffed and ready to be processed. I saw the sunlight catch on the keys that rested on the top of the tire of Samuel's car.

Bingo.

One of the policemen started to make his way to the back of the church and the other to the woods. Now was our only chance. I quickly explained my plan to Macy and Crush to hide in the truck and make a getaway while the policemen searched. They couldn't do anything but agree. We took off for the truck before the cops turned back around and saw us. My plan didn't go any farther than getting in the truck.

I grabbed the keys off the tire and opened the door. Macey and Crush were by my side. The three of us piled into the backseat and got low. Samuel was in the front seat. He turned around and gaped at us. He made a move for the door.

I grabbed a hammer off the floor and stuck the end of it in his back. "This is a gun. If you say anything, I will shoot you. If you turn around, I will shoot you. I shot that janitor dead, and I have no problem doing the same to you. Do you understand? Don't start the car. Just wait."

Samuel nodded.

I handed the hammer to Macey and told her to keep it on his back. I climbed over him and sat in the passenger seat. I looked back and smiled at Macey and Crush. They had most of their bodies under a blanket, but Macey still kept pressure on Samuel's back with the hammer. There were tools all over the floorboard, and there were leaves and sticks on the seats. I brushed them away and sat down. There was also a pink wig on the seat back. If things got really messy, I could disguise myself with that and hope for the best.

"All right, start the car and drive." I handed him the keys. He stared down at them in shock.

"Where did you get those? Oh. The tire. That's where I put them."

I pushed the keys in his hands, thankful for his forgetfulness. Samuel put his foot on the gas, and we slowly started to leave, but not before one of the policemen reappeared and flagged us down. Samuel stopped the truck. I heard Macey and Crush hit the floor, along with my stomach. I grabbed a hat from the floorboard and put it on. I grabbed Samuel's phone and stared at it. I glanced over at Samuel. His hands gripped the steering wheel so hard that they had turned white.

"I'll tell them you were the accomplice. That you were our outside help. You'll get a nice long stay in federal prison. You'll never make it as a preacher. You will bring shame to your family and leave your parents wondering where they went wrong with their kid. Your girlfriend will hate you for life and never speak to you ever again. Or I could just get the gun and shoot you and the policeman. You will tell the police that someone borrowed your phone to call the police and then left. You don't know who it was."

His hands turned whiter.

Samuel rolled down the window and smiled at the officer.

"Yes, Officer?"

"We got a call that three teenagers, two boys and a girl, who recently committed a major crime, were hanging around the church. They were recently seen walking around the neighborhood just down the road. If you don't mind me asking, did you see anyone acting suspicious in the service? Any new faces?"

"Yeah, some guy took my phone and called the police when he saw the kids. But he left."

"Who's your friend?" He glanced at me.

I butted in before Samuel lost his lunch or lost his fear. "He's taking me home. My parents got caught up at work and can't come and get me until late. But I don't think it was the three kids. The girl looked Asian."

Samuel nodded his head, and the policeman seemed to buy it. And why wouldn't he? This was a church. "I'm just going to look around, if you don't mind. And before I forget, you need to change the tint on the windows. I couldn't even see into the backseat." With that, he turned around and started to walk toward the woods.

"Drive," I told Samuel.

Samuel pulled out of the parking lot and turned right.

"Good job. I'm pretty sure they won't follow us now," I told him. "Okay guys, I think it's safe to come out now. Crush, how are you?"

"Not so good," he told me. "I think I need to go to the hospital."

"What's wrong with him?" Samuel asked.

"He was bitten by a dog," Macey said.

"What kind of dog? How?" Samuel asked.

"Does it matter?" I asked. "He was bitten."

"It was a gigantic dog with teeth as long as my thumb. I don't remember what kind it was. I'm choosing to block that day out," Crush said.

"Take us to the nearest hospital, or I'll shoot you and drive there myself." I hated threatening him like this, but we were in a dire situation.

"I'll take you to the hospital, but you guys have to answer all my questions and go to the police after that," Samuel said as he pulled over onto the shoulder of the road.

"Within reason," I informed him and chose to ignore the comment about going to the police. "And I get to go first. Why did you hide in the truck when the police showed?"

"When I called the police, they told me to leave because you three were dangerous. I was looking for my keys. Guess I forgot I put them on the tire."

"We don't look *that* dangerous," Macey grumbled.

"Did you guys really do what that article said? Did you really shoot the guy with your gun?"

"For starters, it's your hammer. Not a gun. And no. We didn't do anything. We were framed." Or had we? Had Ares made us do it? If so, why? And how did they make us forget? This was the first time I'd been in a situation where I didn't know if I was lying or not. I didn't like it. It felt unnatural, like I was two separate people.

"Hurry up," I told him.

"I need names. You guys know mine," he said.

"I'm Chase. That's Macey, and the one that's going to die if you don't get us to a hospital soon is Crush. I'll answer two more questions and then you have to take us to the hospital. Please," I told him.

Samuel pulled back onto the road and started to drive. "How long have you guys been on the run?"

I looked back at Macey for help. "I think it's day two. Maybe. Everything is a bit of a blur. Especially today."

"Why is today especially a blur? What happened?" Samuel asked me.

"Lack of food and water. Among other things."

"Chase," Macey whispered and interrupted another question from Samuel.

I looked back and saw that Crush was completely unconscious.

"Would you mind telling Samuel to go a bit faster?" she asked. She unbuckled Crush's seat belt so his head wasn't at the odd slant it was currently in. He slumped down in his seat, so Macey laid his head across her lap. She ran her fingers through his hair.

"How much longer till we get there?" I asked. We were only going fifty miles per hour.

"About ten minutes. Unless you guys want me to call and get a police escort. I'm going to take a wild guess and say that you don't want that," Samuel said, somehow being able to find humor in this.

When we finally pulled into the hospital parking lot, Crush still hadn't regained consciousness, and I'd pretty much destroyed my fingernails.

"Chase?" Macey asked.

"Yeah?"

"Maybe we should stay in the truck."

"And why would we do that?"

"They'll be looking for three of us."

"The *police* will be looking for three," I mentioned and eyed Samuel. Ares will be looking for any one of us. We needed to stay with Crush to protect him. If Ares found us, I knew that they would kill us or kidnap us again. I wasn't sure which I preferred.

"And let Samuel go alone? I don't think so."

Macey complied. We got out of the car, and I shook Crush by his shoulder. He blinked his eyes. "Come on, Crush. We're at the hospital. All you have to do is make it into the hospital and then you can get a wheelchair or something."

Samuel and I helped Crush support his weight as he stumbled across the parking lot. I looked at Samuel over Crush's bent head. He was probably around twenty years old and was six feet tall with big arms. I hadn't expected to be able to manipulate him so easily.

When we entered the hospital, I told Samuel to take Crush to the front desk and say Crush was a new kid at church who had collapsed. Macey and I walked into the waiting room and sat on a couch in the back.

"Do you think Samuel is telling the nurse who we are? What if the doctor recognizes Crush?"

"I don't think Samuel will tell anyone anything," I said.

"Why not?" Macey asked.

"He wants to know more information about us. We are pretty intriguing, Macey. I don't even know what we're doing next."

Macey laughed. "I hope my parents aren't watching the news."

"Do you miss them?"

"Yeah," Macey said sadly. "I know they're scared half to death."

"Tell me about it. If we ever do get out of this mess alive, we're going to have a lot of talking and explaining to do to the authorities. Not to mention the kids at school," I said and scooted a little closer to her. "We're officially public."

"What about you? Are you thinking about Brandon and your dad?" she asked.

"I mean, it's kind of hard to believe, you know? I went from having no family to having a family. Sort of, anyway. We haven't all been in the same room in a few years."

"I know. We'll make it work out. How do you think we'll get rid of Samuel? He can't come with us. We couldn't make him," Macey said.

"And I suppose you have another vehicle that can get us to the CIA besides his truck?" I asked in all seriousness.

"A plane?"

"Yeah, because we have money," I said. "And I guess hitchhiking is out of the question?" I asked.

"We're being convicted of murder and robbery, in case you forgot. The whole country knows what we look like," Macey said.

"Like people still watch the news."

Macey looked at me for a second and then shook her head. "They watch the news, Chase. They watch the news. None of this would have even happened if our faces weren't plastered on television. We need to disguise ourselves. Fake tans and dyed hair."

"You'd look great as a brunette, but I don't think I can pull that off."

"You are *not* dyeing you hair," Macey told me.

"And why is that?"

She faltered a moment. "It's the hair that makes them stare, right? Like those two girls at the church."

I busted out laughing. "And I guess the spray tan wouldn't work either?"

"I guess you can wear a wig," Macey said.

"That might be smarter. We'd be stuck with the hair if we dyed it, and we can just change wigs."

"Or we could just shave it all off and get it over with," Macey said.

"I don't think Crush could stand that."

Bringing up Crush changed the mood. All humor fell out of the air.

"How do you think Ares got footage of us doing all that stuff to that grocery store and those men? There's no way they have that great of an editing system," Macey said and flipped through a magazine from a few years ago.

"That means we had to have done some of that stuff. Then they probably planted the janitors. What day did we go to the CIA headquarters?" I asked.

"The seventeenth."

"Okay. Okay. So that means we were kidnapped either the eighteenth or the nineteenth, depending on what time it was," I said. "Then I remember the truck ride there, meeting my dad, and then waking up and being tortured by that lady. We escaped that same day, didn't we?"

"Wait. What happened between the time you met your dad and woke up? Maybe Ares knocked all three of us out and, I don't know, forced us to do all that stuff to the grocery store while they rolled the cameras. They probably gave us some wonky drug to make us forget everything. They could have easily done all that stuff to the grocery store in the middle of the night, replaced the real security camera footage with the one of us, shot one of their members and killed another and said it was the janitors."

"So they sneaked us in the grocery store and made us do all that?" I asked.

"Maybe. Or they could have had a set that looked like the grocery store and just gotten our faces and us smashing stuff. I don't think they would have taken us to the actual grocery store. We could have gotten away."

"How did they *make* us do all of that?"

"Simple. Threaten to kill someone we loved."

"It seems highly unlikely," I told her. "We would have had to remember that."

Macey shrugged her shoulders. "All of this seems highly unlikely."

I looked at a digital clock that had the time and date.

June twenty-sixth.

"Macey. Look." I pointed to the clock.

"No way. We were in there for like five and a half days?"

"That's plenty time to ruin our lives," I said. I sunk down in the seat. It seemed like the whole universe wanted us to fail and suffer.

"Why would we do something like that? Did we really kill that man?"

"If they threatened to kill someone one of us loves, then yes. We have to go and tell Crush."

"Definitely. But if that boy is bedridden, I'm going to kill him. We need him." Macey clenched her hands.

We ran into Samuel just outside the waiting room.

"Heard anything?" Macey asked.

"Did you tell the police anything?" I asked.

"No, but I could if I wanted to," Samuel said.

"So, you don't want to?" Macey asked and took a stand beside him.

"I want out of this, and I want out of it now. What did you guys *do*? You're all like, what? Eleven?" Samuel said. "I feel like everyone is staring at us."

"If you ever get this good-looking, you'll get used to it. And I want you out of this too," I said. "What did they say about our friend?"

"The doctors said his infection is bad, and he's dehydrated. He should be fine in two or so days, but they say he needs a lot of rest. They asked me tons of questions, and I had no idea what to say."

My face flushed. "What did you say?"

"I don't even know," Samuel said miserably.

I rolled my eyes. "Just leave. We're fine from here. Go feed the homeless or something, church boy. What room is he in?"

"Second floor. Second door on your right." He looked up at us as we walked toward the elevator. "I'm gonna head out."

We didn't bother to look back at him.

"That went better than I expected," Macey said and turned to me as the elevator doors closed. We were alone.

"It's all on him. He's not getting his twenty bucks I found under the seat. But we need to get Crush and get out of here before he calls the police again."

"We *have* to talk about all this stealing and lying. But after we get out of this mess, because right now, it's all we've got going for us," Macey said and nudged me in the ribs. I turned and tugged her hair.

"Lying and stealing, huh? You forget my dashing good looks, strength, endurance, spy of a dad, and smarts."

"You're so full of it," she joked and took my hat off and put it on her head. I spun her around, took off the sunglasses she'd gotten from Samuel's car, and put them on. I pulled her closer and planned on kissing her. Then the elevator doors opened, and a woman stepped in.

"Is this the floor?" Macey asked and stepped away from me.

"Sadly," I answered. I still felt the heat from her body.

We walked down the hallway until we were at Crush's door. It was closed.

"You do the honors," I told Macey.

She opened the door, and we walked in.

CHAPTER 22

Crush muttered stuff when we walked into the room, but I couldn't make heads or tails of what he talked about.

"What does 'wicked' mean?" Macey asked as she neared Crush.

"No clue," I answered. I sat down on the edge of his bed and noticed an IV in his arm.

"Crush?" Macey went up to him and got the hair out of his face.

He stirred and swatted around his face.

"Wake up, dude," I said.

His eyes fluttered until they opened completely. "Hey, guys."

"How are you?" Macey asked.

"I don't know."

"Do you remember what happened?" I asked him.

"Don't tell me I was talking about the girl I like," he murmured and smiled. He tried to sit up, but the effort looked like it hurt too much. I wondered when he would be able to leave.

"No. But you did admit that you wet the bed until last year," I snickered.

"I'm so sure I did," he muttered. "Where's the intern guy?"

"Samuel? The guy blew the popsicle stand," Macey explained to him. "But get this—it's the twenty-sixth of June."

We quickly explained our new theory to Crush. Although he didn't interrupt us when we told him, he did have a doubtful look on his face. I started to think he just didn't believe anything that he didn't come up with.

"It sure is quite the theory," he commented.

"How else would they have gotten video footage of us?" Macey asked and put a hand on her hip.

"I don't know," Crush admitted. "I just can't believe we were in there for that long. It felt like it was under a day."

Suddenly, Crush's face fell, and I immediately turned around. There was a nurse with her hand on the knob of the door.

"Hide," Crush whispered.

I looked around frantically. There was a closet off to the side of the room, and I grabbed Macey's wrist and pulled her to it. I threw open the door. Thankfully, the closet was empty and had enough room for the two of us. I got in first, pulled her inside, and closed the door just as the nurse walked inside.

"Don't say a word," I whispered.

Macey nodded her head. I could barely see her in the dim light.

"Hello?" the nurse said.

For a few moments, I thought she'd seen us, but then I realized that Crush was acting like he was still asleep. I'd have killed to see what was going on.

Crush moaned, and I heard the hospital bed creak under his weight.

"Are you awake?" the nurse asked sweetly.

"Guess so," Crush muttered, and I hoped against all hope that he'd picked up a thing or two about lying.

"Can you tell me your name?"

"Troy," Crush answered weakly.

"What's your last name, Troy?"

"Johnston," he responded, and his voice sounded convincing, even if he had said only one word.

"Who was the man that brought you here, Troy? Do you know his name?"

"Am I in trouble?" Crush asked in the most innocent voice possible.

"No, honey. You're not in trouble at all. I'm just trying to figure out what happened."

"A dog got me. I was with my friends, and dogs started running after us. We climbed a fence to get away, but one got my arm before I got over.

As I was climbing down, one of the dogs jumped on the fence, and I fell and hit my head, and I guess I passed out. My mom thought I was spending the night at Shane's house, but I hadn't told him about that, so neither of them were expecting me."

I dropped my head. The story sounded all right, but he'd left out major parts, and if the nurse were smart, she'd catch them.

"Wait, how did that man find you?"

"Oh," Crush paused, and I could tell he was searching for the right way to end this. "Turns out they were his dogs."

I cringed.

"Do you know your mom's cell phone number?"

"No."

"We have to find a way to reach your mother. Are you guys in the phone book?" she asked.

I could tell by her voice that her patience was thinning. I suspected that she might have sensed Crush was lying. He needed to get her to leave.

"Yeah, her first name is Jenny."

"So, Jenny Johnston?" the nurse inquired.

"Yeah. Hey, before you leave, can you tell me what's wrong with me?"

"An infection and dehydration. The infection has progressed a lot, considering you were only bitten *yesterday*. You must have been out for some time. We gave you a shot, but you'll need to be on medication for ten days. I'm sure your mother will pick them up for you."

"What about this?" he inquired, pointing at the IV pole.

"Oh, that's just water," the nurse replied, and I heard the door close.

"Well," I whispered to Macey as I leaned in close to her so that our noses touched, and I ran my fingers through her hair. "I guess we can get out now."

"I guess so," Macey said and pushed opened the doors and stumbled out.

Fine. She wanted to play hard to get? I was a professional at that.

Crush laughed at me. "It's about time you came out of the closet."

"You're so funny. Don't forget that I could easily beat you up right now, but I choose not to because I'm a good person."

"I take extreme comfort in the fact that it takes me being in a hospital bed for you to have the slim chance of beating me in a fight." He grinned.

"I guess I should congratulate you on lying without completely and utterly blowing it."

"I try."

Macey chimed in. "We need to get to out of here before we have our eighty-second birthdays."

"Right," Crush said. He eyed his IV, and I wondered if he would be able to take it out himself. Did he know how to do that? *Would* he be able to do that?

The answer was yes.

"I can't watch this," Macey squealed as Crush tore off the tape that held the IV in his arm.

As much as I wanted to, I couldn't tear my eyes away from what he was doing.

He put his hands firmly on the IV and slowly slid it out. Water sprayed out of the end of the IV, and Crush threw it aside. He looked up at me, and I could tell by his face that he was trying not to throw up. Blood dribbled out of the tiny hole on his arm, and within a few seconds, it had reached his wrist. He ripped the hospital sheet in strands and tied it around his arm.

"All right," Macey said as she straightened herself and pulled at her shirt. "Wash the blood off your arm, and let's get out of here. Hospitals reek of death and blood."

After Crush cleaned his arm and changed back to his clothes, we rode the elevator back to the lobby, and all three of us spent about a minute drinking water from the water fountain.

"Do you see the nurse you talked to?" I asked Crush.

"Nope. She's probably still trying to reach my *mom*." He smiled.

"You feel proud?" I asked him.

"Sure do."

"Do you feel any better, Crush?" Macey asked.

Crush shrugged his shoulders. "I guess. My head stopped hurting, and they gave me something for the pain and infection in my arm, so I probably won't pass out again. I just hope we can stay one step ahead of the cops and several steps ahead of Ares. I don't feel like running."

We got into the parking lot, and I didn't see any patrol cars. Which was a plus, I guess.

"Wait," Macey said suddenly. "Look. Is that Samuel's truck? What's he still doing here? I thought he left."

"Apparently not," I said. I regretted involving him, but there had been no way around it.

"Do we walk over there?" Crush asked and walked slowly. I could tell he still didn't feel up to par.

"Yeah. He stayed for a reason, right?" I answered.

"What if he called the cops on us again? What if he is just waiting around to see what happens?" Macey asked.

"He helped fugitives. That's got to be illegal. If he called the cops, he could be arrested too. There's no way he's that stupid," I reassured her.

Samuel's head rested on the steering wheel, and he jumped to high heaven when Macey tapped on his window.

"I want my hat," he said when the window rolled down. A gust of wind blew my hair in my face, and I hoped it wouldn't be too cold tonight. The summer nights could still be chilly.

"Right, of course. Here." Macey handed the hat to Samuel.

He looked at me, and I handed him the sunglasses and made a noise in the back of my throat.

"So that's why you stayed? To get your stuff back?" Crush asked and swayed a little.

He didn't say anything for a few seconds, and my stomach fluttered. Something had happened. "Why is Agent Dotson a traitor, and why do you guys have to get to the other side of the country?" He looked at us, his face set hard.

Sometimes I hated being right.

When we didn't answer, he informed us to get in the truck or he was going to call the police.

"Get in the truck," he said again.

I tried to come up with something as we piled in the truck, but my mind drew a blank. I couldn't come up with anything reasonable that Samuel might believe. Crush must have let something slip while he'd been with Samuel. But if he had, why hadn't he confronted Macey and me in the hospital?

"It's a video game. You have to get from one side of the country to the other, and there's two guys helping you out, but one of them is a traitor, and you don't find out which one it is till the last level when you finally get to the headquarters. It's popular and addicting, and apparently, Crush spent a little too much time playing," I said and hit Crush on his shoulder harder than necessary.

"Really? Sounds fun. It's funny, because both my brothers are crazy about video games, and I've never heard of any game like that. Come on, enough with the lying. Tell me why you guys need to get to the other side of the country, or I'll blow the horn until someone comes over and sees the three fugitives in my backseat. I actually think there's a reward now."

"We can't tell you," I finally said. "If we could tell you, well, we probably wouldn't, but still. It's dangerous for you to be around us. Heck, if I could get away from myself right now, I would in a heartbeat. All three of us would. But we just can't tell you anything, and I'm not sorry about it. Not sorry at all. We know dangerous and fragile information. Trust me, I'd much rather be turned over to the police than the other guys that are after us, but I prefer not to be turned over at all. And I do know another thing—the more stuff I tell you, the more danger you're in."

"Fine. I won't call the police."

"Then will you take off child lock?" I asked and pulled at the door.

"Nope," he said as he stepped on the gas, and we skittered out of the hospital parking lot.

CHAPTER 23

"This is kidnapping! You are a kidnapper," Macey screamed as she reached over me and tried to open the door.

"I said I wasn't going to the call the police, but I'm taking you to the station right now. You guys can't get all the way across the country by yourself. You weren't really going to try, were you?"

"Yeah," Crush muttered.

"No!" I screamed. "You can't take us to the police station. Not after everything. We've worked way too hard."

"Obviously, you guys are in way over your heads. You need help."

"No. You'll be the one that needs help when I throw you out of this truck," Crush warned.

"Oh, please. I saw you walking out of the hospital. You can barely stand upright. Much less push me out. End of the conversation," Samuel clicked on a few buttons and his radio crackled to life.

"I just don't see how it's possible, Mike," a female voice said. "The oldest one isn't even old enough vote. There's no way they're smart enough to commit a crime of this caliber. There are too many missing pieces. Why would they rob a grocery store? Why not a bank?"

"They robbed a grocery store with automatic weapons. These kids are nothing but a bunch of delinquents that need to be thrown in jail for a long time. They still don't know if that man is going to die. You can easily tell that these kids don't have any respect for anyone. Shooting an unarmed man is barbaric. It's horrific that they tied him up near a fire. What was the point of setting the store on fire? These kids have no morals. I'm telling you, Hannah, these kids are serial killers waiting to happen."

"I don't know, Mike. It seems like a lot of planning and work to be done by a couple of teenagers," Hannah defended.

"Don't try to defend them. Don't you remember a few years back? Those kids that robbed all those celebrities? Most of them were just teenagers. They stole over three million dollars' worth of belongings, and they didn't get caught for the longest time."

Samuel cut off the radio and ruffled his hair. "See? Way in over your heads."

"You can't take us to the station," I said. I thought about jerking the wheel from him, but I might have ended up crashing. If I had been him, I would want nothing to do with three kids who supposedly set fire to a store and killed a man.

"Not good," Macey muttered.

"They're going to find us. You guys do know that, right? Ares will pose as someone that has the ability to take custody of us. Then they will kill us," Crush said a little too loudly.

"Shut up," I warned. Samuel didn't need to find out about that.

"Kill you? What are you talking about?" Samuel asked. He pulled off to the side of the road again. I was already sick of him. "The police won't *execute* you."

I checked to see if the doors were locked and was dismayed to see that they still were. If I could only unlock the doors.

"Nothing," I reassured Samuel. "I think the doctors gave Crush something, and he's talking all crazy. Nobody wants to kill us. I'm sure my ex-girlfriend does, but that's beside the point."

"Chase," Crush muttered. "He's right. We are in over our heads."

For an agent, he really didn't have a good attitude. And that was coming from me.

"So you guys really didn't rob that grocery store?" Samuel asked. He turned around and looked at us.

"No," Macey lied. Or maybe she didn't.

"Then who did?"

"We don't know," I muttered.

"Wait," Crush said. A little color had returned to his face. "What's the name of this town?"

Samuel told him the name and more color returned to Crush's face.

"Perfect. And how far away is the interstate?"

"About twenty miles."

"Get on the interstate and go north. Then we will explain things to you."

Surprisingly, Samuel got back on the road and started to drive. Although we still didn't know his destination.

"Where are you getting him to take us?" Macey asked.

"A safe house. I memorized their locations, and I think one isn't too far from here. There will be stuff there that we can use to fight Ares. We can even try to get in touch with the CIA. I'm sure they are doing everything they can to get that story of us off the Internet and news. Man, I really hope they know about Dotson. He's a respected agent, and he can make things happen. Shoot, he's the one that had the idea about the whole junior secret agent thing when he was like twenty. He was an intern for a few years before he got a job as a field agent. He knows a lot of stuff too. We have to warn them."

"Would someone please explain all of this to me?" Samuel asked.

"Just shut your face and drive," Macey told Samuel. She turned back to Crush. "Who can we trust at the CIA? For all we know, they're all backstabbing traitors."

"There is one guy, and he's not fond of Dotson. We can trust him," Crush said.

"Are you sure?" I asked. I had no intentions of being played again.

"No. I'm not sure," Crush confessed. "We can trust my trainer. He probably doesn't have a whole lot of power, but he's someone."

"Isn't that reassuring? So there's pretty much not one person who can help us?" Macey asked.

"Sure there is," he said. "We just need to find them. We'll go back to the CIA, they'll get Chase's dad, and if he wants to tell them what the information is, then he can."

I looked back up at Samuel, who looked in the rearview mirror at us and frowned.

"You forget we're still in New Mexico. Okay, guys. I think it's about time we all shut up." I gestured to Samuel. Crush was quite the blabbermouth.

"So, you guys are involved with the CIA? How in the world did you guys manage that? And who's this Dotson guy?"

No one answered him, and I heard the little church boy cuss under his breath.

I sat back in the chair. Sooner or later, I knew we would have to come clean about everything or there was no way Samuel would drive us all the way to the safe house. There was no way we would be able to get there on foot. We needed him. Or at least, we needed his truck. But who knows? He could still be taking us to the station.

"Maybe we could..." Macey started, but I held up my hand. Samuel didn't need to have anything more to wonder about.

We hit a bump, and the compartment in front of the passenger seat opened, and a small, rectangular object fell out.

"What's that?" Crush asked and rotated the object in his hand after he picked it up.

"I don't know. I've never seen it before," Samuel said.

"There's a button on it."

While Crush and Macey discussed the object, my mind jumped to the worst conclusions. Someone from Ares had tracked and followed us to plant the black object in the truck when we'd all been in the hospital. Somehow, they'd known Samuel wouldn't leave the parking lot. Whatever happened when that button was pressed couldn't be good. This was all a game to them. There was more to this than information. We were pawns in their game. I should have figured that out when there was footage of us at a grocery store. They had known we would escape.

Another thought occurred to me.

They'd *let* us escape.

"Well, aren't you going to press the button?"

Crush pushed the button and proved my instincts had been right, which I wished they hadn't been.

At first, the pain in my shoulder wasn't that bad, but that only lasted for a second. My shoulder and arm started to shake and then progressed to spasms, like the muscles in my arm were on fire and being controlled by a puppet master. I grabbed my shoulder and the pain intensified. I screamed. It felt like flames hugged my arm. I cried out and tried to wipe at my arm, as if this would douse the flame.

"The button! Press the button again!" I felt along the front of my shoulder and stopped where the pain was most intense. There was a bump, maybe the size of an acorn. It hadn't been there before the kidnapping.

Crush pressed the button, and the pain stopped. I leaned back in the chair, covered my face with my hands, and tried to catch my breath. My whole body was wracked with fear.

"What the heck happened?" Macey asked.

"I—I don't know. Just don't press the button again."

The black object started to hum, and there was a flood of fear in my stomach. I didn't think I could handle that again.

The humming stopped. What came next was worse. A voice.

"That's better. Chase? Sydney? Macey? Have you guys been watching the news lately? It seems to me like you guys committed a little crime. It's *amazing* how you three were able to rob a grocery store, shoot a guy, and set it on fire and not get caught. Sadly, you forgot to kill the security tapes. It would have been so easy to override them. I guess we were wrong. You three aren't as smart as we thought. And that janitor. It was weird for him to be working so late, wasn't it? And the bomb that you three planted in the grocery store? Have you heard about that? Lucky, they were able to disarm it before it went off. It really is a shame. Perhaps they didn't want to release that information to the press. Now, before I get too off track, I wanted to ask Chase something.

"Did you find the bump in your shoulder? Can you feel it? I bet your feeling it at this moment. I could make that little pebble in your shoulder go boom with a push of a button. You see, Chase, before you and your friends left, we were able to implant that into your shoulder. It has the capability to send pain signals to your brain, as you might have realized. Everyone at Ares is very proud of the technology.

"But I'm getting off track. We didn't count on Crush knowing about the safe house, so we decided it was the perfect time to say hello. I will make myself very clear. Don't go to the safe house unless you want me to press the button that will cause the device in Chase's shoulder to self-destruct. It's rumored to be painful. I heard that a certain someone told you to go to the CIA headquarters. I'm not sure that's in everyone's best interest. I want the three of you to go to New York City. I want to have a meeting, preferably in person. And I do hate to pay the cost of flying you over. I've called off the search for you three, so now you only have to worry about the police catching up to you. Of course, these rouge agents seem to do what they want. No telling what they might do. It will be fun! Like a game between the four of us. You don't really have a choice. Remember, all I have to do is push a button, and Chase will feel a little more than a cramp."

The black box started to smoke, and Crush dropped it.

"Oh my gosh. Are they serious? How did they—why would they—what are we going to do?" Macey rambled.

"I don't know. They knew we were at the hospital. They must have been following and tracking us," Crush said.

Macey and Crush looked at me.

"What?"

"The bomb—" Crush started.

I cut him off. "Don't call it a bomb."

"Fine. It must be a tracker too. That's how they knew we were here, and that's how they're going to make sure we go to New York City."

"They're messing with us. This is a game to whoever that was, and we're the pieces. We should have realized that when the story about the grocery store came out," I complained, reiterating my thoughts.

"Can they hear us?" I asked.

"Maybe. They knew we were planning to go to the safe house, but now that the black thing smoked, they might not be able to. But it's not like anything we say will make this situation any worse," Macey said. She sank down in her seat and blew hair out of her face. "New York City? None of this makes any sense. If they want us so badly, why don't they just come and get us?"

"I'm not so sure it's as big of a 'they' as we once thought. It sounds like it's a handful of people, maybe less, who are truly involved in everything," I said.

Macey nodded, glanced out of the window, and brought her knees to her chest.

I looked at Crush. Surely, he would have some brilliant plan to get us out of this, but he looked just as stumped as the rest of us. I looked at Samuel, who had been silent this whole time.

Samuel spoke when he noticed I was looking at him. "Look, I know the police are after you guys and all, but wouldn't you be safe from whoever that guy was if you turned yourselves in? That person was psychotic."

The three of us exchanged glances. If we did go to the police, it wouldn't be good.

"There's one thing I don't understand. If this person was close enough to plant this thing in Samuel's car, then why didn't he just kidnap us again?" Crush asked. Apparently, he hadn't been paying any attention to what I'd just said.

"You don't get it yet, do you? There are many levels to this whole situation, and the next level involves us going to New York City. This is the phase two Dotson was talking about. Those people *let* us escape. I don't know why. It's like they want to see what happens, like some kind of study or entertainment on behavior. They're manipulating the heck out of us right now," I said.

"How do we stop it?"

"I don't know."

"So, what do we do?" Crush asked.

Macey looked at me. "We can't let them hurt Chase. We have to go to New York City."

"Guys, no. I'm not making you guys risk your lives for the millionth time. We'll go to the CIA headquarters like we were planning."

"Chase, no. We're not going to risk *your* life like that," Crush said.

"Crush is right. Chase, this isn't your fault. It's Ares's fault for treating our lives like plastic pieces on a board game. We'll figure something out, okay?"

It was then, in that truck, when I realized that Macey and Crush were the only real friends I had.

"Or we could try and cut out the bomb, or whatever the heck it is, out of Chase's shoulder. Then we won't have to listen to anything those jack heads say," Crush speculated.

Maybe Macey was the only real friend.

I stared at him. "I could blow up and die."

Crush shrugged his shoulders.

I rolled my eyes and looked at Samuel. "You wouldn't mind if we borrowed your parents' car for a little road trip, would you?" If they insisted we go to New York City, we weren't walking.

"Sorry, you guys. We're sitting in their truck. Anyway, my dad is probably wondering where I am. I'm going to have to ask you guys to get out of my truck."

He pulled over and unlocked the doors. Great. So now he decided to leave us alone. I stared at Samuel. We needed this truck more than we needed anything. I nudged Crush and whispered, "Any more darts left?"

Sure, it was a little extreme, but we were once again in a dire situation.

Crush smiled and removed one from his pocket. In a flash, he'd stuck it in Samuel's neck. Samuel yelled at us, but only for about seven seconds. Then closed his eyes and slumped down in his seat.

"That was the last dart. I'll just start having to punch people now," Crush said.

Macey's eyes were wide. "I can't believe you guys just did that. Now what are we supposed to do with him? Leave him on the side of the road?"

We left him on the side of the road. Macey protested and said that we were inhumane and lunatics. It didn't make her feel better about the situation when I went back and moved Samuel farther away from the road.

Finally, fed up with us, Macey found Samuel's phone and called his mother. She told her that her son was in need of assistance on the corner of Richmond's Pavilion and First Street. She didn't offer any more information. Crush and I didn't care very much about Samuel, but Macey cared about him, and I cared about Macey. I guess that meant I had to sort of care about Samuel.

"So, I'm driving?" Crush asked as Macey and I got back in the truck.

"Go for it," I told him.

Crush climbed in the driver's seat and fired up the engine.

I took Macey's hand and gave it a reassuring squeeze. She smiled at me.

"Crush might kill us before we get to New York City," I said.

"What do you think will happen when we get there?" Macey muttered and leaned her head on my shoulder.

"We'll just have to figure out a way to kill them all before we get there and then wipe the memory of every American who watched the news. Easy as pie."

"Hmm. I love how the teenage boy brain works."

CHAPTER 24

"Slow down!" Macey screamed.

I woke with a start to all the chaos. Thankfully, it was just Crush's driving that caused Macey's yells. I checked the clock and saw that I'd been asleep for an hour.

We were going eighty miles per hour in a forty-mile-per-hour zone. It might have been a back road, but there was the occasional car, and every time one passed I was sure we would crash into them and die. One car beeped at us for about five seconds. I was also almost certain that a deer would jump out in front of us, and I would be stuck cleaning deer guts off the leather seats.

Crush slowed down to about twenty miles per hour when Macey ordered him to slow down.

"Oh my gosh," Macey groaned. "You're kidding me. Chase was a better driver when we were being shot at by Ares."

"Sorry, I'm trying. You could say I'm under a bit of pressure, with the threat of Chase blowing up if we make a wrong move and everything. I was also in the hospital a few hours ago."

"Do you want one of us to drive?" Macey asked with a slight hint of worry.

"Later. I'm fine for right now."

"Turn on the radio," I told Crush and slumped back in the seat.

Macey and I were in the backseat. Neither of us wanted to have a front-row seat to Crush's madness.

"What? Why? I feel like Mr. Creep will start singing."

"If we're driving halfway across the country to our possible demise, we're listening to music. I'm not listening to you guys the whole time. And we need gas."

"I know, I know." Crush clicked on the radio.

Pop music filled the truck, and I was about to yell at Crush to find something better, but Macey started to sing along.

A few seconds passed. Crush and I made eye contact through the rear-view mirror, and both of us had our eyebrows raised.

"Macey, stop! You're making my ears bleed," I yelled. The opposite was true—Macey had a nice voice, but telling her that would lead to absolutely no fun.

Macey sang louder, and I yelled louder. Crush turned off the radio and yelled at us to shut up, but Macey knew the song by heart and kept singing; therefore, I kept yelling. Crush slammed on the brakes, and we all jutted forward again.

"Can you guys please shut up? I'm trying to drive here," Crush told us.

"Macey's awful singing started it, Dad," I said sarcastically.

"Hey," she protested. "I can sing. My band and I won our school's talent show last year."

"Yeah, you can sing all right," I admitted.

"Thank you."

"Just not to a point anyone would want to listen."

Her jaw dropped, and she shoved me up against the side window and held my face there.

"You also have a face. Just not to a point anyone would want to look."

"Aren't you a clever one?" I asked, still slammed against the glass.

"Sure am," she responded. She pushed her dirty blonde hair back.

Crush started to drive again (after saying offensive things to the both of us) and Macey smirked at me, but she let me go.

For a second, it felt like we were normal teenagers having fun on a normal summer day. Crush broke that spell when he said he was going to look for a station that had talked about us.

"Why?" I complained.

"We need to keep up with what we're doing, that's why. Maybe we sank a yacht or something," Crush told us and clicked to the channel that'd been talking about us before, but they were giving out the license plate number of a stolen vehicle, so Crush kept looking.

"Wait," Macey said. "They aren't talking about us, are they?"

"Why would they be?" I asked her.

"This is a stolen vehicle, and we knocked out Samuel and left him on the side of the road. That would leave a person slightly annoyed. Maybe enough to call the police."

"Not our main problem." We'd been ignoring the terrifying unknown of the situation. I didn't blame them for not wanting to talk about it, but it needed to be done. Although I wasn't too ready to talk about the two janitors. One was dead, and that meant one of us had shot him. But he had to have been an Ares member. Right? Could one of us have shot an innocent man?

"I'm not trying to change the subject to something worse, because I'd much rather talk about the likelihood of the police finding us in a stolen vehicle and everything, but do you guys think Ares let us go?" I asked.

"Yeah. Like you said, this is all a game to them," Macey said. "They wouldn't have any fun if we were just sitting in a cell."

"Why would they put a bomb in my shoulder?"

"To control us. They know there's no way we wouldn't do what they said as long as they threatened to hurt Chase. No matter how annoying he is," Crush offered and continued. "We were probably kidnapped on the nineteenth, right? That means we probably woke up in the truck on the twentieth. They probably put the bomb in you the same day and then let you heal for two days. Then they proceeded to threaten that if we didn't rob that grocery store like we were told, they would make Chase have another attack. It might have taken them a day to edit the footage and get us back to their headquarters. Presuming that we left the headquarters at all. That's when they made us forgot everything. They probably hacked into the security cameras and replaced the footage that made them happy. Or at least that's what I would have done."

I scoffed.

"So what's their motive? Why not kill us? Why go to all this trouble?" Macey questioned.

"Their motive?" Crush said. "I don't even want to know. World domination? Distraction? While the police look for us, they could be pulling something off. Chase, your dad might have told them that the information is in New York City, and that's why they want us to go there. So they can use us as hostages or do their dirty work for them. Who knows? But what could the information be? It stayed so important for so many years. Why not just come and get us and then take us to New York City?" he asked. "Personally, I thought the airfare joke was uncalled for."

"It's a test. To see if we're good enough," I offered. I thought about telling them about the Applied Research Group, but at this point, I wasn't even sure it existed. Dotson had lied about everything else.

"And why did they kidnap me?" Macey questioned. "I mean, I know they got you because you're the son and everything." She gestured to me and then looked at Crush. "And they took you because you're the junior agent with secrets that I'll get out of you later. But why me?" Macey asked.

"I have a good guess," Crush said and cut his eyes toward me. I could hear humor in his voice, and I knew what was coming. He could tell I liked Macey when I could barely tell that I liked her.

"Crush..." I warned, although I had no idea what I would do to him. He *was* driving the car I was in.

"They knew that Chase had a crush on you and thought that they could use that against him."

"Or Dotson just felt like getting rid of all three of us at once," she said, ignoring Crush's comment.

"Or the coward didn't feel like coming up with a lie that clarified why only Crush and I unexpectedly vanished in the middle of the night," I guessed. But I knew Crush was right. Dotson wouldn't have pulled over when we'd seen Macey on the sidewalk if he didn't need to use her. The bobble headman must have told the Ares men on the boat that I was with her.

"Do you guys think he meant for us to hear him?" Crush asked.

"I don't want to talk about him anymore. His name makes me sick, and we're just coming up with questions that we don't have the answers to," I said.

"There's a black car trailing us," Macey said after a few miles.

We turned. The black car turned too.

"This is bad. Oh man, this is bad," I said.

"That's not our only problem," Crush added glumly.

"What? Why?"

"Our friend Samuel apparently didn't believe in a full tank of gas." Crush gestured to the gas gauge.

"Should you stop and see if the guy keeps going?" I asked.

"That reeks of failure, Pretty Boy," Crush informed me.

"Why is that?" I asked.

"Ever heard of a drive-by shooting?"

"We're just going to keep driving and driving until we run out of gas?" Macey asked. "That reeks of failure too."

"Then what do you want me to do?" Crush asked. "We're about to be running on fumes." He tapped the gas gauge, and it bounced up and down. "Or we might be on fumes."

The black car was only two car lengths away.

I shook my head. "Floor it."

"Yeah, 'cause that's not suspicious at all."

"Dude, this guy is about to be in our backseat. I don't think this the time to worry about if we look suspicious," I told him.

Lights in the car started to flash, and I realized that this was either an undercover cop or the CIA. Ares wasn't looking for us anymore. I prayed it was the CIA.

"Don't even think about pulling over," Macey told Crush. She gripped the headrest, and her face lost all color. I felt a wave of guilt wash over me for taking her to the pier that day. I tried to tell myself that Dotson would have found a way to get her even if she had been at home.

We started to slow down.

"Crush? What are you doing? Get away from them," I yelled.

"It's not me, dude. We're out of gas."

We bumped to a stop. "This isn't too good. I recommend we plead insanity." I knew we couldn't run. Crush was still too weak. Besides, the report that Samuel read to me said that we'd killed someone and critically injured another. I wondered if that gave them permission to shoot us. There was no way I was testing these people's patience so soon.

The car pulled up beside us and screeched to a stop. Two men ran up to the truck and opened the doors with their guns up. I really wished we had more darts.

"Get out with your hands up!" they screamed at us.

The three of us gently got out of Samuel's truck. I didn't have my hands up. It felt too much like giving up.

"Hands up!" one of the men yelled again. He gestured with his gun.

Against my better judgment, I put my hands up in the air, only to have them tightly cuffed and pushed against my back.

"Whatever happened to the loosest setting on the cuffs? Don't they teach you anything in cop school? Oh, wait. Is this your first day off of the desk? I'm sorry. Didn't mean to be so unkind. By the way, the truck ran out of gas. We didn't stop for you. Good luck getting it to the station."

The cop wrenched me by my shoulders, put his beefy hands around my neck, and steered me toward the car. I couldn't wipe the grin off my face. I'd broken out of a police station before, and this time I had someone who had been trained for situations like this. It would be a piece of cake.

He told us our rights, and I rolled my eyes. Like I hadn't heard them before. The cop opened the door and shoved me inside. Macey followed, and Crush was shoved in last. He grimaced as the man touched his wound. Only one of the cops got into the car, and I saw the other by the truck. He must be have been stuck waiting for someone to come with gas. More than likely, Samuel told the authorities that the grocery-store kids were the ones that stole his truck. They probably thought we'd hidden the stolen goods there.

The other cop started the car, turned around, and drove.

"Would you believe me if I said that we were innocent?" I asked him and leaned up in my seat. "We didn't rob the grocery store. You guys are being idiots wasting your time with us," I told him.

"Shut your mouth," Macey whispered to me. "Anything you say can and will be held against you."

I leaned in closer to her. "What harm could it do?"

"A lot of harm," she answered back. "We need to get out of here so that bomb in your shoulder doesn't go off. Did you forget about that?"

"Relax—the CIA can get us out of this," I told her, even though I didn't believe the words even as I said them.

"You mean like they stopped Ares from kidnapping us and rescued us from the torture room? Yeah, those were good rescue missions."

I turned my attention back to the officer, unable to resist the urge to make him angry. "Hey, where are you taking us? And don't I get to see a badge or something? We don't even know if you're a legit cop. And it's rude not to introduce yourself."

The officer looked at me in the rearview mirror and scowled. "No talking."

We pulled up in the parking lot of the police station about twenty minutes later. The officer opened the door, and two others were there to grab us by the shoulders and wrench us inside the building.

I was taken roughly into the first interrogation room, and the handcuffs were removed but replaced by shackles that hooked to a steel table. They had never done this to me when I'd been arrested before, but this was different. I wasn't the hungry and troubled orphan who just needed a little guidance to these people. No. I was a possible murderer who needed to be dealt with.

There wasn't a way to jimmy out of these shackles unless I had a key or a lock pick. I needed to start carrying one.

Or a machete. That would have worked nicely.

I looked at the one-way mirror. My face was dirty, and my clothes were in bad condition. I knew there had to be people looking in on me, so I waved (as best as I could) and smiled. Out of all the things I'd been forced to go through in the past few days, this was the least scary.

But I imagined Macey and Crush weren't having such a fun time.

About five minutes went by before a man and a woman that screamed detectives walked in the room and sat on the chairs across from me. The woman threw what I guessed to be my newly printed file on the table.

"Are you guys going to do the whole good-cop-and-bad-cop thing, or is that only in the movies?" I asked.

The detectives seemed a little taken back. They'd probably been anticipating a terrified kid ready to go home to his mother. But that wasn't a problem for me.

"What? Were you guys expecting me to cry and plead for mercy? And doesn't someone have to be in here with me? Like a social worker? You know, to make sure you don't start throwing punches? Or are one of you two the social worker and choosing not to tell me? Smart."

"We've had a look at your file. I would only speak when asked a question," the man told me.

I looked at the man and blinked my eyes. "So, I'm not allowed to spontaneously confess to everything?"

"Listen kid, we can do this the easy way or the hard way. You're already in a lot of trouble, and if you keep smarting off, you're going to be in even more trouble. How would you like that? The crimes you've already committed are enough to land you time in prison. The cases weren't handled properly."

"Please, do read me what's on that fancy little file."

The man picked up the file and leafed through a couple of the papers. He clearly wanted to prove me wrong.

"You're a shoplifter and a runaway. You've skipped school, stolen from a restaurant, and broken out of prison. Then you robbed a grocery store, set it on fire, shot a man and killed another, stole money and other goods, placed a powerful bomb in the store, and stole a truck.

"We have a video of you and your friends, Chase. All we want to know is why and who helped you." The man was inches from my face. I could feel his breath.

"What about the janitor? Did you guys question him?" I wanted to ask if they had the footage of who killed the man, but I wasn't sure I wanted to know the answer.

The man pulled back.

"Of course we did."

"Where is he now?" I asked.

I saw the detective's face drop just a little, and I knew that they had no idea where the guy was. I knew he was back at Ares's headquarters, collecting his paycheck. Or they might have killed him. Or he really might be in the hospital.

"You guys have no clue? Figures. Go ahead and try to find all the witness. I guarantee you won't be able to contact them again."

"We can do this all day, kid," the woman told me.

"So, who gets the reward money?"

The man slammed his hands on the table. "Where did you get the bomb? Who gave you the gun? Who made the bomb? And where's the money?"

"Is this test multiple choice?" I asked him.

"Quit the tough-guy act now."

"It comes naturally. Can't turn it off."

"I would answer the questions if I were you, Chase," the woman told me.

"Or what? What could the two of you possibly do to make my life any worse? Tell me my parents will be disappointed if I don't answer your petty questions?" I asked. I was tired, hungry, and thirsty. I didn't want to talk about something that I didn't remember doing.

"There are kids that have it way worse than you do," the woman told me.

She was wrong there.

"How about this? You answer a question, and I'll let you get water," the man said and seemed to get his temper back under control, but I knew how quickly it could come back.

My lips suddenly felt very dry. If Crush had been dehydrated, Macey and I probably were as well.

"Fine. You want to know where I got the bomb and who made it? I'll tell you. I actually work for Santa Claus. The bomb came from the North Pole, and Rudolph and Comet helped me make it. Mrs. Claus is always worried about the snowmen messing up her garden, so she gave me the gun to scare them off. The money is being shipped via flying reindeer to the North Pole to buy supplies for next Christmas. Times are getting tough. Even for Santa."

I honestly expected to get slapped in the face. Instead, like a first-grade teacher might, they ignored my bad behavior.

"We'll be back when you feel like talking," the woman told me. She left the room.

The man didn't leave. Instead, he put both hands on the table and started to talk quietly. "I could make this place a living hell for you. There's only so much I can do because you're a minor, but listen to this. Not one person cares about your well-being. Not one person. So what does it matter if you're a little uncomfortable or thirsty? No one will come and help you. You're alone."

Okay, that one hurt.

He walked behind me, and I felt the shackles around both my wrists tighten. I winced and tried to jerk my hands free. The man put his cold hands on my arms and squeezed them tightly. I sat there and acknowledged that he had played his cards better than I. On camera, it wouldn't look like he was doing anything to me.

"Hurts, doesn't it? Do you want to answer my questions now? Because they can go tighter. They can always go tighter." To prove that he wasn't kidding, he made them tighter. My wrists stung, and it felt like the bones were being flattened between two concrete slabs.

"I don't know anything! The whole thing was planned. We were framed." I lost my temper, and the pain made me frantic. He couldn't leave them like this, could he?

"Are you really going to stick with that story? Why would anyone frame you for that?" he asked.

I bit my tongue. He'd make the shackles tighter if I told him why. He'd think I was lying.

"I don't know."

"You better figure out why before I come back. I have a meeting with your friends," he told me as he closed the door.

"Wait," I said.

He turned back around.

"I haven't had any water for the better half of the day. I'll consider cooperating if you give me water."

"Answer my questions, and I'll consider cooperating."

He continued out the door.

"Wait."

He turned back around.

"Do you have any kids?" I asked.

He smiled. He knew where I was going with that.

"Thankfully not." He went to slam the door.

"You were right," I said before the door closed completely.

The man poked his head back in. "You'll have to be more specific."

"About no one *really* caring about me. I know that, and I'm okay with it. If you mean to hurt my feelings, tell me I'm ugly or something. I've spent my whole life taking care of myself. I've never depended on anyone. Having someone care would be a surprising change. No one ever cared when I went days without food or could barely manage to walk. They put on those sympathetic faces and told me it would all be okay, but they never did anything to help me in the long run. I was just another hopeless basket case. I'm immune to no one coming and saving me. Life is easier that way."

The man slammed the door shut.

The shackles dug into my skin, and I could do nothing to stop it. I wanted to scream. I felt my shoulder start to vibrate again. At first, I thought I had imagined it, but it gradually started to feel like it had in the truck. Except this time, I also had the pain in my wrists to deal with. I saw black dots form in front of my eyes, and I tried to shake them away, but that seemed to make it worse. I needed water. Was Ares about to set off the bomb in my shoulder? Were they afraid that we would spill what was going on? Should we? It petrified me that my life could be ended by a push of a button.

The pain lasted for about thirty seconds before the two detectives opened the door, but I wasn't fully aware of their presence. I think they told me to shut up, and when I didn't, I think they asked me what was wrong. I didn't answer. I felt like my shoulder was on fire. Ten seconds later, the pain stopped as soon as it had started, just like it had in the truck. I glanced up at the camera mounted on the wall. Could Ares have been watching us?

"What's wrong with you?"

I caught my breath and tried to reply. "I—uh—I'm uh—"

I tried to think of something that could possibly explain why I'd been screaming my head off, but nothing came to mind.

"Well?" the woman asked me.

"Can you loosen the shackles?" I asked and hoped to get her sympathy.

"They're loose enough," she insisted. She opened her mouth again, but I cut her off.

"They *were* fine before Mr. Bad Cop over here tightened them."

The woman walked over to me and looked at the shackles. She took a key out of her pocket, unlocked the shackles, and let them fall to the floor. I raised my eyebrows at her and rubbed my wrists in an attempt to get the blood to flow normally. The cuts had reopened and slowly bled. As if I didn't have enough scars.

"Um, thanks," I told her.

"Brenda, really? No restraints?" the detective asked.

"Relax. He's only fifteen. What's he going to do, John?" Brenda asked. "And look at the boy's wrists. Someone is going to have answer to that. You were instructed to let him free in the first place. He needs water."

John turned to Brenda. "Do you mind if I have some time alone with him?"

Brenda looked at me and then back at her partner. "Just remember that these are recorded. Try not to be too tough on him. I'll get the water."

She left.

"Listen here, kid. I would love nothing more than to see you and your friends rot behind bars for the rest of your natural lives. If I had the authority, I'd throw all three of you in prison right now, but I have rules to follow and bosses to please, and I need to know who shot the two men and who gave you the bomb. The media and public would start a riot if there weren't a follow-up story on the three of you. You and I both don't want to be here, but we're stuck together until you answer my questions. You know you did it. I know you did it. We all know you did it. Just help us out and answer my questions. I'm sure you're hungry and thirsty. You remember our deal, don't you? An answer for water."

"I didn't do anything." I was beginning to wonder if he had authorization to use advanced *integration* methods.

"Oh, I get it. You didn't do anything. One of your alternative personalities did it. Where's that guy? Maybe the security footage shows him? Because it sure isn't you. Nope, it was one of your other personalities, because you didn't do a thing. Right? Or maybe it was one of the reindeer? Or the elves."

"That's right, smarty."

The man's face grew red, and veins in his neck bulged. He reached across the table, grabbed my hair, and slammed my head on the table and kept me there.

"I've dealt with people a whole lot tougher than you. They act just like you are. They think they're tough and untouchable. You've been in trouble before. That's one extra reason for the judge to give you more time. Not to mention that no one here is on your side. You're fighting a losing battle, and all your soldiers are wounded."

He let go of me and left the room.

I was given a bottle of water and a bowl of soup for supper. I've never enjoyed a meal more than I enjoyed that one. The cop who gave me the meal lingered. He was about six feet tall with big arms and a buzz cut. He had a small tattoo on his upper right arm. He looked young. I glanced up at him in between bites, and he immediately looked away.

"What?"

"Nothing."

"Then could you stop staring at me?"

"Sorry. It's just they usually don't bring in kids this young. What did you do?" he asked and walked toward me.

"Seriously? I'm in no mood to be messed with. You know what they're accusing me of doing. The whole country knows," I told him. I saw him glance down at my bloody wrists. I hid them under the table.

"Right. So, how did you do it? How did you break in? And where's the money? Do you know where it is?"

"If they sent you in here to ask me more questions, you might have been better off not asking them all at once. Now, you can leave me alone? I need sleep. What time is it?"

"I'll answer that if you answer me," he asked hopefully.

"I'm not an idiot," I told him flatly.

He frowned. "It's late. Really late."

The man took the bowl and empty water bottle from me. I heard the lock turn as he slammed the door shut. I didn't think they were going to take me out of this interrogation room, but I was wrong. Brenda came back and took me to one of the station's crash rooms. There was a cot, a table, a lamp, and a bathroom. She handed me new clothes. I thought about not wearing them, but I was sick of wearing the Ares-issued clothes.

CHAPTER 25

I'd like to say that I didn't sleep well. I'd like to say that I was so bent on getting out of there that my mind didn't let me go to sleep.

I'd be lying if I said that. And well, we all know how I'm so against lying. I could have slept another six hours, but I was woken up at seven because Mr. and Mrs. Bad Cop wanted to have another round. I was taken to the interrogation room.

"Did you sleep well?" John asked me.

"Like a log, John. Like a log. How about you?"

"You're digging yourself a hole."

"Yeah, to get out of here," I yawned. "Now are you going to ask me the same questions as yesterday? Because I'll give you the same answers. Nothing has changed."

"Actually, we got your friends to talk."

"What?"

"They told us everything."

I let out the breath that I'd been holding. If Macey or Crush had said anything, the detective wouldn't have said that. He'd cry and apologize for everything.

"What did they say?"

Before they could tell me some lie, Brenda's phone rang, and she frowned after a few moments.

"What do you mean it started to talk? What? I'll be there in a second." Her face became red, and she turned and ran out the door.

"Are you going to put the shackles back on?" I asked. Honestly, I didn't think my wrists could handle it anymore.

"I won't if you answer my questions. I want to see if your story matches up with the one I've already heard."

I rolled my eyes. "So, what have Macey and Crush told you guys?" I asked.

"What happened to Crush's arm?"

"He's not talking. I know that. Come on, you don't actually expect me to believe that they told you anything, right? Besides, there's nothing to talk about."

"Of course he did talk. The boy and the girl have already spilled everything. Their stories match up perfectly, and I'll be sure to tell the judge that they worked with us. But you? You better start talking unless you want life in prison."

"I think you're lying to me, John. They wouldn't talk. Mostly because the three of us are completely innocent of all the charges."

"Oh, so you didn't steal that truck?" he asked angrily.

"It was a gift."

"From who? It is the same person that took Crush to the hospital?"

"Now you want me to snitch?" I asked. "Not gonna happen. Look, we were scared out of our minds when we found about the charges."

"And why didn't you turn in yourselves immediately?" he asked.

"I think I'm making your job a little too easy," I told him.

The man threw up his hands and then threw my file across the room. He looked like he was ready to scream his head off, but Brenda came back in the room, and he calmed down.

"What happened?" I asked.

She was at a complete loss for words, and she looked from me back to her partner.

"What happened?" I stood up and walked over to her, and she took a few steps away from me.

"Sit him down," she told John.

"What? Whoa, what happened?" I asked.

John grabbed me, pushed nearly every pressure point in my back, and sat me down in the chair. Once again, he put on the shackles. Brenda took John out of the room and although I couldn't see or hear them, I could imagine that their little talk wasn't going too well.

They came back in, their faces ashen, and stared at me.

"What happened?" I asked for the fourth time.

"There's a black object in the truck. You know which one I'm talking about," John told me.

I did. It couldn't possibly still work! We all assumed it destructed itself. Unless, of course, it was all a trick, and we were supposed to think that it didn't work so Ares could continue to give us little messages of encouragement.

Dang.

They must have been searching the truck for more evidence or money when the black object started to talk. Ares wasn't making this easy for us.

I shrugged my shoulders and looked away.

"Chase, its more impetrative now than ever that you tell us everything you know."

"Did you guys get a little message from the truck?"

"Yes. How did you know?" Brenda asked me.

"I've been told I'm a good guesser. What did the guy say?"

"What's in New York City?" John asked. "Why do these people want you and your friends to get there as quickly as possible?"

"They probably want to kill us."

"Who?" Brenda screamed. "Who wants to kill you?"

I started to count off on my fingers. "Lots of people."

"What are you not telling us? Please, we can help you." Brenda pleaded with me.

"No. No. You really can't," I told her bluntly. "The only way me and my friends and a couple other people won't be brutally tortured and murdered is if you let us go. We need to take that truck and get to New York City now."

"We want to help you, Chase," Brenda told me soothingly. "You're safe here."

"Tell me what the message said, and I'll help you guys. I swear."

"It said that the three of you have four days to get to New York City before someone dies, and then something about a bomb," Brenda told me.

"What bomb are they talking about? Is there another one in the grocery store?" John asked.

I rolled my eyes. "Get over the grocery store, John. This is a little bit bigger than some stupid store. I suggest that you turn your backs, and let us escape."

Ares was making this a little too hard.

"You know we can't do that. The three of you are safer here," Brenda told me again.

I was about to explain how I wasn't safe anywhere and tell them how stupid they were, but both of the adults' radios started to make a high-pitched noise, and they left the room without hesitation. A few seconds passed before the door was thrown open. I half expected Dotson or Ivan Spivakovsky to be on the other side with a gun pointed at my head.

But it was Crush, who wasn't much better.

"Dude, come on. We have to get out of here now," he yelled at me and dangled keys in my face.

"About time you did something useful," I told him as he unlocked the shackles on my wrists with a key he'd surprisingly been able to get his hands on. He opened the door and pulled me into the corridor.

"We have about two minutes to get out of here and find Macey. She should be around this corner..." His voice trailed off as he pulled me down the corridor and toward the exit.

"What did you guys do? How did you get out?"

Macey stumbled out of a room and smiled when she saw us.

"Come on. We have less time than we thought. We can't be here much longer."

The two of them rushed down the hallways, and I had to follow them.

"Which way?" Macey screamed.

"I don't know," Crush yelled. A siren started to wail.

"That way." I pointed the way to the exit, where I guessed we were trying to go. We ran down another corridor, and the front door was just in front of us. It shouldn't have been this easy. Nothing was ever this easy. Where was everybody?

"Wait," Macey said.

"What?" My hand was on the handle of the door, and I wanted nothing more than to get out of this place. Our luck couldn't last for too much longer.

"The key to the truck. Where is it?"

"Check in that desk. There should be some kind of file with all the stuff they took from us in it."

Macey and Crush turned to look at me.

"What? Come on guys, I think we all know this isn't my first time being arrested. It should be the top folder."

All three of us started to rummage through the desk, throwing everything out of our way that wasn't the key.

"It's not in here!" Crush screamed, as if that would help.

Macey pulled a folder off the desk and ripped it open, and a key clattered to the floor. I reached down and grabbed it just as two policemen entered the lobby. They were young and clearly out of their league, which often led to a dangerous situation. We ran out the door, but Crush stopped.

"Dude, come on. The truck is right there," Samuel's truck was parked about twenty feet away from us.

Crush ignored me and ran back to the door, where he produced a pair of handcuffs from his pocket and latched the handles of the two doors together. If there was one thing I had started to appreciate about Crush, it was his habit of taking things that could aid us in the future.

"Now can we go?" Macey asked.

The two policemen shook the door and clearly didn't understand why it didn't open. I waved and smiled at them.

We ran to the back of the police station where our truck had been stored. Crush stuck the key into the door, but it wouldn't even begin to fit. Great. It was the wrong one.

"What now?" Macey asked.

My mind went into overdrive. What could I do? I leaned against a door, about ready to give up.

The rubber around the window was peeling off. The truck was probably made in the late eighties or early nineties. One of my friends used to love to go in parking lots and see how long it would take him to hotwire a car. His name was Dylan. I went with him, mostly because I'd been a homeless eleven-year-old who was scared to stay alone at the warehouse where the two of us lived. I'd never really thought about how he managed to get the car open in order to hotwire it, but I didn't like his method. He took a hammer, knocked out the driver's window, and reached in to unlock it. He did it for fun almost every weekend. Dylan always worked with the older cars. He hardly ever did a newer car because he claimed they were too difficult to hotwire.

He'd taught me how to hotwire a car.

I almost slapped myself. How stupid and oblivious could I possibly be? I looked around for a rock that would be big enough to knock out the car's window. I quickly located one pressed up to the building. I picked it up and hurled it at the driver's window. I pushed Crush out of the way, and I tried to remember the instructions Dylan forced me to memorize.

I swung open the door and attempted to avoid the jagged glass as I ripped off the access cover under the steering wheel, which I was thankful was held in place with layers of tape instead of screws. This truck wasn't in top shape, and I was grateful for it. I saw the wiring harness and knew I could get access to the wires that were behind the ignition. It looked like there were millions of wires, but I was able to locate the ones that looked the same. Dylan said that they were usually red, and this time was no exception. I didn't know what either of them were called, I just knew I needed to connect them. I searched for the ignition wire while Crush yelled at me to move faster. I didn't take the time and concentration to inform him that he wasn't helping.

I found the brown wire and moved down the insulator about half an inch. Man, I hoped I was doing this correctly. I touched the wires together, and the ignition was achieved. I actually had no clue what that meant, but Dylan always said that. He used to clap me on the back when I hotwired correctly. I revved up the engine and twisted the three wires together so they would stay together. Electrical tape would have been nice, but that was asking for too much.

Crush moved me out of the way and got in the driver's seat. I knew there was something I'd forgotten. I had a feeling that it was important. Crush threw the truck into reverse and stepped on the gas.

What was it I forgot? I knew there was something...

Crush tried to yank the steering wheel, but it wouldn't budge. He shot me a murderous look.

Oh, right. The steering wheel.

"Chase!" he screamed at me. "Do something now!"

"We need a screwdriver to put in the lock and twist it," I told him.

We were still in the back of the station and I saw the two policemen running at us, guns up. If they were smart, they would just shoot out the tires.

"Find a screwdriver," I screamed. I remembered all the tools I'd seen the first time I'd been in the truck and prayed a screwdriver was one of them.

Macey held up a screwdriver in her hand. "Is this what you're looking for?"

Crush ripped it out of her hands, stuck it in the lock, and twisted it. I waited for the lock to break off the mounting structure. I heard it crack, but I didn't allow myself to relax just yet.

"Got it." Crush wrenched the steering wheel, and we sputtered onto the busy road the second before the policemen were able to get to us. As Crush pulled away, I felt a slight bump and looked back to see one of the men on the ground. Crush had run over his foot.

Ouch.

We pulled out onto the road, and Crush drove well above the speed limit and passed about seven cars. They all honked loudly at us. He had made three random turns when I saw the entrance to a lake, and I motioned for him to turn. We parked in the parking place closest to the water.

"Why isn't anyone following us? What did you guys do?" I asked and looked at both of them.

They looked sheepishly at each other.

"I asked the two people that interrogated me what happened to the truck, and they were pretty pleased to inform me how quickly they were able to get it into the station's parking lot," Crush said.

"Where did you learn to hotwire?" Macey asked me, as if that was the most pressing matter.

"I'll tell you if you guys tell me how you were able to pull this off."

"I knew that we had a form of escape if the truck was parked in the front. I tried to act scared so they would let their guard down a little bit."

"Oh? You tried to act all scared because you weren't scared in the least, were you?" Macey asked.

"It's a tactic I was taught. Anyway, I got the key to the shackles off of the guy's belt and then it wasn't that hard from there. When they left, I unlocked the shackles and went to find one of you guys. I found Macey and talked to her by pushing that little button outside of the door. I told her that in five minutes she needed to ask to go to the bathroom. I never went back to the room 'cause I was trying to find you. And I guess you know the rest."

"Wait, two questions. How did you get the guy's key?"

"You really want to know?" he asked and raised his eyebrows.

"Yeah."

"It's just another tactic the CIA taught me," he said.

"Fine. How come no one chased after us except for the two cops?"

"I unlocked all the holding cells and let the criminals run loose inside of there. Then I locked every single door except the front door. That's why it took those two cops so long to get outside."

"You let all those criminals loose? Are you insane?"

"It's not insane if it worked."

"How did you unlock all the doors and not get slaughtered by all those criminals?"

"There was a control pad and a ring of keys. The buttons weren't that hard to figure out," he said and shrugged his shoulders as if it was no big deal.

"So, it was just luck?" I asked.

"I mean, yeah, there was skill involved. You couldn't have pulled it off. I did have to knock one guy out," he said, and he showed me his bloody knuckles.

"What would you have done if I had no idea how to hotwire, or they lied about getting the truck fixed? The police lie all the time. They told me they knew where the money was. Too bad there isn't any money." Macey managed a laugh.

"I would have figured something out. But now it's your turn," Crush told me. "I would love to know how you know how to hotwire a truck."

"I wanted to rebel a little bit, so I learned how to hotwire." I paused and took in the looks on their faces. "Kidding. My friend taught me. Against my will, if that counts for anything."

I laughed at their faces. "I was eleven. He was older than me, and the only way I was going to eat was to listen and do what he said. How was I supposed to say no? Anyway, apparently, Ares said we had four days to get to New York City until someone dies. Starting today."

"We have half a tank left, and the cops will be looking for this truck," Macey said. "We have to get rid of it. And this stupid thing." She picked up the black object.

"Oh, so we're just going to walk to New York City?" I asked. "Great idea."

"I don't suppose either of you know how to fly?" she asked sarcastically.

"Sorry, I forgot in the fifth grade," I answered.

"Then I'm out of ideas," she said and leaned back. "We could just sleep. I didn't sleep well last night."

"Let's talk about how we slept later," Crush said. "We have to move."

We got out of the truck and slammed the doors shut. This whole situation made me feel like I was retaking a math test. I had no clue what to do, even when I was given a chance to correct my mistakes.

"Macey's right. We need to get rid of the truck."

"How?" Crush asked.

"I have a pretty good idea," I said.

I located a cinder block that was near a boat ramp and lugged it over into the truck and placed it on the gas pedal. I started the truck for one last time and slammed the door shut. I stepped back as the truck flew into the lake, and a waterfall erupted upward. The truck disappeared into the lake, and a few bubbles escaped as the seconds ticked.

"Whoa," Macey breathed.

"This really stinks for Samuel," I muttered.

"We need to move. Now," Crush said, effactually killing the moment.

Macey and Crush walked away. I stayed a few extra seconds and watched the last few bubbles reach the surface and the ripples die. Macey yelled at me to hurry. We walked in the opposite direction of the police station.

The calmness didn't last long. We heard sirens coming toward us, and we immediately made for the cover of the woods.

I looked around the small area of woods we were in. There wasn't much space between the lake area and the road. I ran to the edge of the woods and saw a ratty two-story house across the street with a couple of trucks in the front yard, but I doubted any of them would start. We could still hide in the house until it was safe. I just hoped we could get across the road without the cops seeing us.

"Come on." Without waiting for a response, I looked across the road and ran once I was sure it was clear. I hid behind a thick pine tree and caught my breath. I peeked around the tree as a car passed. The sirens from the police cars grew louder. Macey and Crush waited until a car went around the bend in the road before running across.

"Your plan better not end here, Pretty Boy. The police are getting close."

"This better not end up like the river house did," Macey told me.

"You guys can think of something too, you know."

I knew we had about ten seconds before the police car passed us, and if the driver saw us, we were done. I turned around and looked at our options, which were limited.

"Let's hide under the house."

"What?" Crush asked.

I didn't bother to answer. The porch jutted out about twelve feet, and about every ten feet or so there was a cement pole. The poles were connected by wooden lattice that looked rotten, and I knew I could easily kick it out. It was the perfect hiding place. I grabbed each of my friends' wrists, and we took off toward the house. I kicked out a section of the lattice. I threw myself in between the space of the cement and the broken lattice and landed under the porch. A cloud of dirt flew everywhere.

Macey and Crush followed.

"Gross," Macey whispered.

"Why didn't we just run?" Crush asked. "If we get caught under here, there's no way out." He looked at my face closely in the dim light. His dark eyes were intimidating. "Or did you not think it through?"

I didn't have time to come back with something smart because an unmarked car pulled into the driveway, and the three of us scooted back as far as we could. Two policemen I didn't recognize got out of the car and made their way toward the house. I could see their guns.

"These kids are making us look like a bunch of monkeys," I heard one of them say.

"They got lucky, Hightower," the other one said.

"And you could have broken out of a police station when you were a teenager? They let seven criminals break loose so we would be distracted, and they could make a clean getaway. These kids are smart," Hightower said to his partner.

"So their truck turned into the lake entrance? Are you sure?"

"Of course I'm sure," Hightower said. They were about twenty feet away from the steps.

"Then why aren't we searching the lake?" the other one said. He clearly hadn't been at this job long.

"They could have run over here to hide," Hightower answered, clearly annoyed. "And we're stuck warning people that a couple of murderous teenagers and seven other criminals escaped from our custody and are on the loose. I'm glad I wasn't assigned to look after them."

"Why haven't they radioed us? They should have found the truck by now."

Hightower climbed the steps, and his partner followed. I heard one of the policemen knock on the door, but I doubted anyone lived here, and even if people did, I didn't think they were home. They would have seen us.

"If the kids came here, they might be hiding inside. I say we take a look." one of them said.

The policemen disappeared inside.

Macey nudged me. "Hey, let's go see if they left the keys in the car. I didn't see any in the guy's hands."

"No, there's no way they left the keys in the car. They're not stupid."

Macey thought otherwise. "Come on," she whispered. "What are we supposed to do? Wait around here until we get caught? We have to get to New York City, and we're not going to unless we get a car."

"Well, who's going to run and see if they left the keys?" Crush asked.

No one said anything.

Macey rolled her eyes and groaned. "Fine. I'll do it, but you guys better be ready to tackle those guys if they see me." She got out from under the porch, glanced back at the house, and ran toward the car. She crouched by the car and peeked through the windows, and I saw her smile from fifty feet away. She motioned for us.

"She's a genius," I said with a laugh as Crush and I came out from under the porch and ran toward the car.

"The keys are on the dashboard." Macey pointed as the three of us piled in.

"Hurry up," I urged Crush as he fumbled to find the right key.

"If something went right, I'm glad it was this," Crush said as he put the car in reverse and floored it. We were speeding down the road in no time.

"I know it was my idea and everything, but how soon is it going to take before they're looking for this car?"

"It shouldn't take long," Crush muttered.

There was calmness on the road. No one was chasing us. It seemed we'd escaped the police. For now.

"Where am I going?" Crush asked after a few miles. He momentarily turned the blinker on and off.

"We need to get food. I have money in my pocket," I told Crush.

"We'll need to go a few more miles and then we'll get something to eat," Crush said.

Crush slowly made his way down a road, and no one said a word. I was too exhausted to talk about anything. To fill the silence, Crush turned on the radio. I half expected for someone from Ares to come on and make threats, but some country singer came on. Macey sang along, and I didn't mind. Her voice calmed my nerves.

We drove forty miles before Crush finally agreed that we'd gone far enough and that we could stop and get something to eat. We pulled into the McDonald's parking lot, and Crush and I fought about going in or not. Crush looked like he was ready to punch me in the face, but I knew he wouldn't. The three of us were going to be in each other's company for a long time, and he had to get used to it. The drive from where we were to New York City would take about twenty-seven hours.

Crush had done the math.

If we drove about nine hours a day, we could get there in about three days, but we didn't have that kind of gas money. Anyway, we all knew we couldn't take this car. Crush, being the agent-in-training that he was, had attempted to dismantle all the police features of the unmarked car. He hoped that would delay the police.

We had seventy-five dollars. Thankfully, the police hadn't bothered to take our money, and we'd managed to get a lot from the car.

"Macey? What do you say we do?" Crush asked.

"I suggest we go in. It's McDonalds. People aren't exactly brilliant in there, and I need to go to the bathroom. But before we go anywhere, I suggest the two of you kiss and make up. I'm sick of you guys fighting."

"We're not fighting," Crush told her. The freckles on his nose scrunched together.

"But we're not exactly on great terms," I butted in.

"Yes we are," Crush said. "You just need to stop overreacting to stuff and start helping out. You haven't done much of anything."

"What?" I asked.

"Be real, Chase. You haven't done anything to help out." He looked to Macey.

"Keep me out of this," she cautioned.

"Are you serious? Are you forgetting that I was the one that saved our butts when I hotwired the truck?" I fired back.

"Let's not forget that I was the one that got us out of there in the first place," he told me.

"We would have gotten caught before we even stepped out of the parking lot if it wasn't for me."

"And why is that?" Crush asked. His voice was bitter and hard.

"Good kids like you don't know how to hotwire trucks in under two minutes," I told him and smiled.

"It was not under two minutes," he snarled. "And Macey and I wouldn't even be involved with Ares if it wasn't for you."

My face reddened.

"You got involved with Ares the second you signed up to be some stupid junior agent."

"Oh my gosh, both of you, shut up!" Macey screamed at us. She kept her blue eyes closed. "We're stuck with each other, so it would be best if we got along. Chase did not mean for us to become involved with Ares. If the police catch up with us just because you two are going at it, I'm going to kill both of you. Chase, how much money do we have?"

"Seventy-five."

"And that's not near enough money to make it to New York City, right?" Macey asked.

"If we sleep in the truck, eat McDonalds, marry water fountains, and don't mind walking a couple hundred miles," I answered.

We ended up going inside. Mostly because we all smelled terrible. I planned to take a minishower in the sink. We got a couple of sandwiches and drinks and devoured the food in the corner of the restaurant with no problem. We'd spent ten dollars, but we had leftovers.

"I found a hair in the sandwich," Crush said with a twisted face as we walked back to the car.

"That's lovely," Macey said as she opened the door and got in.

"How many miles until we are on empty?" I asked.

Crush turned up the truck and started to pull out. "About seventy. I think we should get out of this state and into the next one. We can get gas there."

"Do you know where to go, Crush?" Macey asked.

"I'm a trained CIA operative. I think I can get to the next state," he said.

"Which is?" she asked him.

"We're in Oklahoma right now, but we're close to the border of Kansas. So I guess Kansas. I just want to get out of Oklahoma. I hate it here."

"I second that," I said.

"Me too," Macey finished.

CHAPTER 26

Thirty minutes later, Crush pulled into one of the stations and announced he was going to put twenty dollars' worth of gasoline in the car. That left us with about forty-five dollars.

Crush stuck his head in the window. "I have to pay inside. If I'm not back in five minutes, come and check that I'm not dead. Okay?" As he left, Crush smiled at me and looked at Macey and raised his eyebrows.

I wanted to punch him.

Macey leaned her head against the window, her eyes slightly squinted and lips in a straight line.

"So, Macey. What are you thinking about?"

"You," she said in a low and slow voice.

"Really?"

"You were holding that shard of glass in your hand when we met," she said and turned to me. "And now I'm in a truck alone with you."

"You know I would have never have used that on anyone," I told her. "Unless they were trying to kill me."

Crush was back and pumped the gas.

"I have a hard time believing you. You lie about a lot of stuff." She smiled.

"Only when I'm trying to save our butts," I said and laughed.

Our faces were inches from each other. My face felt hot, and my heart started to go a little crazy. It was too bad an angry cashier decided to run out of the station. He came straight for us.

Macey leaned over me and put the keys in the ignition as Crush hastily put up the pump and flung himself in the truck. I noticed a map in Crush's back pocket. Macey turned the keys, but the engine didn't catch. She turned the key again, but to no avail. Finally, the engine caught, and Crush flung the truck in reverse and stepped on the gas without even looking back. I was glad the girl behind us had fast reflexes.

"What did you do?" I screamed at him.

"I stole a map," he answered and whipped onto the road at an alarming speed.

"And they saw you?" I asked, astonished.

"That guy wouldn't be after us if he hadn't," he said and gripped the steering wheel.

"They're going to call the police, and we're going to get caught because you stole a *map*," I told him.

"I'm aware of that," he yelled back.

I turned to see if we were being followed, but the cashier was stopped in the middle of the road.

"And you paid for the gas?" Macey asked.

"Yeah."

"So let me get this straight," Macey started. "You spent twenty dollars on gas and then stole a three-dollar map?"

"It's a four-dollar map."

"Oh, then that makes it better," Macey finished and punched him in the shoulder.

"You should have let me steal it. You would have distracted the guy, and I would have stolen it."

"I'm so incredibly sorry. Okay? I didn't mean for the guy to see me." His apology was a bit insincere.

"It's all right. It doesn't look like anyone is after us," Macey said and took another look back.

"Let me see the map," I said.

Crush handed me the map, and I unfolded it and tried to make sense of all the roads.

"Okay, I think we're on this road," I said. I showed Macey so she could verify.

Macey took the map from me and turned it the other way. I'd been holding it upside down.

"Okay, we need to head northeast. So, in about ten miles there should be a turn. You need to take that one. At least, I think you do. Man, I wish we had a GPS," Macey said. "You couldn't have stolen one of those?"

Crush made a noise that sounded close to a growl.

———

We drove for a few hours. We constantly looked at the map and fought about which way we had to go. Finally, we were on a road that we would have to stay on for the next thirty miles, so we relaxed a little. We had been going at a constant speed almost the entire way.

Everything was fine until the engine started to make noises. The engine light came on.

Crush started to slow down.

Macey had been asleep, but the change in speed woke her.

"What's going on?" she asked and yawned.

"The engine," Crush muttered. "It's dying on us. Cheap police."

"Really?"

"Yeah, really."

Crush pulled off onto the shoulder of the road and got out. Macey and I followed him.

He pulled up the hood and propped it open.

"Do you know how to fix it?" Macey asked.

"Of course I do."

"Good. So, get to it," Macey told him and sat down.

"But there's a problem," he said.

"What would that be?" she asked.

"I'm going to need a brand-new engine to do it."

"So we're stuck?" Macey asked.

"Pretty much," he said sullenly.

I felt a small vibration in shoulder, and my stomach dropped.

"Uh-oh," I said.

"What now?" Macey asked.

"My arm. It's vibrating."

"Are they going to communicate in Morse code or something?" Crush laughed.

I looked blankly at him. "That might kill me."

"Right," he muttered.

"Let me feel the chip. Or bomb. Whatever you want to call it," Macey said.

"Sure," I told her. The vibrating was light. They were taunting me.

She walked behind me and put her hand on my shoulder. "Is this it?" she asked.

"Yup," I answered, attempting to keep my wincing to a minimum.

"Ouch."

"You have no clue," I muttered.

The vibrating ceased.

We started to walk. It was important that no one found us by an unmarked car. That would only raise questions.

"We could walk until we found some other car," Crush offered.

"Ha! That's funny. Crush, if you haven't forgotten, you were in the hospital yesterday. I don't really think walking miles would do you so good," Macey said. "Anyway, it's about to be dark."

"Hitchhiking might work." It wasn't my favorite means of transportation, but it was sufficient.

"I don't think that's going to work, Chase. There hasn't been another car since we got here," Crush said.

As if on cue, I heard the sound of an engine.

Crush and I started to wave our arms, and I took a couple steps in the road so they would stop. They were going in the direction that we needed to go.

The car pulled over to the shoulder of the road about ten yards away from us, and we walked over to the car.

"Y'all need help?" a woman asked us, who looked to be about twenty-seven. There was a little girl in the backseat peeking at us.

"Please," I asked. "Can you please give us a ride? Our car broke down a little ways back, and we don't have cell phones."

"Where are you guys headed?" the lady inquired.

"In this direction."

"Um, sure. Hop in," she answered a little reluctantly.

"Thank you," I said and climbed in the truck. I waved to the little girl, and she smiled.

"I like your hair," she told me.

"Thank you," I said and grinned. It had gotten considerably lighter in the past month.

"What's your name?" she asked in a high-pitched voice.

"Chase Miners."

Macey and Crush tensed, and I immediately realized what I'd done. I'd said my name.

The lady pulled back onto the road and continued to drive. "You know, the first thing they tell you when you get your license is to never pick up any hitchhikers."

"Yeah, but I bet you've never had hitchhikers as adorable as us," I tried and hoped she hadn't heard me say my name.

"Mommy?" the little girl asked.

"Yes, Samantha?"

"Am I going to miss my show?" she asked.

"The TV is broken, remember? It has been for the past four days," the mother said, slightly annoyed.

"Your TV is broken? So you haven't watched any TV?" Crush asked. As always, he was in the front and asking questions.

Maybe this lady didn't know about us. I hoped she didn't listen to the radio. We'd probably made the news again with the stunts we'd pulled today. I wondered if some of the inmates Crush let out hurt anybody. I hoped not.

"I haven't been out of the house in four days. Samantha's been sick. But you're all better now. Aren't you, sweetie?"

The little girl smiled and nodded her head. She took my hand, and I couldn't help but grin.

"Now you hold that girl's hand," she said to me and pointed to Macey.

Macey looked over at us, and her cheeks flushed red. But there was *no way* I could disappoint this little girl. I took Macey's hand in mine and kissed it.

"Ewww," the little girl said and took her hand away. "I didn't think he would give you cooties."

"It's okay," Macey said and squeezed my hand.

We were in the car with the lady about thirty minutes. I planned to let her take us as far as possible. We made small talk, but I could see Crush trying to catch some sleep. I wondered how he really felt.

"Okay, I live just down the next road. Do you want to call your mom?"

"Sure," Macey said. I shot her a look, but I knew to trust her. She had a plan.

Macey dialed a phone number on the woman's phone. A real phone number.

"Hey, Mom, don't tell Alex, but his truck broke down. Don't worry about us. We're fine. We're getting a ride from a lady, but she lives like right where we are, so she's just going to drop us off at the gas station where Dad works, okay? Right. Yep. I know. I'll do it when it I get home. Yes, Mom. I love you too. I'll be fine. Don't worry. I'm with the guys. Yes, I understand. Look, I have to go. Bye. Oh, and don't call this number again." Macey hung up the phone, handed it back to the lady, and thanked her.

"Could you drive us to the gas station up the road? My dad works there."

"Sure," the lady said and laughed. "Was your mother mad that you three hitchhiked?"

"Nah. But she is a little mad about the car breaking down," Macey said.

No one spoke the rest of the way.

"Is this the gas station?" the lady asked after a few more miles. There was a busy Marathon to the right.

"Yes," Macey answered and seemed a little relieved.

She pulled into the gas station parking lot. The three of us thanked her, hopped out, and walked into the gas station, where we used the restroom and then made our way to the woods and began to walk. Again.

"Guys, not to rain on anyone's parade, but it's getting dark. We need to find shelter." I looked up at dark clouds that brewed. The wind picked up a bit, and I knew the bottom of the storm was about to drop.

"Great," Macey said. "Rain."

"I don't know. It might be a good thing. We all stink pretty badly. The woman was crinkling her nose the entire time," Crush snickered.

It started to rain, a drizzle really, and it was almost calming. Then it progressed to the kind of rain that you would get out and dance in. Except when it started to thunder and lightning started to strike, we didn't have the option to run back inside and dry off.

The wind picked up and made the rain feel like tiny bullets.

"I. Hate. This," Macey grumbled as she pushed tangled and wet hair out of her face.

"I can't even tell if that's a vine or a deadly snake," Crush said and squinted his eyes to the right of a tree. The sun had set, and I found it harder to navigate.

"It's a vine," I assured him. Just to make sure, I stared a little longer at it—maybe six seconds—and it started to look like a snake.

Thunder rumbled, and I shivered in the cold rain.

"No way," Macey breathed after another fifteen minutes of walking. "It's a barn."

"About time," Crush breathed.

I looked up from my feet. We'd come upon a barn. I might have walked straight by it if Macey hadn't said anything. There was a house with rotten shutters about one hundred yards in front. A dull light came from inside the house, but I couldn't see any other activity. Normally, I would never stay in a place so close to other people. But I wasn't in a normal situation. And I was quite ready to be out of the rain.

"That is the most beautiful thing I've ever seen," Macey said. She smiled at me and took off toward the front of the barn. Crush and I followed her.

The barn was dry inside, which was good enough for me.

"All right, we can have a quick rest, but we really need to keep moving," Crush said and cracked his knuckles.

Macey and I turned around and started to scream at Crush. It was a mix of, "Are you kidding me?" and "I'm going to hurt you."

"Guys, I was kidding." Even in the dim light, I could see his grin. "I'm probably more tired than the two of you, with this raging infection and all."

I sat down. The barn was really more of an oversized shed. There were tools, hay, and dirt all over the walls and on the ground. There was an old green tractor parallel to the back wall. The ceiling leaked a little, which wasn't that comforting. It would be a real damper if the roof caved in on us.

"This is heaven," Macey said.

"Yeah, it is," I said. Thunder boomed again, and I felt the barn shake.

"I'm exhausted. No one talk till morning," Macey said tiredly. She blew the dirt and hay out of the way and lay down on the rigid floor.

My clothes were soaked, but no one else complained, so I decided to keep my mouth shut this time. I took off my shirt and saw Crush doing the same. I balled it up so I could use it as a pillow. A wet and cold pillow, but a pillow all the same. Then I looked over at Macey. She had her arm cocked under her head. Another wave of guilt washed over me.

I tossed her my shirt.

It landed on the back of her head, and she sat up.

"What's this?"

"Just sleep on it for tonight."

Macey smiled and gave me a quick kiss on the cheek. It was nothing, really. It was sort of like a kiss that a sister would give to a brother.

Sort of.

I don't exactly remember falling asleep. One would think with the storm that raged outside, it would have been hard to fall asleep. Or maybe the hunger and thirst that gnawed at me would keep me up like it usually did. But like Macey, I was exhausted.

———

When I woke up, Macey was busying herself trying to rake the tangles out of her hair. She tossed me my shirt.

Then the complaining started.

"I really wish the police had let us brush our teeth."

"I wish they would have let me take a shower," Crush complained.

They looked at me.

"I would have been happy with more water," I said. "But let's not forget that we only have three days," I stared. "That's how much time Ares is giving us to get to New York City. Or someone dies. That's probably me."

Macey and Crush bobbed their heads and averted their eyes. The grim reality that there was no way we could possibly get to New York City was sinking in. It was idiotic of Ares to think we could get there. They had made us an enemy of the public.

"Can you think of a CIA safe house anywhere else?" Macey asked.

"No," Crush said sadly. "If I remember where one is, you guys will be the first to know."

I heard the door being pulled open and immediately whipped around. Someone was coming in the barn. There was no exchange of words or looks between the three of us. That would waste too much time. Time that we didn't have. The three of us ran to the back of the barn and hid behind the old tractor. It felt like our breathing was louder than a stampede.

I turned my head so it couldn't be seen between the wheel and the seat. I heard music blaring from someone's iPod. "Wrench. Where is the wrench? I swear I put it here the other day…"

I peeked over the side of the tractor and saw that the person was overweight, had bad acne, and wore camouflage overalls. His brown hair stuck up at odd angles. He was probably in his early twenties.

Not one of us breathed a word.

"Maybe it's by the tractor," he said.

The three of us stared at one another. He was coming over. We were done for. There was nothing we could do.

He slowly approached us, and his weight wore him down. Maybe we could overpower him and get away. We'd broken out of the police station; surely, we could break out of an old barn.

The fat guy found us. He let out a shrill scream and stumbled back a few feet. The three of us stood up. We only had one exit. The wall eliminated one escape, and the fat guy eliminated the other. We would have to climb over the tractor.

We began to scale the tractor. The fat guy burst into action and yanked on my ankle with more force than I thought he could manage. I crashed to the ground. I landed on my chin first and felt my teeth sink into my tongue. Blood immediately filled my mouth.

"Chase!" I heard Macey scream.

"Go! I'll catch up!" I screamed.

I stood up and saw Macey and Crush running toward me, completely ignoring my order to flee. I balled up my fist to deliver a blow to this guy's oversized stomach, but I stopped when I saw he held a rifle. Where had *that* come from?

"Freeze!" the guy yelled.

I gulped.

"Who are you?"

"Who are you?" I shot back.

"The guy that's gonna put a bullet in your knee if you don't tell me what you're doing here." He turned to Macey and Crush. "You two. Get over here right now."

Macey and Crush walked over to me.

"You're bluffing. You won't shoot."

"I ain't."

"Then do it. Shoot me," I told him.

He aimed at my leg and pulled the trigger. I immediately flinched. I expected to feel pain, but there wasn't any. I looked down at my leg. There was no blood.

"No bullets?" My breath was shaky. If there had been bullets, well, I would be in a bit of a pickle.

The guy frowned. "Safety was on."

"How lucky am I?" I asked.

"I'm gonna call the police. You broke and entered my barn. Sit against the wall and don't move. I took the safety off."

The three of us slowly sat down. This guy wasn't bluffing.

He walked backward out of the barn, rifle still trained on us. He shut the door firmly behind himself. As soon as he was gone, Macey ran up and tried to push the door open. It only opened a few inches.

"He's locked it."

"I'm surprised he remembered," Crush said as he kicked an empty can across the room.

"How do we get out?" I asked.

We all looked around. Nothing came to mind. We were trapped.

"So the fat dude is going to be the death of us? Really?" Crush asked.

"No," Macey said with a slight smile.

"Do you have a plan?" I asked.

"Only if he left the keys to the tractor in here."

She walked back to the tractor and looked around it. "The idiot left them on the seat. What is it with people leaving their keys in the most convenient places?"

"Are you really going to ram down the door with the tractor?" I asked and spit blood out of my mouth.

"No. Crush is."

Crush's head shot up at this remark. "Why me?"

"I'm the one that came up with the last plan and the one who executed it. It's someone else's turn."

"Why can't Chase do it?"

"Because you're the one that's been trained by the CIA. Not too well, I'm afraid. It's time to put some of that into action. Besides, Chase is hurt."

I stuck my tongue out at Crush, who frowned.

"Fine. Move out of the way."

Crush mounted the tractor and told us to move back. He cranked up the engine, and I was surprised it even worked. But would it be enough to knock down the door?

Crush took a few seconds to figure out how to work the thing and an even longer amount of time to turn it so that it faced the exit. He slowly picked up speed and headed toward the door. When the tractor hit the door, I could hear the already weak wood creak under the force.

"Cover your head," I yelled. I didn't want the door to break and hit him. That was the last thing we needed.

Crush covered his head with one arm, but it wasn't needed. I heard more wood crack, and there was now a gap large enough for us to get out.

"Stop," Macey instructed.

Crush cut the engine. "I can't believe that worked."

"Me either," I said over the dying engine.

Macey pursed her lips. "Thanks, guys."

"We need to go now," Crush said. He hopped off the tractor seat, and the three of us squeezed through the gap and took off for the woods. I vaguely heard the fat guy yelling after us, but there was no way he would be able to catch up.

We ran until we couldn't see the house anymore.

"Good driving, Crush," Macey said.

"Good plan," he responded.

We walked for about ten minutes before Crush raised the question that we were all wondering. "What do we do next?"

"I guess we need to get some food first. I'm famished," Macey said.

Immediately, I felt for the money in my pocket. I didn't feel anything. Yesterday, Macey had handed me the money.

"Problem," I said.

"What?" they both asked at the same time.

"Either of you wouldn't happen to know where the money is?"

"You're kidding me." Crush said. He did a face palm.

"I guess—I guess it fell out in the barn. Maybe. I'm sorry."

"You do realize what this means, right? Ares won't even get a chance to try and kill us. Or do whatever the heck they want to do with us. We'll die because of starvation!" Crush yelled at me.

"Crush, we're not going to die. My ego would never permit it," I assured him.

"Chill yourself. We're not going to die out here. All we have to do is get to a town and shake some people down for money. We'll pull a puppy-dog face. You can't turn down kids," Macey said.

"I wouldn't put money on that, Macey," I grumbled. I'd been denied money countless times.

"Well, to do that, I would need money in the first place, right?" she said in a fake cheery voice. They were both fairly annoyed.

We started to follow the road. I wasn't sure I wanted it to lead to a town. Towns were where you got caught. Crush and Macey didn't know that yet.

There was a string of houses at the end of the road, and we stopped to take a rest at the last one. The lights in the house were off, and I couldn't see any cars. I made the suggestion that we could stop and use the hose to get water.

The water was cool and felt great for my parched throat. As I watched Macey soak her hair, I thought about how we all knew it would be impossible to get to New York City in three days, but none of us could bring ourselves to say anything about our dreaded fate. We still hung onto the last shred of hope, which was withering. I walked around to the front of the house. The garage was slightly ajar, maybe a foot and a half off the ground, probably to let the cat in and out. I decided to slip under to see if there was anything useful, like a small self-flying plane. There wasn't. But there was the next best thing.

Two beautiful four-wheelers.

I smiled, shimmied back under the door, and ran back to Macey and Crush. I knew they couldn't get us very far, but we needed to get as far away from this town as quickly as we could.

"I think I may have solved our little transportation issue. For a little while, anyway." I beckoned them to follow, and they did without a question. Not a complaint was made, even when they had to squeeze under the door. We had made progress.

"We don't even know if they have gas. Much less if they even work," Crush said, killing the mood. He walked over and grabbed the key that rested on the seat, stuck it in the ignition, and gave it a twist. The engine roared to life, and I smiled.

"How much gas is left?" I asked.

"Full tank," Crush muttered as he walked over to the next one and checked how much gas was in that one. "Full tank in this one too."

"I feel bad about this. These things cost a lot of money, and we're taking two," Macey said to me after we had mounted the two four-wheelers. She was driving, and I was behind her. It didn't seem like a good idea for me to drive, with the out-of-control arm and everything.

I didn't feel bad about it. I knew I should, but I didn't. We needed these four-wheelers way more than these people did.

"It's not our fault these idiots left the door open and the keys just laying around," I responded.

"Well, they probably weren't expecting three accused criminals to come and steal them."

"You want to leave a note or something?" I asked.

"Chase, that is probably the sweetest thing I've ever heard you say. Come on, there's some paper and a few pencils over there."

Crush groaned and started to laugh when he saw what we were doing.

Macey wrote the note on a crumpled piece of paper. It said how sorry we were to take the four-wheelers, but we needed them, blah, blah, blah. We signed our initials at the bottom. CM. MM. CD. We would be long gone by the time they saw this.

Or dead.

"Can we please leave now?" Crush asked. "The map doesn't go for too many more miles, but I can probably get us the next twenty-five miles."

"What would we do without the great and powerful Crush…" Macey's voice trailed off. "Crush…um, what's your last name?" Macey asked as she fired up the four-wheeler and pulled her hair into a tighter ponytail.

"Daysort."

The exchange was small, and it was going to be forgotten by the both of them within the next few hours. It had no real significance, but it reminded me of how little we knew each other. We'd been thrown together by chance and been through so many hardships, yet we barely knew each other's full name.

We rode for about an hour and a half until Macey slowed down and came to a stop.

"What's wrong?"

"We're out of gas."

"Already?" I complained. It didn't feel like we had gone far enough to empty the tank.

"Yup." She flagged Crush down.

"Are you guys out?" he asked.

"Yeah. How much do you have left?" I asked.

"Not a whole lot. Almost on empty."

"Why did ours run out first?"

"Extra weight?" he speculated, but he seemed unconcerned. "But it's okay, because I don't where we're going anymore."

"Great. No gas and no money. We have no clue where we are going, and I'm starving," Macey said.

"That's a railroad up ahead, right?" I asked and pointed.

"Yeah," Crush said. "So what?"

"There was always talk about train yards being like an airport for run-aways. It's free, fast, and there are always trains going somewhere. We could find a train heading in the direction of New York City and hop on."

"But that's not a train yard. It's a railroad crossing," Crush, the ever-so-observant teenage spy, told me.

"I know that, Crush. But maybe if we walk awhile, we can find one."

"Our luck isn't that strong. We need a plan that doesn't rely on the slim chance that there's a train yard."

"I don't know," Macey said. "Our good-luck streak might continue. The lady gave us a ride, and we got away with it. We found that barn and slept. Chase doesn't have a bullet in his knee, and we got out of the barn. We found the hose and the four-wheelers. I'm planning to ride this streak of luck to New York."

Macey got off the four-wheeler and started to walk. She didn't even check to make sure we were going to follow her. Crush and I glanced at each other. I smiled. Crush didn't. We dismounted the four-wheelers and followed Macey.

"Right or left?" I asked when we arrived at the tracks.

Macey looked down both directions. "Right."

So we went to the right with absolutely no proof that it was the right way to go. Even Crush didn't object.

We walked for the better half of the day. The heat was sweltering, and sweat poured into my eyes, which made the walk even more inconvenient. When we came up to a body of water, I was always the first one to jump in and cool off. It wasn't much fun to walk while soaked, but I was fine with it. It was better than overheating, having a heat stroke, and dying.

Actually, pretty much everything was better than that.

It didn't take too long until I felt the tracks rumble under my feet. I eyed Macey, and I could tell by her facial expression that she felt it too.

"All right, kids," she said. "Let's get off this death trap before we become pancakes. Who's with me?"

The train was going the opposite way we were headed, but it wasn't going that fast, which probably meant it had just departed. We had to wait a long time until the train passed. We got back on the tracks and walked another two miles. My legs felt like Jell-O, and I wanted to go to sleep.

But what else was new?

Then we found a train yard.

I couldn't believe it. But there it was.

"No way," I breathed.

"This was an act of God," Macey said and covered her face with her hands.

"Divine intervention at its best."

"Okay, let's find a train that's going where we're *trying* to go," Crush said and killed the mood for the billionth time. He walked over to one of the trains—there were three in all. One didn't have any carts attached, and I doubted that the other two would offer us too much help. It would be a really bad thing if we got on a train and it took us the wrong way.

"A train schedule would be nice," Macey whispered to me.

We walked around the trains for a little while and searched for an open boxcar. Right now, it didn't matter that we didn't know which one to get on. If we couldn't find an opening in one of the cars, we would have walked miles for nothing.

We got to the front of one of the trains when we heard whom I guessed to be the conductor talking on the phone.

"Yeah honey, I'll be home in a few days. I know it's on such short notice, but they really need this delivery. Right. Yeah. It's still going to Pennsylvania. Yeah, it has to. Right. I love you too. I know. I will when I get home. I got it. Right. Okay. I love you too. No, that didn't have a tone. Bye."

We were hidden, and I was fairly certain the conductor couldn't see us. We all smiled at each other. Pennsylvania was closer to New York City than we were right now. A lot closer.

We found a boxcar in the back of the train and vaulted ourselves in.

"It would be a stupid thing if I asked if you guys thought that Ares set this all up so we could get to New York City in time? The guy said it was on short notice," Macey said as she settled down next to me. We were all pretty happy to be off our feet. The walk had exhausted all of us. It had been a whole day since we'd had food. We couldn't keep up this pace much longer.

"Of course not," I said as I took her hand in mine. "Those people apparently have agents in high places."

The train started to move.

"Hey, Macey?" I asked.

"Who did you call when the lady gave you her phone?"

"Oh, I called my mom."

"What did she say?"

"I got her voicemail."

"Oh, she'll be happy to hear from you."

"I hope so."

CHAPTER 27

I wondered if we were going to drive all night, which would fall in about three hours. I'd never really thought about that. Where did the conductor sleep? Where did they get food and water? When did he go to the bathroom? Was there more than one conductor up there? And if so, did they take shifts?

I wasn't sure why I cared.

I learned early on that there was no way I would get any sleep because the noise from the train sounded like an atomic bomb detonating every few seconds. I was exhausted to a point where I was seeing things. There was a vague blue haze out of the corner of my eye.

I was half asleep and half awake, which was the recipe for the world's worst dream. I sat in a chair in a completely dark room. I wasn't tied down, but I couldn't move. Two men walked in. The director of Ares and Dotson. My father, on his knees, appeared in front of them.

"Are you ready to give up?" Agent Dotson asked.

"You know the information. What more do you want from me?" my dad asked.

"Are you ready to give up?" the director of Ares asked.

"You know what the information is. What more do you want from me?" my dad repeated.

"Are you ready to give up?" Dotson asked.

That's how the whole dream went. My dad and the evil guys repeated the same conversation over and over until I forced my subconscious to wake up. It wasn't scary, more along the lines of disturbing and unnerving.

I was beyond ready for this ordeal to be over. I wouldn't even bother to go to New York City if I couldn't be killed with a touch of a button.

The train was still going strong, and the landscape went by quickly. We went over a river where people were swimming. I would have given my right hand to be one of them and the other hand for a bottle of water and a hamburger. I yawned, sat up, and tuned into Macey and Crush's conversation.

"I swear," Crush said and put his hands up in the air.

"I don't believe it. I mean, it sounds awesome, but it seems really weird. Too weird to be true."

"What?" I asked, groggily.

"Nothing important," Crush assured me.

"If it isn't Sleeping Beauty," Macey said.

"How much longer until we get to Pennsylvania? We don't have a lot of time left," I reminded them. I couldn't help but feel like the person Ares was going to kill was yours truly, even though they had no reason at all. My father was insane. My death wouldn't affect him more than the drop of hat.

"Oh yeah. Let me just go and check the GPS and the clock. Chase, no offense, but that was a stupid question," Crush said.

I rolled my eyes. I knew the hunger and dehydration had put everyone in a sucky mood. "I didn't know if we passed a sign or something, you jerk."

"Either Missouri or Illinois. Indiana, if we're lucky," Crush said.

"So you did have an idea," I told him.

"I always have an idea. I'm training to be part of the CIA."

"Are you sure?" I asked.

He snickered and laughed sarcastically. "It's either that or the Boy Scouts."

"Or the ARG," I muttered.

"The what?" Crush asked.

"Nothing," I said and instantly regretted it. If I'd learned one thing, it was that knowledge was dangerous and intelligence was vital. You didn't just go around sputtering knowledge about one of the most secret groups in the world while trapped in a boxcar with a slightly unstable teenager superhuman.

I might have been lacking intelligence.

"What's the ARG? Why would you even say that?" Crush stood.

"I'm not supposed to say anything."

He walked over to me. "You better spill it before I spill your brains. Like the first day we met."

I rolled my eyes again. "ARG. The Applied Research Group. After the Red Scare, all the intelligence agencies were worried that their power might be limited, so some of the members of the CIA, FBI, and the NSA formed the ARG to share information and to serve as a backup in case something happened. Or at least that's what I got from Dotson."

Crush laughed. "Oh, you got it from Dotson. The man who screwed us over."

"I thought about that too. But no one really questioned me when I showed at the headquarters. Dotson said it was because the superior also worked with the ARG."

"Why didn't he just take you to this *Applied Research Group's* headquarters?"

Dotson's story began to seem less and less believable. "Um, because they don't have headquarters good enough to house a teenager."

"Oh, so one of the most secret organizations in the world doesn't have a sufficient bedroom for you to stay in?"

"I didn't make it up," I defended.

"Oh, I know you didn't. Dotson just lied to you about the whole thing, and you were stupid enough to believe it. Of course, I'm training to be a part of the CIA. They would have told me otherwise."

"Just thought I'd make you aware of the situation, Crush."

"And thanks for that."

Macey raised her eyebrows. "Um, it's a little obvious why he brought us to the headquarters. And it had nothing to do with a sufficient bedroom."

"And why is that?" Crush asked.

"You should be able to figure it out, spy boy. He wanted to kidnap all three of us, but he also wanted the CIA to know that the kidnapper was powerful. The man wants a show, something he can mess and toy with. He's a control freak."

"And we're his pawns."

"No. I think we are a bigger deal than that. Chase, you're the one he cares about the most," Crush said.

"Whatever we are," I said, "I'm getting sick of it."

"I'm done trying to figure it out," Macey said. "All I really want is water."

"Yeah, well. We're in a boxcar," I said. "Not a mall."

We rode for a few more hours, and the thirst really started to get to me. I would have settled for a glass of blood. Okay, not really. But even a capful of water would have been nice. Finally, the train started to slow down and came to a stop.

"Why are we stopping?" Macey asked. "There's no way we're there yet."

"I guess to refuel," Crush said.

"That's going to take forever. Let's get out and walk around."

So we did. We didn't see anybody, but we could hear them on the other side of the train. If they saw us, I had a feeling things would go badly very quickly. We were in another train yard in the middle of nowhere. There was a small building about fifty yards away. We ran behind the building so the owners of the voices wouldn't spot us.

"You think there's someone in there?" I asked, referring to the building. I could hear the air conditioning.

"Someone needs to go and check in that window to make sure," Crush said, constantly looking around and keeping low. In moments like this, I could see a bit of his training shining through. Not much. Just a bit.

When nobody made a move, Macey groaned, crawled over to the window, and slowly rose up. She took an extremely fast peek and ducked back down.

"Anybody there?"

"I don't know. I looked too quickly."

I rolled my eyes. "Look again."

She did, slower this time, and gave us the thumbs up. "There's no one in there, but there's half a sub sandwich. Looks like turkey."

The door to the building remained locked for a total of five seconds after we discovered the handle wouldn't turn. Crush declared he was hungry and kicked the door down. Macey and I didn't even bother saying anything. The damage was done. We stepped inside. The building was really just an extremely small office, a little bigger than the kind they had at dumps. But it had a fully functional bathroom, so no one complained.

After a much-needed bathroom break, we gawked at the sandwich like it was a nugget of gold. We didn't have anything to cut it with, so we all just took turns taking bites. There was no whisper of spreading germs, which I expected out of Crush. It was a little stale, and the meat was hot, but I didn't care. None of us did. We didn't have that luxury.

"Is anyone coming?" Crush asked as he finished off the last of the sandwich.

"No," Macey said as she checked out the window. "But we need to leave in case someone does."

I grabbed a couple pens and a notepad off the desk. A game or two of hangman wouldn't hurt. I bent down to grab a dropped pen when I saw the most beautiful thing in the world. A white and shiny minifridge. I immediately opened it and was beyond delighted to see three gleaming water bottles on the top shelf.

I brought them out and sat them on the table. "Look what I found."

"Water!" Macey yelled as she took off the cap, and she drank the whole thing in about fifteen seconds. Crush and I did the same. We'd all consumed a bit of water from the sink, but it had been too metallic and too warm to be enjoyable. After we'd emptied the water bottles, I took the bottles to the sink and filled them back up. Macey and Crush would be thankful in an hour or so.

———

"What could possibly be taking them five million hours?" Macey asked. She blew her hair out of her face. We'd sat in the boxcar for an eternity, and I was going to scream if the train didn't start moving. Sweat caked all three of us, coating us in its hot and sticky embrace.

"We could have stayed in that air conditioning a lot longer than we did," I complained quietly.

"What happens after this? If we survive, that is. What happens?" Macey asked, not bothering to look at me or Crush.

"I suppose the CIA will make up some story about how we didn't do all that we're being accused of and broadcast it. Or give us new identities," Crush told us, which didn't make us feel any better.

"Do you think you'll still get to be a junior secret agent, or whatever you prefer to be called?" Macey asked. "It might be too dangerous for them. And you."

Crush's face stiffened, and I realized how much that job meant to him, even though it was what got him into this mess. It was what he did and who he was. As much as the guy got on my nerves, I didn't want him to lose the job because of some crazy guy's obsession with world domination.

"Hope so," he answered.

About an hour later, the train finally started to pick up speed, and we were back on our way to Pennsylvania. I felt my body relax. It felt safer to move. We were moving away from and toward danger.

"Anybody hear that?" Crush asked, obviously startled. He sat up and looked around.

"Hear what?" Macey asked. "All I hear is the train."

"That beeping noise. What is it?"

Macey and I eyed each other and frowned. What was Crush talking about? Had the stress finally gotten to him? Was he going crazy?

"You guys don't hear it? There's no way you guys don't hear that! It's so high pitched. It must be somewhere in here." Crush got up and started to look around the boxcar, which was completely empty, excluding the

CAUGHT

stuff we'd brought. He paced around the boxcar, screamed a bit, and covered his head with his hands.

Yup. He'd definitely lost it.

Macey tried to calm him down, but he wasn't having any of it.

"It feels like—it feels like it's inside of my head!" he screamed.

"It's not inside your head. You've just gone crazy," I told him.

Macey turned to me and scowled. Her face told me I wasn't helping.

"It's inside my head!" Crush yelled.

"Why would your head beep?" Macey asked.

"I don't know. Oh, make it stop!" Crush screamed.

"Okay. Okay. Just tell me where it sounds like it's coming from," Macey coaxed. She put her hands on his shoulders.

"Heads don't beep," I told him, simply to annoy.

"Mine does!" he yelled.

"Okay. Okay. What if Ares implanted something in you too? We don't remember a lot of what happened," Macey tried. "We think they knocked us out for days, right? Erased our memories? They had enough time to implant something in Chase. Why not you?"

Maybe," he said, obviously trying to get himself in order.

"They already implanted something in me. Why implant something in you too? And in your head?" I said.

"The CIA," Crush whispered and sat down.

"What?" I asked.

"It must have been the CIA."

"How would they make your head beep?" I asked.

"They must have put a tracking device in my head. It was probably Dotson."

"Why would they do that?" I asked. "And why would they just now be trying to find us?"

"I don't know," Crush yelled, and panic rose in his voice again.

"Let's try to be rational about this. They didn't cut your head open. Too risky. Is there anything you can remember that the CIA made you do that you thought was weird?" Macey asked.

245

Crush looked at her. "There are about a million things that the CIA made me do that I thought was weird."

"Pick one," I told him.

"They made me go to the dentist one time."

I didn't even have to think about that one, but I had started to wonder why Crush was so dang trusting of the CIA. "They could have put the tracking device in your tooth."

Crush felt around his mouth with his tongue, and his face cringed. "My tooth is vibrating."

"Now you know how my shoulder feels. Except multiply that little vibrating feeling by a thousand and one," I told Crush. "You'll just have to wait for it to stop." I tried not to let the panic I felt creep into my voice.

About ten minutes later, Crush announced that the beeping had stopped. His face relaxed. I breathed a sigh of relief. Still, I felt like a sniper might jump into the moving boxcar at any given minute.

"So, the CIA should pop up soon? Because that would great." Macey stood to stretch her legs.

"Or Ares still might blow me up," I said. I felt the bump on my shoulder and shuddered.

"We have to be close to Pennsylvania by now. That's pretty close to the headquarters. We could get there within the next few hours," Crush said. "Someone could get the bomb out of you there. Cut you open in a parking lot or something. And I could pull out this stupid tooth."

"Thank you for that wonderful image, Crush," I grumbled. "Anyway, they would blow me up before that could happen."

"Just saying."

We rode a few more hours until I saw a sign that told us that we had entered Pennsylvania, but by that time it was the middle of the night, probably around two or something. But I wasn't tired. We'd been taking turns going to sleep.

We hopped off the train, which had slowed down, and ran as fast as we could into the woods. We probably could have walked and not been seen, but we'd made it this far, and I saw no reason in taking a chance. It was a cloudy night, and the sky was black.

"This is creepy," Macey said as the lights from the train broke through the trees and slowly faded.

We came up the side of a hill and could see the haze of lights, which we hoped belonged to a town.

"How many more days do we have?" I asked and moved a limb out of my way. I stepped over what I thought to be a broken glass bottle.

"Okay. Um, say yesterday was day two. So it's the end of day three. Or it might be the start of day four? I honestly have no clue. My mind feels like mush," Macey said.

"We have about a day left?" I asked. I could almost feel the pain in my shoulder.

"Seems about right," Crush said. "We can get to New York City in a day, right?"

"I hope so. I really hope so," Macey said, cutting her eyes toward me.

As we crossed the creek, I got both my feet wet, and one of Crush's shoes got stuck in mud. Macey couldn't stop laughing at the both of us. She hadn't had a problem crossing the creek. I shot her a look, but I didn't think she even saw me.

We made it into the town about two hours later. It was slow going. I couldn't count how many times I'd tripped over a branch in the last hour. I just wanted sleep and a cheeseburger. We were on the outskirts of town, and I was ready to pass out right where I stood. It was unquestionably past my bedtime. We tottered down a few streets before I concluded that this tired town we'd entered was extremely small, which made it even more dangerous. As far as I could tell, there was a library, a small park in the middle of the square, a thrift shop, a few small restaurants, a tearoom, a clothing and furniture store, and a bank.

We stood in the middle of the town square, unsure of what to do.

The moonlight was scattered on the ground. It reminded me of the view out the window of my room in the Haneys' house.

"We can't stay here," Macey said.

"Why not?" Crush asked.

"It's too public. Everyone is going to come out in the morning, and we're not going to be awake, and boom. We get attacked for being the kids that blew up the grocery store, stole a bunch of money, and killed a guy."

We walked through the park in the middle of the square. There was a vintage passenger train car, but if I looked at it for too long, I could almost hear the rumble of the train. There was a statue in the middle of the park of some guy that fought in some war.

We walked past a bench, and Crush stumbled in the dark but caught himself (like the talented and skillful spy he was) by putting his hand on the bench. I heard something clatter on the sidewalk. I bent down and felt around for the object and discovered that it was a phone. I pressed the power button, in hopes of using it as a flashlight. It had about 20 percent left on the battery.

Then curiosity took hold of me.

I entered our names in Google and clicked on the first website. There was a report about our escape from the police station, but it said that we knocked several people out with a fire extinguisher and held people at gunpoint. That was the only reason we had escaped. Crush and Macey laughed at that.

I read the rest of the report, and I almost dropped the phone.

"What?" Macey asked, alarmed.

"They're saying that the other 'janitor' died. The good news? They don't know which one of us did it."

Great. Now we were being accused of killing two people.

"I wonder how much the guy got paid to do that job," Crush wondered. "Not that it matters now. He can't spend the money. Was it like a punishment or a reward? Getting to sacrifice yourself for Ares. Or do they draw out of a hat...?"

"I'm so not going to a good college," Macey muttered. "What else does it say?"

"It keeps talking about how horrible we are and our parents should be ashamed of themselves. It talks about how we were caught in Samuel's truck, and you broke that rookie's foot. Nice," I said and paused. "I wonder how long it will take them to find the truck."

"This sucks," Macey said.

"You know what's going to suck? When you guys have to carry me. Can we please find somewhere to sleep?" Crush asked.

"That passenger cart probably still has seats with cushions," Macey said. "As big as my newly acquired hate for trains is, it's better than nothing, which is what we have."

"But when we wake up, we have to go and find something to eat," I said. I knew we couldn't run on an empty tank. We had to find food, no matter the danger. I took the cell phone with me and set an alarm. Hopefully, the battery would last.

We turned and walked back to the passenger car. We climbed in, and I was hit with the smell of mold. I couldn't see how bad the condition of the seats were, but I guessed it wasn't exactly top-rate material. I sat down in the back of the car and leaned against the cool window.

"You know what gets on my nerves?" Macey asked after we were settled.

"What?" I mumbled.

"Being a human," she told me.

"I've got the same problem."

"Not what I meant. I mean humans have to eat three times a day or else you feel sick, you have to get so many hours of sleep a day, and a whole bunch of *other* annoying stuff."

"I know people that are like that as well. Now go to sleep. Big day tomorrow," I told her.

CHAPTER 28

I woke up with a hand over my mouth, which was my least favorite way to wake. At first, I thought it was either Macey or Crush playing some sick joke on me, but they wouldn't do that. I started to freak out. I expected a gun to pop out and end my life right there. But I wasn't that lucky.

The person with her hand over my mouth stood me on my feet and told me not to scream. I planned to do just that when I got the chance. She spun me around and relief and panic immediately entered my system, which was emotionally and physically exhausting. I recognized this lady. She was the one who almost shot Crush back at the CIA headquarters when we took the shortcut through the walls.

"My name is Elizabeth McDowell. I work for the CIA. We've already met. Now, I'm going to take my hand off your mouth, and you will not scream. Then we are going to wake up your friends. You three have some explaining to do."

That's how Macey, Crush, and I ended up in the back of Elizabeth McDowell's car with McDonald's food in our hands.

"What do you mean? We have explaining to do? Do you have any idea what we've been through?" I asked the woman as I stuffed a cheeseburger in my mouth.

She pulled off to the side of the road. I sucked in a breath and got ready for a lecture.

"I'm sure what you guys went through was traumatic, but right now the whole country believes that you three killed two men, blew up a grocery store, let convicts escape custody, and broke a guy's foot. That's a problem for us."

"It's a problem for you? Are you kidding? It all might be true," Macey said. "Chase is right. We don't have any explaining to do. You people need to answer our questions and inform the public that we're not maniacs."

"It doesn't matter what the truth is. It matters what the public believes," Elizabeth McDowell said. "Now tell me what you know."

"We know where Ares headquarter is," Crush offered.

The lady looked back at us and frowned. "They took you three there?" she asked.

"No. They took us to Disneyland," I said. I wanted to yell that they should have known that. They put a tracking device in Crush's tooth. They should have known where we were at every step.

"It's in New Mexico," Crush said.

"Where we were tortured, if you care," I added.

Elizabeth McDowell pulled back on the road.

"How did you find us?" Macey asked.

"Sydney has a tracking device in one of his teeth," Elizabeth McDowell said, as if it were no big deal.

Anger flashed across Crush's face. "Why?"

"You're young, right? We had to know where you were at all times."

"If you were tracking us, then why in the world didn't you rescue us sooner?" I asked. "Like a week ago?"

"Some things are too difficult to understand."

"Fine. Then I guess we won't tell you that there's a bomb in my shoulder. If we don't get there by today, someone is going to die. Most likely me. Oh, and my dad is alive."

"We know. That's why I'm taking you three to New York City right now. You were taking too long to get there on your own, so we were forced to interfere. We didn't want Ares to know we know where you guys were and what's happening. Ares thinks you're hitching a ride to New York City. We don't exactly know what they have in store for the three of you, but the CIA has agents in New York City right now trying to put a stop to what's happening. You three are going to enter New York City in a cab and walk around until someone from Ares approaches you, which I've been informed they will. When this person approaches you, the CIA will handle it from there. There will be agents surrounding you. You won't be in any danger."

"Well, that makes me all bubbly inside," I said. "No offense, but that's the worst plan I've ever heard. In my whole life. That's awful. Whoever came up with that should be publicly humiliated and fired."

"It is," Crush agreed. "Worse than the Friar's."

Elizabeth McDowell clenched the steering wheel. "Is there anything else you three would like to inform me?"

"Um, Dotson works for Ares," Macey said. "Just a minor detail."

She sped up. "We are aware of that."

"How?"

She took a sharp breath. "I wasn't authorized to tell you this, but Dotson is the one that called and told us what to do with you three when we arrive in New York City. He's the one that told us that he put the tracking device in Sydney and how to find you three. The people that implanted it in Sydney's tooth died. I'm going to go out on a limb and say Dotson killed them. They were the only ones that knew about the tracking device, excluding Dotson. That's why we weren't able to find you three earlier. We had as much information as the public. Dotson gave us the tracking number, and we were able to find you in less than ten minutes. We were then instructed to take you three to New York City via cab and not accompany you or..."

Elizabeth McDowell didn't say anything else, but she'd just pretty much contradicted everything she had said before about Ares thinking we were hitching a ride to New York City. She didn't think we knew about Dotson and had planned to leave us in the dark.

"Or what?" Macey asked and put her hand on the back of seat.

Silence.

"They'll kill us, right? We'll follow Dotson's plan for you, but the second something goes wrong, I'm screaming so loud that the deaf cringe," Macey said.

"Dotson said he would blow up the tracking device in Crush's tooth and the device in Chase's shoulder if we didn't comply," the woman told us.

"So get this stuff out of us!" Crush screamed.

"If we tried, he would just press the button, and the two of you would be dead." She glanced at the clock. "We will be in New York City in about three hours. I suggest you three get some rest before we arrive."

I didn't bother to tell the lady that when facing your death, it's not simple to go to sleep.

My stomach was in knots. This lady wasn't telling us the whole story. Or maybe she had but manipulated parts until they pleased her. Either way, something big was about to happen, and she had lied to us. Or she might not know she had lied to us. The truth was hardly known as a whole. She might have told us what she thought to be true. I thought about jumping out of the car. I didn't want to go through with this. Then I remembered the thing in my shoulder.

Dotson proved to be devious and cunning. I just wanted to know why he cared to go to so much trouble with us. Why did he need us? This surely had to go beyond some dumb information.

Elizabeth gave us new clothes to change into, which was quite difficult to do in the back of a car with two other people. She handed us listening devices to wear at the bottoms of our shirts, out of sight. When we arrived in New York City, Elizabeth gave us forty dollars and told us to take a cab to the middle of Times Square. This was supposed to be the place where someone from Ares would approach us. My hands shook. The CIA was simply handing a bunch of teenagers off to crazy men.

We got in a cab, and the driver didn't seem to think it was strange that we were by ourselves or smelled like a dirty passenger car. He didn't even speak to us during the drive or when he dropped us off. Or when I handed him the money Elizabeth had given to us. I vaguely wondered if he was CIA. Or ARG.

Time Square was bigger than I thought it would be. The streets were packed with people of all different races, and I could hear foreign languages being shouted. There was a guy with a guitar in front of an Olive Garden, and one of the workers attempted to get him to leave. Skyscrapers towered over me, and huge posters that featured upcoming movies attacked me at every angle. Cars crowded the streets, and jaywalkers ran in between them in hopes of getting to the other side before the traffic started to move.

"How is Ares supposed to find us here? There are so many people," Macey said and dodged a man with a backpack. "And is anyone else mad at little Ms. Elizabeth?"

"I'm guessing that they're just going to use the tracking device in my tooth to find us," Crush said.

"Maybe the beeping means it's tracking you," Macey offered.

"Or my shoulder might start vibrating," I muttered.

"Or that," Crush said.

We stood in front of a store and patiently waited for someone to approach us. Waiting was more nerve-racking than running. At least when you were running, you were attempting to save yourself. We were about to deliver ourselves on a gold platter. This went against my nature. My legs itched to run. Or maybe they just itched. There had been a lot of mosquitoes.

I knew any one of the people around us could have been Ares. A key point of being a criminal is not to appear to be a criminal.

The vibrating in my shoulder and the beeping in Crush's head started at the same time. The pain in my shoulder wasn't as bad as it usually was, but it was enough to make me wince and bite the inside of my mouth to keep silent.

Macey grabbed my good shoulder. "Look!"

I turned around, and I felt like I needed to throw up.

Dotson.

"Do we run?" I asked. Every fiber in my being wanted to turn and run and never look back.

"No, he'll blow up your shoulder," Macey said.

He got closer to us and smiled. A scary and horrid smile.

"Hello, kids. How have the last few days been?" he asked.

"Superb," Macey said.

The pain in my shoulder stopped, and Crush let out a breath.

Dotson put his hand on my shoulder and applied pressure. I tried to back away, but he held me where I was. "Chase. You're looking little tense there. Is your shoulder hurt? Sydney, didn't anybody ever tell you that it's not good to grind your teeth? Such a bad habit. Now come along, we don't want to be overheard, and I hear that the three of you are wanted for murder and arson. Messy business. Can't be good to stay in public for too long. Follow me. I believe I owe you three some type of explanation."

He led us out of the busiest area of Times Square and to a building. We walked inside, and he led us downstairs.

Macey grabbed my hand.

Where were the other CIA agents? Elizabeth told us they would handle it from there.

"Is something wrong, Chase?" Dotson asked.

I eyed Macey and then looked back at Dotson, who now had a knife in his hand to intimidate us.

"No."

"Then I don't see the point in the listening devices."

He took the three listening devices, stepped on them with his foot, clicked his tongue, and cursed at the CIA. He opened the door and ushered us inside.

The room was a bit smaller than a classroom, but a lot more sinister. There were a couple of long and black rectangular tables with books, computers, and stacks of paper on them. I saw a sleek black gun on the table next to Dotson, easily within arm's reach of both of us. The room was painted a dull gray, and the floor was concrete, and if I had to take a guess, I'd say the walls were soundproof. The ceiling was about ten feet tall. There were three wooden chairs in the front of the room, and we were instructed to sit in them. I couldn't take my eyes off the gun.

"Why did you want us to come to New York City?" Crush asked. "Did you want us to see your ratty little office? Honestly, I'm not that impressed. And what's with the tracking device in my tooth? I want it out. It's not well made if I could hear it beeping the whole time. I'm guessing you made it?"

"The beeping is optional, but if you really want it out, I would be honored to do the job. I do have a pair of tweezers around here somewhere," Dotson said menacingly and began to rummage around in cabinets.

"Um…" Crush started.

"Never mind that. This isn't my real office. What I have is *much* grander. I wanted you three here to talk and congratulate you. We just need to talk."

"And you couldn't have done that without making us criminals?" I asked. What did he mean? Congratulate us?

"You three had to prove yourselves first. Then we could talk."

"We have nothing to prove," Macey said.

"He does." Dotson looked at Crush, who shifted uncomfortably. "They're disappointed in you, Crush. They thought you could find a way out of this mess." Dotson moved around the countertops. "I've found what Ares, ARG, and the CIA have been after all these years. You see? I knew if I worked for Ares and the CIA, then I would have access to more information. There's a method behind my madness. It's rather senseless of Ares and the CIA not to have worked together. They could have achieved so much. They both knew a small portion of the information. I just needed to work my way up." Dotson stood about ten feet in front of me.

"I thought my dad was the only one that knew what the information," I said, hopelessly confused.

"The ARG is real?" Crush muttered.

"You're right, Chase. Your father is the only one that knows what the information is. And it's right here." He motioned to a piece of paper.

"My father's here?" How had he gotten out of the headquarters and here as quickly as we did? I looked around, as if I'd been stupid enough not to have noticed him before. "Where is he?"

Dotson smiled and spread his hands out. "Standing right in front of you, Chase."

"What?" I asked. I didn't trust myself to say anymore. My stomach erupted into a ball of flames, and it took all I had and a little more not to throw up. But suddenly, everything made a little more sense.

"You're lying," Crush said for me. I chose to believe that he was referring to the part about Dotson being my father and not the bit about the Applied Research Group being a real thing. "You're not his father. He's a prisoner at the Ares headquarters. We all know that."

"Sadly, no. I'm not lying." He switched his attention to me. "I thought there would be more hope for you rather than Brandon. You're the only one that committed more than one crime. I'll have to contact my partner to discuss the results. Your whole life was preparing you for this, and I think you did a pretty good job. I needed you to acquire a certain set of skills. You proved yourself once when you escaped juvie. I just needed to impress a few more people, and I knew you were up to it. This past week was to prove that you were capable of handling the kind of life that is ahead. There was no hope for Brandon at any time, which I predicted years ago."

"Hope for what?" I asked, my muscles tense.

"I need help, Chase. You can give it to me. You've proven to be very resourceful and capable. I want you to join me. With this," Dotson gestured to the piece of paper. "Chase, we can have and do anything we want."

"*Join* you? Are you kidding? I would rather die."

"Would you really? You've never belonged anywhere. With my friends and me, you will belong. I can give you everything you need and want. Doesn't that sound nice? You won't be the pitiful orphan anymore. You will have a future with me. Without me, you are nothing. I am the one who constructed everything about you and your life."

"I belong in Florida. Not with you. And why would I want to spend my life with someone who made it awful? Telling me that everything that happened to me was because of you probably wasn't the best move."

"You think the Haneys will want you back? Chase, I'm your last hope."

"I ran out of hope a long time ago."

Dotson seemed to shrug my response off, like he'd expected it. He went back to his speech like our conversation never happened.

"I did learn more in my experiment. About Crush. No matter the training or cost, a teenager will always confess secrets. But that can be fixed." He smiled at Crush. "And you are training for the ARG. The "corrupted" part. My part. By the time you're twenty-one, you're going to be lethal. The CIA thinks you're training only for them. Ninety-eight percent of them don't know about the ARG. There is nothing you can do about it. If you say anything to anyone about your training or the ARG, we will kill them. I think you already knew that."

My mind was in overdrive. Had Ares interrogated Crush? Were they looking for information? Why? Dotson could have easily supplied the information. Unless some of the higher officials for Ares didn't know he was working for the CIA. Or was he a triple agent? It all seemed too strange. I understood that this whole thing had been some test, but what exactly was he testing? What were the results? Why was he choosing, especially now, to tell Crush about the ARG?

And had he really orchestrated everything about my life?

"You made sure I wasn't adopted?"

"I presumed if I had children that they might as well be of some use to me. This experiment and the torture techniques will be of use to many individuals and groups."

There it was. Our pain was for someone else's gain. My whole life had been set up. It had been organized to fit this man's needs, and it had sucked majorly. Emotion overcame me, and I stood up and dove for the gun. I wasn't sure what I planned to do with it, but it didn't matter because Dotson was able to reach it before I did. He kicked it aside and lunged, grabbed my wrist, and yanked me toward him.

He noticed the scars on the inside of my wrist.

Something flashed across his face.

"Interesting. Very interesting."

I didn't say anything. Instead, I tried to jerk my wrist away; he just held it tighter and pulled me closer to him.

"I don't think you're doing it correctly. The cuts aren't deep enough."

He slammed my wrist against the table and held me down. He took the knife again and placed it about five inches away from my hand. He put pressure on the tip of the knife, and I watched a bubble of blood come from the cut.

I tried to pull my wrist away.

Crush and Macey quickly moved toward us. Dotson, who didn't bother to lift his head, told them if they took another step, then the next cut would be across my throat. They stopped in their tracks.

Dotson continued the slash until it was the width of my arm. Blood gushed from the cut.

"I gave you life, Chase. You should have taken better care of yourself. You should be more grateful. You will still join me. Be my legacy. I can still use you, even like this."

I bit the inside of my mouth. "Stop. Please. Stop it." I didn't care what he said about me.

"Why? You do it to yourself. I've watched your every move over the years. I know everything about you. I know who your friends are, your grades, what sports you play. Everything that a father should. I did a lot for you over the years. Who do you think offered the judge assigned to your case enough money so he could retire early if he let you go? That was me. It was me. It was all me. Me."

"You didn't do anything for me. You did everything *to* me," I muttered through clenched teeth.

He replaced the knife about half an inch away from the first cut. I thought he was going to make the next cut slow like he did the first one, but he just ripped the knife across my arm. Blood poured from the cut. He repeated the process about an inch from my hand.

My knees felt weak as I watched the thick, red blood gush down my arm. I think I screamed.

"Stop! Stop it!" Macey shrieked. There wasn't much else to do.

He took the knife and placed it a little farther up on my arm and held it like a pencil. He pressed down hard on my skin and cut a vertical line about five inches long. I felt like throwing up. The blood poured down my arm and dripped onto the floor and my shoes. I took my other hand and tried to staunch the flow of blood, but it hardly did any good. Tears burned my eyes.

He pushed my hand away and started to cut me again, but I grabbed his wrist and shoved his arm away.

He backhanded me hard across the face, and I vaguely heard Macey and Crush protest. I eyed them, and they stood still. They looked like they were about to cry.

He put the knife where the vertical cut ended closest to my hand and cut a diagonal line that faced downward. Then he cut another vertical line on my arm. The three cuts came together to look like an N. Then he connected the cuts. It looked strangely like a bow tie with sharp edges.

More blood gushed down my arm, and I turned my head away. I fell to my knees as he made another cut below the one that looked like a bow tie.

That was cut number eight, and it didn't look like he would stop anytime soon.

And he wasn't.

I threw up when he cut a vertical line that went the entire length of my arm and shoulder, all the way up to my neck. I fell to my knees, only to be jerked roughly up by my hair.

"Stop!" This time it was Crush that screamed.

He hurled himself at Dotson and knocked him over.

The bloody knife was flung out of his hand, and the clatter of the metal hurt my head. The room felt cold.

Dotson slung Crush off before I got to the door. Macey was trying frantically to get the door open. I looked back at Crush, who had a bloody lip. I desperately tried to get my head around what was happening, but to no avail. I grabbed my injured arm again. It was completely covered in blood, which pooled around my feet. I tried to staunch the flow.

Dotson produced the gun out of thin air and had it pointed right at my heart.

"Sit down."

I didn't sit down.

"Do it. Shoot me. I don't care. What's another death on you? You already killed me once. Just do it again and get over with." Adrenaline raced through me.

He seemed to consider this, and while he did, Crush leaped again and tackled the man around his legs, and they both fell to the floor. The gun scattered about ten feet away. Within seconds, I had the gun in my good arm. It was pointed at Dotson as blood from the cuts dripped on the floor and created a new red puddle. Dotson shoved Crush off of him and stood.

Crush straightened, backed away, and got out of the shot.

Dotson smiled at me. He didn't think I would do it.

"Who was the man that said I was his son? Where is Brandon? What's the information? What does the ARG have to do with anything?"

"The man?" Dotson had a crazed look in his eyes, and I knew he'd lost his mind a long time ago. "I brainwashed him to believe he was your father. A little medication and torture can go a long way. I was the *only* one that knew he wasn't your father. He was kept prisoner for a long time to convince the others that worked for Ares, and it worked. Everyone believed it. No one had the slightest clue what was really happening. Except my partner. My wonderful partner. The director thought he was in on the secret, but he wasn't. My partner and the director never knew about the ARG or anything. They both played their parts perfectly. Nothing went wrong. The CIA and Ares would have never found the information without me. Never!"

I shifted the gun in my hands.

"All these years, you were going on the assumption that you would find the information. If you hadn't, you would have made my life a nightmare for no reason at all."

He didn't acknowledge that I'd talked.

"I knew more to the story because my father worked for the group that had the information in the first place. That group didn't have the resources to make use of the secret, and their priorities changed with time. But my father saw the importance and worked hard to get the information. After years, all he had managed to get was the first coordinate. Now, *I* have them all to the farthest decimal point necessary. Ares got drift of some of the coordinates, as did the CIA. When I first started working for the CIA, I told them that there was important information that could give them power. That was about twenty-five years ago. It would just take some time to find it. They thought I knew more than I let on, which was true. That was one of the reasons I was called to be a part of the Applied Research Group. It took me years and years to find out the coordinates from both organizations. But I'd never stopped working on my experiment I'd started with my sons. So I captured the man and brainwashed him until he believed that he was your father. Not an easy task," he said and laughed.

"Coordinates? Coordinates to what?" Macey asked.

He gestured to a folder next to him, and I knew that must have been a copy of the document that contained the information. How could coordinates stay important for so long? Was there information that Dotson added?

Crush eyed it.

"Where's Brandon?" I asked.

"He's alive. I have more to busy myself with than the likes of your pathetic brother. I decided he was weak a long time ago, and when he showed up at the pier and wasn't able to save you, my assumptions were proved even more true. You're the one that interested me the most because of your rebellious blood, which happens to be all over my floor. You will join me, along with your friends. You will help me use the information to the greatest extent. They both showed great skills and bravery throughout the past few days. They will be of great help in the future," he said, again with a laugh.

"What's the information?" I asked.

"I told you. All the coordinates." He giggled and started to nod his head uncontrollably.

"Coordinates to what?"

"The submarine! What else? That's all I need. I just needed the coordinates to the shipwreck."

"What submarine? The *Juggernaut*?" Crush asked and raised his eyebrows.

Dotson couldn't hide the shock on his face. "Yes. The *Juggernaut*. It was used in the forties and fifties to transport information during and after the Second World War."

"I knew that," Crush said. "Everyone with any type of clearance at the CIA knows about the *Juggernaut*. It was carrying a lot of precious jewels when it sank. No one knows where it sunk exactly."

Dotson smiled, as if he was mocking a child. "And when you get a higher clearance, you will learn that the *Juggernaut* wasn't just carrying millions in regular jewels."

"What else was it carrying?"

"Nothing is known for certain. But after years of research, I have concluded that the *Juggernaut* was carrying priceless sculptures and artifacts from the Amber Room."

"The Amber Room?" Crush asked, uncertainty in his voice. "The thing from World War Two? I thought that thing was underground somewhere."

Dotson's face scrunched in annoyance, almost like a child's. "Yes. The *thing* from World War Two. It was stolen in 1941 by the Nazis from Peter the Great's Palace and costs and millions of millions dollars. It was thought to have been destroyed. But the Americans recovered bits and pieces of the Amber Room after the war, and it was the *Juggernaut*'s job to transport the artifacts. But it sank. There are amber plates on the *Juggernaut*, which was airtight. Nothing has happened to those plates or the other artifacts. Crates upon crates of priceless artifacts! All thought to have been lost."

"So this was all about money?" Macey asked. "Besides, who knows what kind of condition the amber is in? The submarine could be flooded for all you know."

"And the fame and glory of being the one who found artifacts from the Amber Room! Even if the amber isn't salvageable, I'll make my millions off the sculptures and paintings!" Dotson screamed and slammed his hand on his chest.

His voice shook as he spoke. "You can still join me. Think of what we could do together! Think about how much money people would pay for this stuff on the black market!"

"No," I told him flatly. "You don't even have the stuff." My vision blurred, and my arm went numb. If I was going to do it, I was going to have to do it soon.

During Dotson's rant, Crush had crawled over to the document, and I'd watched him read it.

"I get it. Macey would think badly of you if joined me. You really shouldn't be pressured like that, Chase," Dotson told me. He grabbed Macey by her neck. "I'll get rid of her, and that won't be a problem. Then you and Sydney can join me."

He was going to kill Macey.

He was going to break her neck right in front of me.

I wasn't going to let that happen.

I couldn't shoot him—I might have shot Macey instead. I could always—

Macey acted first. She kicked Dotson in the leg, and his grip loosened. She grabbed his hand and bent back two fingers, and he let out a yelp. With her other hand, she punched him in the face, and he stumbled backward. She threw a wooden chair at his back and then ran across the room toward me.

Dotson was more furious than injured. Furious and insane were not a good combination.

"I'm going to kill all of you!" he screamed, pulling a gun from a holster on his leg and pointing it right at me.

I pulled the trigger before he did.

The bullet hit him in the chest.

The three of us screamed as blood poured out of the bullet wound. He fell to his knees, his eyes wide. I saw his eyes roll back, and he clattered to the ground.

I threw the gun across the room, and it smashed against the wall and fell to the ground.

"Let's leave," I said, my voice trembling. My whole body quivered, and I felt lightheaded.

Macey and Crush nodded.

Before we left, Crush took a lighter from one of the tables and lit the document on fire. He said he'd memorized it and that the information was to stay between the three of us. He said that this had already caused too many deaths and needed to be destroyed. I was fine with that. We all tried to ignore the smell of blood as it filled the room. As the adrenaline died in my bloodstream, the pain set in. It was a piercing pain that affected my whole body and my mind. I fell to my knees and fought to stay awake. I was afraid if I fell asleep, I might not wake up.

I didn't even have to say anything. Crush and Macey supported me.

Crush didn't stop with the information. He knocked the door down and set the rest of the room on fire. In that instant, we didn't care too much about the surrounding buildings.

Crush and Macey more or less carried me out of the room and up the stairs, and we didn't look back once.

EPILOGUE

We stood in the busy airport, my arm in a sling, and the crowd parted around us. I'd spent three days in the hospital high on drugs. I was still in a lot of pain, but I had been relieved when I was allowed to leave.

All three of us were eager to get home. Crush and Macey were both ready to see their families again. I was just as glad that I was going to the Haneys' house. Dotson had been wrong about them not wanting me. I wondered if they knew I would be arriving in the middle of the night with a (real) CIA agent in the car with me. I wasn't looking forward to explaining everything.

It had been about a week since I'd shot and killed Dotson.

The CIA was having a difficult time covering up and fixing the mess that the press had made out of all three of our lives. They released a fairly convincing story about us not being guilty and blah, blah, blah. They had covered stuff up that was much worse than this. It was too bad that it hardly mattered what was on the news. People were going to believe what they wanted. I kept telling myself that something big would happen, and all the attention would be off of us soon.

We'd spent the last few days explaining everything to people at the CIA. They wanted to know every detail, and I attempted to give it to them. More or less. Macey and I didn't tell them that Crush knew the information. No one mentioned the Applied Research Group. We didn't say a word about any coordinates, the *Juggernaut*, the Amber Room, or priceless paintings or artifacts. Acting like we were ignorant was the safest option.

Now that Dotson was dead and gone, the three of us assumed that Crush would get a job with the CIA when he was old enough, not the ARG. With Dotson gone, the whole organization would hopefully crumble, and Ares would find something else to obsess over. Hopefully, it would have nothing to do with us. The CIA told Crush that Ares had shown interest in the whereabouts of certain notorious terrorists. With any luck, they would concentrate all their efforts on that for a while.

I'd informed them that Dotson was mentally insane and that he'd insisted that he was my father. They didn't believe it, so they took some DNA they had from him and some of mine and sent it off to the lab.

The tests came back positive.

Hooray.

I was the son of a terrorist. A criminal. Breaking the law was in my blood, but most of my blood was still in his "office."

The CIA suggested that the three of us go and see some of their therapists. The three of us refused. None of us wanted to talk about anything. At all.

"Are you ready?" Macey asked Crush.

"Yeah," he answered. Because he lived in Virginia, he wouldn't be going home by plane, but he insisted on coming to the airport with us. Someone from the CIA was escorting each one of us for two reasons.

First of all, there was a lot of explaining to tell our families, and I knew a lie wasn't going to cut it. They needed the truth, and the CIA was willing to give it to them. (Sort of.) The second reason was protection from anyone who didn't believe the story about our innocence. But why would anyone? We did all of that stuff we were accused of, except we had no memory of it. The CIA did multiple tests on all three of us but couldn't find anything out of the ordinary. Someone told us that our memories might return. I wasn't looking forward to that day.

"Chase?" Crush asked. "Sorry I gave you a hard time about the ARG."

"And about a lot of other stuff. But don't worry about it. We were pretty stressed."

Crush was determined to find out who in the CIA was part of the ARG and see if it was true that he had been training to join them. He mentioned something about a fourth panel of a sculpture in the courtyard of the CIA, but I hadn't been paying too close attention then. We made him promise to keep us updated.

"Hey, what did you say to me in Spanish when we were in the woods?"

He smiled. "I think I called you ugly and tiny. Something along those lines, anyway."

"Oh, I love being insulted in languages I don't understand."

Crush laughed. "You guys know what really sucks about all of this? The Amber Room was already in bad condition *before* the Nazis stole it. Who knows what kind of condition it's in now, wherever it is. Dotson would have had a difficult time making money off of it."

Macey snickered. "That is a considerable downside. I wish he had gone down there, and the submarine had blown up in his face."

"Still, who knows what else was really on the *Juggernaut*. There could have been more information too delicate to talk about in front of teenagers. Like information gathered from doctors at concentration camps. Or crimes committed at internment camps."

Something in Crush's eyes flickered, and I knew he wanted us to ask more questions. The answers could have cleared up questions I still had about Dotson's motive. The answers might have brought some relief. I wanted to ask what else was being transported when the *Juggernaut* sank. But I didn't. Too much went along with knowing that.

"One more thing," he muttered when he realized Macey and I had no interest in learning more.

"Yeah?"

"Do you think Dotson was gay?"

I blinked at him a few times.

"What does that have to do with anything?"

"He kept talking about his partner. I didn't know what he meant."

"Lab partner? Psycho partner? Business partner? What does it matter?"

"I was just wondering."

We had learned from the CIA that Dotson had a master's degree in psychology. He'd written a few strange papers and had them published. Ares probably recruited him because they needed someone that could get inside the mind of their CIA prisoners (I guessed one to be the man who was brainwashed to believe that I was his son) and make them give up their secrets. Dotson thought that he could bypass the trouble of prying secrets out of people by getting a job at the CIA and having the information and secrets given to him, which he gave to Ares. He got access to a lot this way. And got paid. A lot.

The CIA speculated that Dotson wanted to know how people handled secrets, how far they would go to protect them, and how your lifestyle affected how well you kept secrets. That's why he wanted Crush. Crush didn't remember telling any secrets.

We wanted to know more. Of course, they told us that if we hadn't burned the place to the ground, then they would have had more information on Dotson.

"How's your arm?" Macey asked.

"Still really sore. These bandages itch. I still feel a little woozy."

I was wearing a loose long sleeve to cover up my injured arm, along with a sling. I didn't care about the heat. I didn't want anyone to see it. My arm was healing. I'd lost a lot of blood and received transfusions. Thankfully, I had type AB. I had to have a lot of stitches, but they would come out soon. I'd been rushed to the hospital by the CIA operatives who had been assigned to make sure nothing like that happened, in and out of consciousness the whole time. I was going to have to live with those deep scars for the rest of my life. They would be an ugly reminder of everything that happened.

The doctors had been warned (heavily, I might add) to keep their mouths shut about all of this. They had been forbidden to ask questions, and there was to be an operative with me the whole time. The doctors knew I was with the CIA, but they didn't know the details of the incident.

That's what they called it.

The incident.

They didn't know I had almost died a million times just so Dotson could make sure I was fit for following in his footsteps. I had decided Macey had been sent there as a distraction. He needed to see if I could stay focused.

The CIA's excuse for not stopping Dotson in time to save us was that the tracking and listening devices had stopped working. Of course, they blamed it on Dotson. I expected nothing less. It was an organization run by prideful, hotheaded people.

The fire that Crush started was put out before it caused any damage to the surrounding buildings. Operatives went back in the building to see if there had been any remains.

They found bones.

Of course, the CIA had gone to Ares's headquarters after getting the vague directions from us. We hadn't heard much, just that the place was empty. Completely empty. Everything was gone, much like the Amber Room was rumored to be. I suggested that they tried to find the owner of the grocery store that we supposedly blew up and see if his bank account had received any deposits recently.

"So this it?" I asked. I rubbed my aching shoulder, and it wasn't just from the cut that ran the length of my arm. The mini bomb had been removed after a two-hour surgery. A doctor that worked within the CIA did it. Crush was equally glad that the tracking device was out of him. Needless to say, I didn't have any use of my arm. Every tiny movement sent a thick, electric, and hot pain up my arm. I was on so many painkillers that I'd lost count.

———

Among countless other things, there was still one big issue that wouldn't leave me alone.

My blood relatives.

The CIA hadn't been happy to look into it for me, but they owed me. I didn't care too much about Dotson's family, but I wanted to know if the lady who had given birth to me was equally as crazy as Dotson. They didn't find much on her either. It seemed like Dotson had wiped anything that would be helpful off the Internet. He had been crazy but shockingly smart. Although they did find her grave site. I declined when they asked if I wanted to visit.

Brandon Patterson, my supposed brother, was also another person of interest. Apparently, the Pattersons had been locked away in a safe house during the whole ordeal. They had been safe. Completely and utterly safe.

They were under the impression that they were being targeted because of Brandon and Justin's uncle, who was a high-ranking officer in the air force. They were to be released when the flames calmed down and the news stopped running the bit about the three of us being allowed to run loose in society. Brandon was the only one who knew what was going on, but he hadn't said a word to his family about it as far as the CIA was concerned. He knew nothing of the *Juggernaut* or the Amber Room.

———

"I guess this is it. But we'll see each other again. We'll Skype. You don't go through something as crazy as this and not stay friends," Crush said.

"Hopefully, there won't be any bombs or train rides the next time we see each other. Which will be soon, right?" Macey asked. "We will do something normal. Like see a movie or something."

"Of course. At least you two have each other," Crush said. "I'll have to homeschool. The CIA wants to increase my training, so I'll have to go to the headquarters during weekends and all the holidays. I'll live as a hermit. You two are lucky."

"Yeah. I know." Macey took my hand in hers.

"Gross," Crush grumbled.

"Do you think your parents are going to freak about your *internship*?" I asked and ignored his comment.

"They would freak more if they found out about what I was *really* training for."

The CIA was going to tell Crush's parents that their son was going to work as an intern at the headquarters. They weren't exactly going to tell them what he was training for—just that he was working. The CIA refused to tell Crush's parents about the training, which came as no surprise. Crush wouldn't even tell us what he did at training when we asked him. He closed his eyes, shook his head, and pleaded with us not to ask him again. I understood. Some subjects should be left alone.

"Good luck," Macey told him.

He smiled, and one of the agents told him it was time to leave. He took a breath, said another good-bye, and turned away. He walked toward the door with his escort right behind him. Before he'd gone twenty feet, he looked back and waved again.

Macey and I watched him go until he was lost in the huge mass of people. We both knew that it wasn't the last time we would see him. He was right. We had gone through too much together to just forget about one another—even though Crush claimed he would love nothing more than to forget about me and my tendency to make his life hard.

Still holding my hand, Macey and I turned around and headed toward the gate, hidden beneath hats and sunglasses. I couldn't help but think that if I ever went on another adventure just as crazy as this one, I wanted both of them by my side.

And maybe Iron Man.

ACKNOWLEDGEMENTS

I would like to thank my parents and sister for putting up with me for four years while I wrote and worked out the kinks in *Caught* and my grandmother for encouraging me since day one. A special thanks goes out to my friends, who always responded when I texted them at odd hours. Most of these texts included strange questions (which would help me finish the book) or sentences that I didn't like and didn't know how to fix. You guys are the reason the word "cooties" is still in the book.

46695549R00169

Made in the USA
Lexington, KY
18 November 2015